One Tenth
of the Law

"KELLI —
HOPE YOU ENJOY,

Ray

RAY PEDEN

DEDICATION

This novel is for Layne and the unconditional love that exists eternal between father and daughter. Without that magical bond and the paranoia of a dad's fertile imagination the seeds for this tale would never have germinated.

Those who find their way through these pages will understand.

Somewhere along the way all of us lie.
Not the dead.
They have things to say.

So we listen to the dead for their honesty.
And we listen to the living for their lies,
because they always tell them for a reason.

Chapter 1

THE ASSAULT on Patrick Grainger lasted less than three seconds. A deafening explosion, the Humvee rising into the air, a rush of flames through the floorboard, the powerful blast wave that slung him like a piece of overhead luggage through the driver's side door.

As his body went airborne he cursed fate that his number had finally been called, an instant before he slammed back-first onto the gravel shoulder, plowing through limestone aggregate, shredding uniform and skin. The brutal impact emptied his lungs, and life functions ceased for a moment in a desperate, convulsive struggle for air. Only after he managed to gulp a first new breath did he feel the searing pain compliments of the roofing nails, ballbearings, and scalding shards of undercarriage buried in his butchered right leg.

In the fog of chaos he watched a pair of hands, apparently his own, slapping silently at the patches of flame that swarmed the right side of his desert fatigues. A quick roll onto his stomach, scorched hands pressing into the coarse desert scrub, he pushed himself up with a tortured scream but he heard nothing. The roar from the roadside bomb had disappeared, replaced by a hollowed-out silence and a faint high-pitched tone from somewhere deep in his skull.

Within seconds blisters sprouted on his face and neck from

the inferno twenty feet away. In a desperate scramble to drag his body away from agonizing heat his leading hand fell against something soft, spongy, covered in coarse cloth. Even in his daze he recognized the 100th Division patch on the sleeve of an arm no longer attached to a person.

His eyes frantically scoured his own body and he cringed at the bloody canvas of shredded and charred flesh, but no major parts missing. Then the only explanation came to him and he twisted toward the Humvee, a mangled carcass of metal and glass canted on its side in an asphalt crater, engulfed in a silent movie of flames.

No one heard his howl of anguish at the sight of two half-formed silhouettes, Harrelson and Willis, enlisted men like him who had not been thrown free by the blast. They'd stopped thrashing, their bodies swallowed in a raging coffin of yellow and orange while an angry plume of smoke billowed out of control, carrying their ashes and private dreams away into a desert air thick with the flavor of burning diesel fuel.

As he fought the pain his world shifted into slow motion and for the briefest of moments he pictured two mothers, distraught in front of closed caskets somewhere back in Kentucky desperate to believe their sons had not suffered.

He never heard the other soldiers' approach from the convoy, only a mute rush of shadows and boots. He felt the rough tug under his arms while they dragged him away from the burn. When his head flopped backward his face took the full brunt of the sun, blinding even during a Kuwaiti winter, and he tried to turn away. Then a powerful shudder—a second blast wave from an exploding fuel tank. Arms that had been dragging him lost their grip.

Minutes or seconds, he had no idea, and out of desperation a second sense forced his hand down to his belt. The satellite phone had survived the ordeal, battered but still secure in its leather holster. The veil of blood streaming down his face made it impossible to see but it didn't stop his fingers as they fumbled to release the leather strap. His index finger guided itself to the keypad, painstaking jabs as he entered a familiar number.

With his head packed in virtual silence he knew he would hear no ring tone so he forced himself to be still, feel the vibrations. *Middle of the night. Asleep.* After four rings the vibrations stopped. He willed his arm to raise the phone to his ear and began stammering a stream-of-consciousness ramble to a wife he prayed was on the other end.

The false swagger he carried into every firefight and followed them around every suspicious corner was swept away now and he broke down, words pouring out unguarded while the crackle of flames flooded the background.

When shock finally took him over his eyes rolled back in his head and the SAT phone fell to the sand, the connection still alive, while the scratchy sound of Allison Grainger's panicked cries streamed through the static and stifling desert air.

* * * * *

From a low-rise rocky hillside two hundred meters away a pair of high-powered binoculars observed the carnage playing out below. The truck's passenger noted the time on a titanium watch. He dropped the remote device onto the seat and hit his cell phone's speed dial. On the other end of the call a pair of hands laid a manifest for field rations on his desk blotter and retrieved the vibrating phone from his breast pocket.

"It's done," said the caller. He issued an order to the driver and the battered Toyota pickup truck disappeared into the barren mountain landscape.

Chapter 2

THE STEADY SNOWFALL that settled overnight onto the county road had turned nasty, a gritty slush tracked through by morning traffic. The coroner's SUV took its time easing through the last sharp curve. Patrick Grainger sat heavy in the passenger seat slumped against the door, his vacant stare lost out the window while woven wire fences and bare-naked trees streamed past.

An hour earlier in the Judge-Executive's office he half-heard the sincere condolences. He did his best to wade through the official reports while a cup of coffee in front of him turned cold. Vivid forensic analyses by experienced professionals, void of personal sentiment, as always. Now, as they pulled through one final familiar bend he couldn't avoid the inevitable any longer. Through a melting lacework of ice in the tree canopy that crowded the right shoulder he got his first glimpse of what was left of the farmhouse.

His eyes closed in self-defense and he tried to block out haunting images he knew would follow—what that night must have been like. But scenes flared alive before he could stop them: empty pastures under a blanket of fresh snow; a black sky, shot-gunned with stars, alight in an orgy of yellow; a towering blaze spewing sparks and cinders like fireworks. He cringed as he watched feather-light pieces of his life carried away in a crackle of flame and smoke the color of night.

Charlie Reed, the County Coroner, spoke from the driver's seat, his eyes fixed on the road. "Pat, you sure you're up for this?"

The words were barely audible over the roar of the inferno. When Grainger opened his eyes the images and sounds vanished as quickly as they had come. He blinked back at Reed, no response other than an unconscious tic.

Ten months earlier he'd left behind a satisfying parcel of ground with a wife and daughter on it, brave and fortified with hope. All the trappings of a fine life that for so long had seemed out of reach, maybe even undeserved considering his sins. She'd stood there on the front porch waving gamely, chin held high, manipulating their baby daughter's arm in a tiny wave of her own, bracing for the next long year to come and go. A fine life.

Gone.

The Explorer skidded on an icy patch as it turned into the entrance. Its tire tracks would be the first to mark the driveway's virgin snow. Fifty yards in they pulled to a stop in the gravel turnaround and Reed rolled down his window. When he shut off the engine the stark silence of down-country winter filled the cockpit. No sounds other than shallow breathing and bodies shifting in leather seats as they stared at the blackened skeleton.

Remnants of the long covered porch and the front wall of the parlor leaned forward, defying gravity—for now. A brick fireplace and chimney stood at attention, naked at the far end, a testament to its unwillingness to yield. Grainger surveyed the few charred walls still standing, walls once adorned with wallpaper and family pictures, now empty and desolate other than a few clinging scraps of horsehair plaster. A tall single-paned window, its glass shattered and jagged, hung alone, conspicuous in its isolation, waiting for the right moment to release its grip.

In the center, mounded ingloriously in a bleak testament to that terrifying night, was a tangled pile of rafters, charred plank sheathing and tar paper, twisted sheets of metal roofing, dozens of shapes barely recognizable, all collapsed onto itself in the crawl space. Strands of ancient knob-and-tube wiring snaked in and out of the drifts like vines. Hard lines in black and gray, the edges softened with highlights of fresh fallen snow. A once colorful life reduced to a bleak rendering in monochrome.

Grainger was the first to break the awkward silence. "Who got here first?"

Freddie Winters answered from the back seat. "Volunteer fire department was first on the scene. My EMS guys maybe twenty minutes after that."

"By the time I arrived," Reed said quietly, "it was pretty much out." He didn't try to disguise the pain in his voice. "The back half of the house . . . was already gone."

Grainger stared, motionless, his lips moving without sound. After a long breath he opened the car door and lingered by the vehicle for a long time before he began a slow, pronounced limp through the snow to the farmhouse. He circled around a large sugar maple tree in the front yard, fatally scorched from the fire.

When Reed opened his door Winters stopped him with a question, "What are we doing here, Charlie?"

Reed closed the door. "It's a miracle the man's even alive. Unconscious for, what, six weeks? When he woke up, his wife and kid were already in the ground. I think he's entitled to some closure."

"Him running over that IED and his house catching on fire back home, less than a day apart. I mean, what's the odds? I couldn't handle that."

"I'm not sure he's doing much better."

They got out of the car and trudged through the snow toward the house where Grainger was hugging a post topped with an antique dinner bell, one of the few survivors.

Reed recognized the unmistakable stale odor of char clinging like a rotting carcass to the rubble. After eight weeks of winter gusting through the valley the worst of it had drifted off into the woods that rose up behind the house, but not all. Not enough to erase the details of that night.

"Fire Marshall got here maybe an hour after I did," Reed volunteered. "Arson detectives a little later." He turned to Grainger staring at the porch. After a conspicuous stretch of silence he measured his words. "How much do you really want to know?"

Pat Grainger was focused on the wicker settee and table overturned on the porch, stained gray from the unholy mixture of soot and water and peppered with slivers of splintered porch ceiling that had given ground during the battle. His eyes closed and his grim stare slowly drifted into a weak smile.

During that first year he and Allison had spent hours on the porch, spring evenings, long weekends, just the two of them at first, legs and arms tangled, bare feet propped on the table, a cooler of beer on the floor, amazed at their simple good fortune as their eyes swept lazy across a summer-glazed yard shaded with maples and oaks that had watched families before them come and go. Jokes were told, novels read, plans made.

Then later after Aimee was born, the three of them drawn back to the comfortable peace of the porch, the baby carrier perched proudly on the wicker table, two gushing parents waving away flies, gently poking, spouting ridiculous noises and fake baby words they were certain their daughter would understand. It was all there in front of him like it was yesterday. Pat smiled one final time at this warm glimpse of a magical life, gone forever, and opened his eyes.

"All of it," he said.

Reed sighed and touched Grainger's arm. "Come on." He led the three of them through the snow into the side yard.

"It started here," Reed said. "Went up quick. The Army

teach you anything about 'flashover'?"

Grainger's eyes never left the ruins, his response seeping out in a slow, lifeless monotone. "Flames spread across the ceiling, roll down the walls, hot gasses ignite . . . boom."

Reed nodded. "Probably reached eleven hundred degrees, maybe more. Found fragments of wood and glass out past the fence. Neighbors a mile down the valley heard the explosion."

Reed rested his hand on Grainger's shoulder. "It was over fast, Pat. They didn't suffer."

Grainger squatted, staring at the space that had once been the nursery. His head dipped and he balanced himself for awhile, then stood and limped to the edge of the shallow crawl space and dropped in. "Where'd you find them?"

Reed braced his arm on the top of the stone foundation wall and gingerly lowered himself into the crawl space with Grainger.

"Baby was about here," he said, pointing to a spot under a snow-covered pile of shingles and waterlogged mineral wool insulation, the frozen crystals glistening in the sun.

Grainger looked away into the forested hillside beyond, trying to purge the images that flooded in. His voice cracked. "Allison?"

"Over by the door to her bedroom." Reed said as he turned toward a spot buried under the rubble. "Looked like she was trying to get to the nursery and didn't make it."

Pat's memory of his house was perfect and he winced at the next thought, his voice weak. "The explosion didn't take her?"

Reed hesitated. "No."

"Smoke?"

"Yes."

"How bad?"

Charlie Reed threw a nervous glance at Winters.

"Just tell me, Charlie," Grainger whispered.

"Come on, Pat, don't torture yourself. You know what a

thousand degrees does to a body. We had to pull dental records."

Grainger fought back the images: her body tucked into a pugilistic curl, clothing burned away, the charred tissue. Unrecognizable. He felt his bad leg buckle and he stumbled over to the stone foundation. He took several deep breaths until the demons backed off and questions began to reform.

"So she only made it to the door?" he said to himself. He cocked his head, puzzled, as bits and pieces rattled loose in his head.

"Pat, maybe we should go?"

"They know how it started?" Pat persisted.

Reed looked at Winters, then gave in. "They found the metal works of an electric space heater over there on the outside wall," he said, pointing to a spot behind Grainger. "Shattered glass all around so it was under a window. They assumed curtains."

"Space heater?" Grainger flinched at the answer. He clasped both hands on top of his stocking cap. "But we talked about that. There's no way she would have . . ."

The sound of a vehicle pulling into the front yard interrupted their conversation. When the headlights went out an older man in denim coveralls and a worn Carhartt work coat got out of a farm truck and trudged toward them. A woman followed behind. Fred Winters met him.

"We help you?"

"Neighbors," the man said, pointing to the next farm.

"You the ones that called it in?"

"Yeah. McCormick." He pawed the snow with a work boot as he stared at the ruins. "It weren't right," he said, "a baby having to die like that. Allison neither."

"Now's probably not the best time, Mr. McCormick," Winters said, placing his hand gently on the man's elbow. "The Coroner and I are going over the accident scene with the husband."

The man nodded once, then looked off toward his house and continued, answering questions that weren't being asked.

"The explosion's what woke us up. The wife called 9-1-1 but I knew there weren't enough time to get it put out." His brow furrowed and a helpless expression came over him. "You think if we'd called it in quicker they'd made it out?"

"No," Reed answered politely from the crawl space, "too much old wood in the place. You did all you could."

After a forgiving silence, Reed thanked the man and turned back toward the rubble when the woman spoke to his back in a soft voice, "There was a car in the driveway."

Reed patiently acknowledged her. "Yes ma'am, she had a car."

"No, another one, driving out."

Grainger's head jerked up.

"When?"

"Soon as the fire started. One of them big station wagons, like what churches use to carry folks. A black one, looked like. Dark blue, maybe."

"Probably somebody driving by," Winters said. "Saw the fire, knew they couldn't do anything and turned around to go call the fire department."

"Could be," she said, "but we don't get much traffic out this way at three in the morning. Especially not no churches."

Grainger and Reed exchanged puzzled looks when the woman offered another question. "Did they call it in?"

"Who?" Reed answered.

"Them people in the station wagon. Did they call it in too?"

Charlie Reed's face fell silent.

Chapter 3

12 Years Later
Central Georgia, USA

SEVENTY MILES south of Macon, a lone motorcycle packed with army-issue duffle bags drifted into the northbound rest area on I-75. The distinctive rumble from its Cobra tailpipes went unnoticed.

The rider adjusted his sunglasses with an index finger. Even as he slowed, the air wash cascading around the windshield swirled shocks of gray hair that leaked out from under a purple bandana.

He took the fork to the right and motored around to the back of the island. An older woman sitting alone on a concrete bench, a cigarette dangling from her hand, sized up his rugged features with undisguised disapproval: the untrimmed week-old beard, denim shirt with sleeves cut away, jeans and work boots salted with two days of road grime.

He chose an isolated parking spot at the curb in the shade of a time-tested water oak and dismounted, a few light stretches before he dug into his left saddlebag for a spray bottle and a stained cotton rag. Pat Grainger moved to the front of his Harley

Davidson, took a quick inventory of the yellow bug entrails plastered across the windshield, and triggered a few squirts of diluted peroxide.

As the afternoon sun glinted through slits in the leafy branches of the oak he soaked up this brief interlude of calm. It was a welcome respite from the drone and hustle of the interstate and the swarming herd that had been jockeying for position with him over the last two hours.

While he waited for the peroxide to do its work he paid no attention to the travelers dribbling into the parking lot on the front side of the island, slamming doors, their idle chatter evaporating into a cloudless July afternoon. He found it more difficult to ignore the gathering sound of a worn out panel van barreling into the rest area, winding down too fast off the interstate. He raised only his eyes to the squeal of tires on hot pavement, brakes grinding, metal against metal, and the low-pitched growl of gears downshifting inside a worn out transmission.

He lowered the spray bottle and tracked the van. It aimed for the far side of the truck lot, cutting across empty parking spaces and lurched to a stop alongside the curb. Grainger made a mental note and delivered a second shot from the spray bottle before he studied the van again, out of place against the evergreen backdrop of the pine forest. No movement, no one getting out to dump trash, stretch, take a leak.

The dissolving insect residue had begun a slow ooze down the windshield. He wiped the slurry away with the cloth and gave a final cautionary glance at the rusted-out van two hundred feet away before he returned the plastic bottle to the saddlebag and turned toward the restrooms.

He'd taken only a few steps when he saw her stepping off the curb. Twelve, maybe thirteen. Her bright yellow t-shirt with the Florida graphic outlined in glitter was the first thing to catch his eye. Then a tiny shot of contrast, black and white, an animated, long-haired Chihuahua trailing on leash behind her.

He stopped cold and caught himself staring. His discomfort was conspicuous. The girl didn't notice him and gave the dog a light tug and took off splay-legged across the broad expanse of the concrete parking lot heading for a patch of grass on the far curb. Watching her brought a wistful smile, followed immediately by an almost imperceptible shake of his head. Then the melancholy that always seemed to come. As he'd learned so many times before he forced himself to let it go.

He threw another glance back at the rusty van, isolated on the back curb like a ghost ship waiting at an empty dock, before he continued toward the welcome center.

When he emerged from the restroom he didn't waste time with a soft drink. The mingling crowd was babbling, the sea of words unintelligible, but the silent voices in his head were clear and they hadn't stopped nagging him. He hurried down the entry walk and scanned the rear parking lot. Two hundred feet away the girl's head was still visible on the down-slope past the far curb while her dog pulled her along looking for the right spot.

The parked van still showed no signs of life. He felt an uneasy tension as he ambled down the sidewalk and settled on a bench next to his cycle. Then an impulsive glance back at the girl dueling with the hyperactive Chihuahua. He couldn't suppress a cautious smile as he tried to rise above the lingering sadness that lived just beneath the surface.

As he pondered the circumstances he heard an ignition turning over. Then movement when the van began creeping along the curb line. His smile vanished. He flashed to the girl. She and the dog had turned back toward the parking lot and were waiting to let the van pass.

"Just keep on going," Grainger said under his breath, as he edged forward on his seat. But the van stopped, blocking her from view. Grainger bolted upright. His muscles tightened. At the sound of the faint, clipped scream he lunged off the bench in a full-out sprint across the concrete pavement.

He was halfway through the lot when the van screeched away from the curb, accelerating toward the on-ramp. When he stopped, his eyes swung back to a tiny speck of jittery black-and-white alone on the curb, barking.

Chapter 4

GRAINGER'S EYES swept the rest area. Other than one trucker stepping off the curb, the entire population of Rest Area 10 was inside or milling around the front sidewalk. The call to action was instant, born purely from instinct, on his bike in seconds, accelerating across the parking lot, the 1600-cc motor of his Harley Davidson full throttle.

By the time he reached the interstate the needle on his speedometer was inching past sixty-five and he leaned into the natural sweep of the ramp. The van was in sight less than a half mile ahead. It would be no problem to overtake it but then what? Steadying the handlebars with his right hand, he fished a smart phone out of his jeans pocket, touched the green icon, and tapped three numbers on the screen with his left thumb.

Two rings. "9-1-1, what is your location?"

The road wind buffeted the mouthpiece, and the throaty rumble from his tailpipes all but drowned out the operator's voice.

"I-75," he yelled into the phone, spacing each word for clarity, "south of Macon . . . following gray panel van . . . someone kidnapped from rest area . . . near mile marker . . ." He waited for the next green marker stake. ". . . mile–marker 85."

"Mile marker 85 on I-75. You say a kidnapping?"

"10-4," he said, straining to hear over the noise. "A girl. I'm following. Alert state patrol."

"Stay on the line, sir, so we can track your location."

He slipped the live phone into his shirt pocket. He was within fifty yards of the van and reduced his speed to match it. His phone's GPS would give them a fix. *The license plate number might help.* He closed the gap. With his free left hand he reached into his shirt pocket. As he retrieved the live phone the wind currents whipping around the windshield ripped at it, dragging it out of his hand and he juggled it twice, trying to catch it in mid air with one hand before it bounced away and shattered on the pavement at 85 mph.

"Shit!"

* * * * *

Randy Oliver leaned over the middle seat of their blue and gray Suburban, filling up the plastic grocery bag with trash when he felt several pats on his rear end.

"Uh, pardon me," he said sternly without looking back, "my wife is coming back from the bathroom soon and she would *not* be amused."

"Your wife *is* amused," replied Karen Oliver. "You're actually cleaning something."

Randy backed out of the car and shot her a smirk.

"Where's Julie?" she asked.

"Back there," he said, waving his hand dismissively across the island's picnic area toward the far back side of the parking lot. "Took Winnie to poop."

Their conversation was interrupted by an engine revving in the distance and they turned toward the sound of a gray panel van speeding away, engine wound tight.

"Idiot." Karen muttered.

Before he could acknowledge her their conversation was interrupted again, this time by a motorcycle with loud tailpipes accelerating across the lot. They followed the path of the biker as he sped past.

"Hey, did you see that guy!" Brad Oliver said as he approached the Suburban from the restrooms. He motioned toward the motorcycle racing wide open down the ramp. "That's one kickass bike. Dad, when you gonna let me get one of those?"

"When you're 40," said Randy. "And don't say 'kickass' in front of your mother."

"Funny. Come on, Dad, let's get *two*. Father-son bonding time." He flashed a broad fake smile.

"Forty," Randy replied with a firm grin.

"Brad," Karen interrupted, "get your sister. We've got to get on the road."

"Where is she?"

"Walking Winnie," Randy said as he pointed toward the rear of the parking area.

Brad turned toward the back of the rest area, then stopped short. He didn't move for several seconds before he spoke.

"Dad? Mom?"

Randy and Karen Oliver joined their son as they stared at Winnie, a tiny speck barking on the back curb alone.

* * * * *

The largest of three men had dragged Julie Oliver into the van. Now, speeding down the interstate at 85 miles an hour his huge frame was planted on the second seat holding the struggling girl on his lap, beefy arms locked around her, one huge hand covering her mouth like a catcher's mitt.

He looked over his shoulder into the back of the van, a jumbled clutter of grimy duffel bags, blankets, discarded wrappers, bags of stale cookies and chips, a nicked-up Styrofoam cooler with beer and ice long melted. He growled at the lanky companion on the seat beside him. "Make a place for our girlfriend here."

Lavon cleared out a space behind the bench seat and spread a musty blanket on the floor. The giant rose with the girl into a stooped position, fighting to keep his balance in the speeding van. As he shuffled around behind the seat the girl writhed in his powerful grip, her legs kicking wild, hunting for traction but all she found was air. He released her to the blanket where she curled face-down into a protective cocoon.

Over the road noise he screamed at the driver. "Get off the fucking road. We get picked up with this little bitch we're dead."

The driver had already considered the implications. Despite his unchallenged position as *lider* of the Northside Latin Lords, a ruthless band of homegrown renegades that ruled a 20-block neighborhood in the projects of Tampa, Carlos sometimes let mistakes bite him in the ass, especially ones fed by careless arrogance. Like today.

He was already cursing their decision to pick up the hitchhiker nine exits back. It had been a poor one. All for a lousy bag of weed. As soon as the body was discovered in the dumpster under a stack of cardboard boxes the Georgia State Patrol would be out in force, an all-out manhunt. Grabbing the girl, he realized now, was another careless decision.

Their impulsive moves weren't that surprising considering that all three men were swimming in a chemically-altered world of their own making, steeped in a cloud of marijuana and high on their daily diet of crystal methamphetamine, an unpredictable cocktail that sent mixed messages to their central nervous systems.

"Somebody tell me where the fuck we are," Carlos commanded from the driver's seat.

Lavon unfolded a crumpled road map while his eyes scanned the interstate shoulder for the next mile marker. "Some county road up ahead before we get to Cordelle," he finally shouted.

"Some hick road out in the sticks."

"Where it go?"

Lavon traced the white county road on the map with his index finger. "If we cross over we be heading toward some big-ass lake. Gotta be some back roads we could slip in and hide."

"What exit?"

Lavon located the number on the map. "92."

A hundred yards behind the motorcycle followed.

Chapter 5

RANDY AND KAREN OLIVER found one of Julie's sandals and fresh blood splatters on the pavement, the result of her struggle when the men dragged her across sharp edges of the rusted door sill. Hysterical, Randy called 9-1-1 on his cell phone and within two minutes a trooper from the Georgia State Patrol cruising I-75 arrived at the scene.

The GSP put out an immediate BOLO alert and called for roadblocks on all I-75 exits between the rest area and Macon but by the time most of them were in place 18 minutes had elapsed since Julie Oliver was abducted. The gray van had already left the interstate at Exit 92 on its way toward Lake Baxter.

* * * * *

The two-lane county road wound through acres of remote, rural farmland—cotton, soybeans, peanuts—marked only by an occasional tenant house or double-wide trailer with cars and work trucks parked in front yards. Carlos' eyes darted between both sides of the road.

Finally he slowed and came to a full stop in the empty roadway. Off to his left 150 feet away the abandoned farmhouse was barely visible, hiding behind a yard overrun with years of knee-high prairie grass, uncontrolled native underbrush, dozens of volunteer scrub trees. Through spotty gaps in the foliage he saw no signs of life, only decay: white paint blistered on curling clapboard siding, gaping holes in a rusted green tin roof, Americana gingerbread rotted or missing altogether, a front porch swallowed by Kudzu. An overgrown dirt driveway that in years past had curled around behind the house into dense woods was virtually undetectable. A log had been rolled across the dirt driveway to discourage visitors and a rotten fence post with a rusted "No Trespassing" sign had fallen unceremoniously in the dirt beside it.

Carlos pulled off the pavement and eased around the right end of the log and followed the faint path of the lane into the tree canopy behind.

The deeper into the woods they went the more rutted the lane became. An undistinguished habitat of undergrowth, untended for years, had nearly filled the passage, limiting their visibility to a few feet. Branches scraped the sides of the van as it crawled its way through the tangle.

After 40 yards the thick woods abruptly opened and the lane spilled out into an empty field, rocky and overtaken by Johnson grass and blue thistle. Carlos made out the faint shape of the former lane that curved around a small stagnant pond lined with cattails and bull rush, heading toward an abandoned barn. Faded, broken-down sections of plank fencing peeked out above the knee-high grasses in the field, a bleak reminder of a farm long since left to ruin.

He eased the van through the weed-choked field around to the back of the old barn and got out. Both barn doors had rotted and fallen away from their rollers. Slabs of plank siding were split and badly weathered, and the dark rust that crusted over the original tin roof made it clear there was no prospect for recovery.

A quick reconnaissance inside revealed the stale remains of a farmer's previous life. An ancient pickup truck, a prime candidate for restoration in some earlier day, was parked at the far end of the center aisle, windows cracked, four tires flat from dry-rot. A haphazard inventory of household items had been discarded randomly throughout the stalls: an old wringer washing machine, the cabinet shell of a console TV, derelict furniture picked clean by varmints looking for nesting material. Vintage hand tools, harnesses, mule tack, all abandoned, hanging on stall posts, infested with rot or blue mold. A long-ago life had simply given up.

The stillness of the barn unnerved him, the dead silence a stark contrast to the ragged clamor of the ride along the rutted lane. Once the ringing in his ears dissipated he returned to the van and switched on the ignition. He leaned back against the seat and released a long sigh as he analyzed their prospects.

Finding an out-of-the-way spot like this with good cover was a temporary solution. If they got caught now with a kidnapped girl their fate was sealed, a death sentence—lethal injection, electric chair, or whatever method the great state of Georgia used to legally take a life. He was not interested in testing any of them. As his eyes made one final sweep back across the field toward the tree line and the county road beyond, a grin crawled onto his lips when his view settled on the stagnant pond a hundred feet away.

Chapter 6

GRAINGER FOLLOWED the van along the county road at a safe interval. As the road narrowed and the curves drew closer together, the guttural roar of his Harley Davidson was becoming more of a problem, resonating off isolated stands of forest.

When he rounded one tight bend he tensed. The van was stopped in the road less than the length of a football field away, red brake lights glowing like a warning flare. Grainger braked hard and steered his bike off the right shoulder into a fence line choked with honeysuckle, and hit the kill switch. He held his breath for several seconds until the van's brake lights went out and it pulled left off the road.

He waited before he eased his bike back onto the pavement. When he got close enough he made out the remains of the abandoned farmhouse. The van had disappeared. He stopped on the yellow centerline of the road and picked out the trail of broken knee-high grass in the lane. His squinting eyes traced the van's path as it curved around the house and disappeared into the woods. Finally he caught what he was looking for: a brief glimpse of brake lights blinking through the undergrowth.

He pulled into the yard and nosed the front wheel of his bike into an overgrown honeysuckle thicket growing wild at the base of a stately loblolly pine. When he switched off the ignition the sound of his cycle evaporated into the stillness of rural Georgia.

Quarters were getting closer and he couldn't afford to ride up on them. Communications were shot. Even if he could flag down a random motorist on this remote county road, alerting the police would take time. The girl in the van was out of time.

The unfolding crisis had taken on a life of its own, un-choreographed, feeding on its own energy like others he had observed before in a life past. As he pictured her, helpless and vulnerable, his eyes closed against his will and vivid scenes from an earlier time began to rush in—sights, sounds, smells, one after the other, all of them unbidden, ghosts flaring alive, familiar figures parading out of a former life in living color, until finally a devious jolt of energy completely took him over and he was back there with them, as if he'd never left.

There was no way he could have done anything more to save them.

He adjusted the focus on his binoculars from the safety of a rocky hillside while he observed the young men of the village 120 meters away, playing volleyball in spotty patches of snow beside the makeshift mosque.

The intelligence he sent back was accurate. Quandil was not an enemy haven. A rural village, families, nothing more.

His binoculars drifted: Shamal trouncing his cousin at dominoes next to a barrel fire while kerosene and wood smoke offered modest protection against the mountain chill.

It was logical for Command to suspect Saddam's deserters might seek refuge in a remote location this far up in Kurdistan, but his intelligence proved them wrong.

His favorites, Hanifa and Sabeen, the youngest with whom he had grown so close during his week-long reconnaissance carefully disguised with lies, were inside with the rest of the women in smoky rooms preparing a meal of yogurt and flatbread with fresh honey.

His report was detailed, precise. No trace of Republican Guard. No soldiers. No equipment. No weapons.

But jaded men in safe rooms, comforted by cold drinks and warm meat, found it easier to play it safe, their strategic war games staged on a colorful map board. It was too convenient convincing themselves that blood and flesh were collateral damage.

He did all he could. Still he should warn them.

They were simple people. They had honor. Better than him.

At least give them time to run.

He weighed duty and orders and balanced them against life. Then a shudder at the swoosh of the drone when it wiped out the village while he watched safely 120 meters away. Once the dust and smoke settled, the stone and mud homes reduced to rubble, the clothing and rugs and pottery and animals and people all reduced to cinders, returned to the earth, it was too late to decide anything. He and they, made different forever.

When he blinked open, he was sitting on his motorcycle. Hanifa and Sabeen smiled at him from a distance offering comforting reassurance, no longer in judgment. Still, their message was clear: with forgiveness came responsibility.

He unbuckled his left saddlebag and dug to the bottom. His hands found the comfortable shape of the Colt 1911 45-caliber semi-automatic pistol, a treasured gift from his grandfather, stained with memories from that hero's own war. A loose 8-round magazine in the rosewood grip was loaded, as always, with hollow-point rounds. He firmed it home and retracted the bolt, chambering the first round and tucked the pistol into the back of his jeans. One extra magazine went into his pocket.

He had already turned over necessary questions. Was she still alive? Number of captors? Weapons? How to divide them? Everything an unknown. He'd have to take whatever the situation presented, like they trained him. The element of surprise was his but if it came down to a gun fight a showdown with bullets flying could be dangerous. Collateral damage. *Maybe the Colt shouldn't be his only response.*

He unzipped one duffle bag strapped to the back of his seat. He rummaged around for a moment and fished out a wrapped object. He laid it on the bike seat and unfolded the cloth covering. The survival knife slid willingly out of its sheath. He admired it briefly, an old friend he had not visited in awhile. The 8-inch long stainless steel blade, hollow-ground with sawback serrations on the spine glinted in the late afternoon sunlight. Its stock handle was wrapped with layers of abrasive tape to improve the grip. The cutting edge had been honed razor-sharp during empty nights as he stared into a campfire lost in despair.

It had taken lives before. Holding it again renewed his resolve. Hanifa and Sabeen had not chosen their destiny, yet he had failed them. The girl in the van was too young to have to meet them so soon.

Grainger pulled his dog tags over his head and dropped them into the saddlebag. They would be too noisy. Unfastening his wide leather belt he fished it through the twin slits in the knife sheath and closed the snap that held the weapon in place. A dozen long strides and he disappeared into the woods.

Chapter 7

THE GIANT STARED at the girl cowering face down on the blanket. He was ready.

Carlos fished a warm beer out of the styrofoam cooler and killed it, then grabbed another. It would make his job easier. As he raised the can for another swallow the giant took it out of Carlos' hand and dribbled some on the back of Julie Oliver's neck. The liquid startled her and she swung around to brush it away. As her eyes adjusted to the filtered light in the van she saw the three men standing over her.

"Guess you picked the wrong time to be walking yo' dog," Carlos said, a crooked smile coming to him.

The girl looked away to get her bearings and scanned the back of the van: cold steel side panels with vulgar images and graffiti scrawled in magic marker, personal items hanging on metal side ribs like ghoulish Halloween accessories, food bags and wrappers scattered. Graphic reminders that there was no escape. A chamber of despair. Something terrible was going to happen, she sensed that now, and she couldn't imagine how she was going to endure it.

Carlos knelt down in front of the girl. "You have a name?" he said as he reached to stroke her hair. She jerked away, terrified at his touch. She looked at him for the first time, a leather-toned young man with coarse angular features, his shoulders and neck a cluttered canvas of crudely inked tattoos. A mop of spiked hair bleached white was held aloft by a red leather headband. She avoided his wild eyes and the darting tic of nervous energy that telegraphed chemical overload.

Carlos withdrew a black-handle knife from his pocket. When he pressed the button the blade switched out of the base with a frightening click. Her eyes widened, almost beyond their capacity. He inched toward her, the knife blade in front of her face. She tried to back away but the walls of the van left her no room for escape. In vain she turned her face sideways to gain some distance from the blade. Carlos moved the knife closer and asked again, "Do . . . you . . . have . . . a . . . name?"

Breath rushed out of her body. She tried to speak but her lips only quivered. Her mouth formed the word but the sound wouldn't come. Finally, fueled by fear and desperation she focused on the knife blade and closed her eyes. "J-Julie," she whispered, followed by an uncontrolled trembling.

"Julie!" exclaimed Carlos, smiling and backing away as if he had just been given the correct answer in class. He allowed the blade to swing back into the handle and stood up. "Whaddya think," he said, arms crossed, a smug look at the large man, "you like that name?"

"Yeah, I like the name," said the giant, his eyes fixed on the girl. He kneeled down, planting three hundred seventy pounds of loosely bundled fat in front of her.

The man who grabbed her. She smelled him now. For the first time she got a clear look: an oversized, misshapen bald head, black mustache and goatee, an enormous, glandular body, and like the driver, his arms and neck blighted with crude, vulgar tattoos. As he leaned his face, scarred by acne, closer to her she recoiled from his breath. With a sweaty hand he pulled one of her legs out in front of her and removed the one remaining sandal and tossed it aside.

Lavon fidgeted, dreading the tortuous ordeal he knew was coming. He never had the stomach for this kind of torment, not the way it came so easily for the other two. Still, it was the price he had to pay for being a Lord. He nervously shifted his weight and looked away at the walls and ceiling of the van.

The giant reached two large hands toward her belly and pulled at the button of her cutoff jeans. She tried to push him away but his strength was indefensible. She felt a nauseous wave roiling through her, screaming for him to stop, kicking, her hands scratching and clawing at his. Useless. He unzipped her and hooked his fingers into the top of her shorts and yanked on them, violently jerking her whole body away from the side of the van. The force flung her neck backward. He made several quick, rough yanks, finally tugging her jeans down to her knees. Rough hands and fingernails scratched her legs. Then he stood up, lifting her in the air, and yanked her pants off in a final wrenching motion. As soon as she dropped to the floor she pulled her bare legs, bloody and scratched, back under her body and coiled into a ball on the blanket.

He moved on her again, a clumsy reach toward her stomach. Again she tried to fend off huge hands, flailing with her arms, frantic, but her efforts were useless. He jerked the bottom of her yellow t-shirt upward, enshrouding her face and binding her arms. With one powerful stroke, he ripped the shirt in half, tearing it away from her body, along with one of her earrings. Her ear began to bleed.

She grabbed at one edge of the blanket and tried to cover herself while three animals watched.

The giant stood up, hovering over her and reached for his zipper when Carlos' voice stopped him. "What you doing?"

The giant hesitated, his eyes fixed on the girl, then he glanced at Carlos. Meek uncertainty flooded his face. Carlos glared back with the dominant presence that had carried him to the top of a ruthless street gang. He said nothing, his sinister charisma on full display. He knew how to manipulate them all, especially the ones with a limited capacity for thought. Even now he felt no intimidation at the prospect of confronting a man-child more than twice his size.

"You'll get your turn," he said flatly.

The giant sullenly moved aside. After a few seconds a smile crept onto Carlos' lips like venom. "Hold her down."

A blade of despair ran through her. She tried to avoid their grasp and as Lavon and the large man slid her out into the van's floor her screams flooded the barn. When Carlos began to unbuckle his belt Julie Oliver whimpered a brief muted cry, then bellowed one final primal scream for help, one she knew would not be answered.

Chapter 8

GRAINGER RACED in a running crouch across the final 40 yards of open field. An overgrown thicket of briar snagged his jeans with every stride. When he reached the barn he stooped and squinted through gaps in the warped oak siding as his eyes adjusted from sunlight to shade—no movement, no one in the driver's seat. He pulled out the Colt and slipped around the back.

Inside the barn door he scooted along the left side of the van and darted his head into the bottom corner of the open driver's window. In the back of the van two men were staring at the floor while a bald head bobbed behind the rear seat. *Three.* When the tall one gave an order the girl's screams exploded into the silence of the barn. *No more time.*

He whirled and grabbed a loose tobacco stick in the stall behind him, then stepped back and flung it into the loft where it clattered on the oak plank floor.

Carlos was unbuttoning his jeans when he heard the rattle overhead, barely audible over the girl's screams. "What the fuck was that?" He looked up toward the sound even though all he could see was metal roof.

"What?" Lavon yelled, as he held the struggling girl. "Some fucking cat or owl or somethin'. Get this over with!"

Carlos' instincts wouldn't let him ignore the sound. They *were* out in the sticks. But even if it was a barn animal, he hadn't fought his way up the chain to become *lider* by taking chances.

"Lavon. Check it out. Make it quick."

"Check it out? You want me to go chasing a fucking barn cat?" he said, as the girl continued to struggle. "Ain't nothing out there."

"Just do it," he said, zipping his pants back up and wiping the back of his arm across his mouth.

Lavon relinquished his grip to the giant and sullenly slinked over to the side door and rolled it back. He stepped out onto the dirt floor and craned his neck up toward the loft, sparsely stocked with broken piles of mildewed hay. A galaxy of swirling dust motes glittered in shafts of sunlight streaming through the gaps in the barn roof. He cursed and glanced back in the direction of the open barn door where a worn 2x4 slat ladder was anchored to the first stall. He stalked over to the ladder and started to climb.

He never saw the knife when it plunged into his side. A powerful hand covered his mouth from behind to muffle the cry. Grainger forced the blade deeper, manipulating it with surgical precision, the razor edge slicing through the sides of the stomach, blood vessels, kidney, until the tip severed the vena cava. The struggle was brief. Within seconds the victim lost consciousness while blood pulsed and filled his abdominal cavity until his heart stopped pumping. Grainger dragged the flaccid body around the back of the van into an empty stall. With a discarded feed sack he brushed out the drag marks and the blood trail.

"Lavon! What's the fuck's taking you so long?" Carlos yelled out the open van door. No response. A second call, again greeted with the silence of the barn.

"What the fuck? . . ."

He glared at the giant holding the girl down, glassy eyes fixed on her half naked body. "Don't do *nothin'* 'till I get Lavon's ass back in here," he said, buckling his belt. "*Nothin', you hear me!*"

He stepped out of the van and looked left into the shadowy midsection of the barn. Through the dusty haze he saw only stall fronts and broken-down reminders of a farmer's life. It was all foreign to him, the stale, organic smell of rough sawn timbers, moldy hay, rotting leather, abandoned to the years. He stepped back and looked up into the loft. No sign of Lavon.

"Motherfucker!"

He wheeled and headed outside. The instant he emerged into sunlight the ratcheted click of a pistol hammer locking into place resonated in his left ear. He stopped still. Then a slow turn toward the sound. He was staring down the barrel of a semi-automatic pistol, hammer cocked, brushed steel inches from his eye. So close he could almost see the leading end of the hollow-point bullet in the pistol's oiled chamber, a tiny rocket capable of bringing his life to a messy end.

Patrick Grainger's expression was as hard as his weapon. No trace of emotion. After a moment of mutual understanding he brought his free index finger in front of his lips and slowly wagged his head side to side. Carlos watched as Grainger deftly transferred the gun to his left hand and reached down to his belt with his right. He unsnapped the knife and brought it up alongside his face, the sunlight highlighting the blood-stained blade, an announcement. He didn't blink nor change his expression.

"Turn around," Grainger whispered.

Carlos hesitated. Rotating only his eyeballs in the sockets of his skull he glanced at the knife, then back to Grainger. "You gonna cut me anyway?"

Grainger raised one eyebrow and moved the end of the pistol barrel closer to Carlos' right eye. "I won't ask you twice." He indicated, this time with the knife, to turn around. Carlos complied, then felt the end of the gun barrel seated against his head as Grainger closed the gap between them.

When Grainger raised the knife edge to Carlos' throat the razor edge against the man's Adam's apple drew a trickle of blood.

"It's sharper than it looks," he whispered into Carlos' ear. "If you want to live . . . on the ground." He released the hammer on the Colt and tucked it into the small of his back.

* * * * *

The bloody violence from Carlos' past, the turf wars and power struggles, the psychotic hatred between unbalanced adversaries with nothing to lose, had already exposed firsthand the gory power of a sharp blade, slicing through flesh. Carlos knew exactly what the knife could do. But the drugs coursing through his system powered a false sense of invincibility and emboldened his decision.

He had already sized up his opponent—an older man, possibly a hunter or farmer, or from the bandana, a glory-seeking biker. The man would be no match for Carlos' own deceptive strength and sharper reflexes.

More importantly, Carlos couldn't ignore the inevitable consequences of a kidnapping and attempted rape on his resume. There was no way he was willing to sit strapped into an industrial-sized chair while reporters and friends of the family on the other side of the glass flashed fake sympathy or cheered with blood lust for revenge as they watched him take his last breath.

As he knelt, his left arm sprang upward. In that split-second he seized the wrist holding the knife and locked onto it with a vice-like grip. As his two hands pulled against one he slowly drew the knife away from his own throat, his biceps straining and winning against the weakening leverage of his assailant's arm.

* * * * *

Grainger's reactions were immediate—and unanticipated—a lesson learned too late by former adversaries that no longer lived to recount the events. His left hand grabbed a handful of blonde hair and jerked Carlos' head backward. In a simultaneous motion he hooked his left leg around Carlos' ankles as a pivot and lurched forward, a violent surge, forcing his own body hard against the younger man.

Separate, distinct movements, each one like an isolated instrument in a symphony. When played individually they offered little value to the performance. When joined together in a complete score they delivered concordant perfection in this concert of death.

As Carlos lost his balance and stumbled forward, the laws of physics and the mechanical relationships of both bodies took on new dimensions. Angles of arms and legs were altered, points of leverage shifted, interactive positions between body parts transformed, until Carlos' iron grip on Grainger's right arm began to loosen, as Grainger knew it would, and he fell forward, releasing his hold completely.

In that instant the blade once again came alive, a free-floating instrument of carnage recalling old memories stained with blood and chaos. In one swift, unrepentant swipe Grainger drew the knife across the rapist's throat. A savage cut, severing carotid arteries and slicing through the trachea. No cry for help, only the gurgle of blood filling his throat.

As he felt the man's final tremors Grainger remained stoic, his eyes empty, betraying no emotion when the wave from the past appeared and washed over him. The smell of fear, the sensation of warm blood pulsing over his hands, a desperate last gasp, the one final breath that would never come, all triggers powerful enough to birth a metamorphic flashback he hadn't prepared for. In one ruthless instant the familiar rush of the kill had again taken him back to a dangerous place and another time.

Now the final struggle was nearly over, this Fedayeen fighter writhing beneath him. Nothing but the predictable last reflexes, legs kicking through the sand and rubble. Grainger despised these medieval zealots, animals with no conscience. Still he had given this one a chance. All the coward had to do was comply with a soldier's simple order and he could live. The traitor had refused his generous offer.

Grainger held the terrorist's face down in the hot sand with his free hand, suppressing all sounds. Finally he rose up from the twitching body as it released one last gasp and went still. Sergeant Patrick Grainger, Special Forces 82nd Airborne Division, wiped his hands on the dead man's pants, then did the same with the bloody knife blade before he sheathed it, and turned toward the last combatant.

Chapter 9

GRAINGER PULLED OUT his Colt and took slow, measured steps through the rock and sand as he approached the last remaining enemy fighter from the rear.

As he neared the open door he heard grunting sounds, the heavy breathing of a man laboring, primitive noises mixed with the hysterical screaming of a young voice. He darted his head into the open doorway. An enormous man with a misshapen bald head stood with his back to the door—naked.

Animals! Barbarians, all of them!

Grainger leveled the Colt at the back of the heathen's head, his finger against the trigger, when he caught a flash of motion, a girl in the shadows, screaming. Her eyes were closed, refusing to look at the ponderous body hovering over her, layered with obscene tattoos and a fresh film of sweat. But it was the unusual tattooed words on the man's neck that made Grainger flinch.

Florida State?

He felt a jolt. One peculiar body marking on the heretic in front of him, clearly a gross aberration in their cauldron of religious fanatics. It forced a hard blink and a second look.

A young girl.

Another discomforting shot, edgier than the first, and he gave his head a vigorous shake. Then his eyes darted to another object that didn't belong.

A styrofoam cooler?

He faltered and surveyed his surroundings, another jolt, hard-hitting this time as a vaguely familiar shape and color began to fill the picture.

A gray van.

His eyes swept the scene and a full-throated reality emerged, shocking him back to the present and a dimly lit, musty barn. He glanced down at his dusty jeans, then back at the stage set in front of him. His mind swirled while rational thoughts settled into place until it finally made sense again, why he was here.

He cleared his head and stepped into the open doorway, his pistol leveled, and cocked the hammer. It drew no reaction. His first impulse was to fire. But the thought of the girl having to witness a cold-blooded killing made him stop. He heard his own voice shouting.

"Gun aimed at your head. Back away from the girl."

The giant had worked himself into a lust-filled frenzy but the warning stopped him. He slowly turned around, still stooped under the van roof, his erection in full view. He stared at the pistol pointed at his head and raised his hands as much as the metal roof would allow.

Grainger wagged the gun. "Out."

The giant stared at the gun for a moment, more in surprise than fear, then inched toward the door of the van. As he stepped out onto the dirt floor the van's chassis rose with a metallic creak. Grainger backed away, the Colt leveled at the large man's forehead, and allowed him to circle away from the vehicle until they were facing each other beside the stall walls.

The giant had regained his senses and his erection was shrinking. "What now, big man?" he finally asked. He looked over Grainger's shoulder toward the open barn door. "Where's Carlos?"

"Gone to a better place."

"You kill him?"

"Suicide. He was feeling guilty." He shot a quick glance left at the girl, curled in a fetal position on the floor of the van. Then back at the man. Pat Grainger searched for words but none came. "Her name's Julie," the giant said finally, a hateful grin crawling across his face. "It don't matter to me how old they are. They say I'm crazy, you know."

The giant smirked, bolder now. His hands were still up in a sign of mock surrender when Grainger raised the aim on his pistol to the man's forehead. His right index finger found the trigger.

The huge man dropped his smirk. "You don't want to do that, pal. Even a psycho like me it'd still be murder. You wanna go to the goddamn pen to keep me from fucking somebody's daughter?"

Patrick Grainger reflected on the consequences. But his decision had been made long before this moment. Just not the details.

Until now.

"Somehow," he said, his demeanor calm, "I believe I could convince a jury of loving parents that this was the right thing to do."

Everything happened quickly. In one fluid motion Grainger lowered his aim on his pistol toward the giant's mid-section. The man's eyes followed the path of the gun barrel, then opened wide. Grainger smiled when he pulled the trigger, four times in rapid succession. The bullet pattern was tight, accurate, a near-perfect square. Four hollow-point rounds tore into the giant's male anatomy and it exploded in a gore of blood and flesh. The larger pieces dropped onto the dirt floor while smaller scraps of tissue sprayed onto the stall walls or plastered themselves in bright red on his hairy, corpulent legs.

Despite the early pain the man looked down in shock at the blood flowing freely from his groin, pulsing in even spurts while his heart emptied him. He dropped to his knees and grabbed at the large hole in his crotch with fleshy hands. It didn't register at first why he was finding nothing but blood, bone, and shredded flesh. As the intensity of the pain finally ratcheted up, signaling the certainty of it all, he uttered a submissive whimper and reached down to the dirt floor and picked up something familiar. Life continued to gush from his body, spilling through his fingers, pulsing out onto the dirt in a pool of dark crimson. A grand opening, some might say, one that seemed appropriate for the occasion.

The giant looked one last time at the fleshy object in his hand, puzzled, then back up at Grainger, the helplessness of the young girl mirrored in his own eyes just before he toppled face down onto the blood soaked dirt.

Chapter 10

HE WATCHED the man's final breaths with cold detachment. Sergeant Patrick Grainger, Special Forces 82nd Airborne Division, showed no sign of remorse, embracing the raw satisfaction that always came from the kill. His breathing was calm, steady. Another successful mission. He stood over the body, eyes empty, feeling nothing.

The sharp crack of the pistol's four rounds was the post-traumatic trigger this time. It had taken him over again in an instant, transforming him, and like minutes earlier, he had not seen it coming. Despite his training and his ruthless approach to combat and the violence that goes with it, like all the rest of them his subconscious was no match for the indefensible mind games that war had played on him over time. It overpowered him, summoning primordial energy from memories he spent years trying to leave behind.

Now the energy was growing unchecked, his surroundings once again taking on new properties, no longer stale dirt on the barn floor but powdery sand, stringing across the sun-baked desert of northern Iraq. Aging oak timbers and plank siding of the barn had vanished altogether, replaced by a barren landscape: rock-strewn mountains, desert scrub, withering heat, and a blinding clear sky. He approached the twitching body and his desert combat boots nudged it, one final check.

A sound from behind caught his attention. A whimper.

Maybe a local they had missed in the first sweep.

Their orders were harsh but clear—eliminate them all. No survivors meant no witnesses. No witnesses meant fewer American soldiers would die. Cold-hearted decisions, but necessary, even for a professional like him.

He turned and followed the sound toward the open door of the enemy vehicle. His pistol hung loose at his side, his finger laid flat against the trigger guard.

Duty.

At the van door he raised his pistol and darted into the line of sight.

They had missed one. A local. Partially clothed, on the floor of the vehicle. Crying.

He felt a pang of guilt. She seemed too young. It was times like this when he felt the gut check. Sometimes his own chain of command was barely more civilized than the archaic barbarians that roamed this country justifying death and oppression in their blind, self-serving quest to appease Allah. Still, duty. His finger instinctively moved to the trigger.

Then a bright flash of color on the floor in front of her interrupted the flow.

Yellow.

He blinked.

Glitter in the folds.

The girl was cowering, her eyes wide as headlights at the pistol pointed at her face. Through the fog the sounds engaged him. A girl's frantic voice, begging.

Yellow.

Black-and-white.

Tiny dog.

A vigorous shake of the head. The energy inside him refused

to let go, relentless, viral, a toxic spirit determined to keep itself alive.

Something not right.

Another shake of his head, an uncomfortable hitch, scenes darting, out of focus. The negative energy fluttered, then faded as the baking desert dissolved, replaced once again by the soft shadows and cool, musty haze of the barn. The girl's pleas for mercy came at him now in gasping English.

Pure reflex, a product of his training, he surveyed his surroundings, glancing left out the door of the barn—a body lying in the dirt. Then to his right—a huge man, bloated and naked, soaking in a pool of blood. And past the giant, in the shadows of the barn, moldy tools, an old truck.

The maelstrom inside his head fought back, a last-ditch resistance to his attempts to exorcise it. The hated adversaries—the then and the now—battled for control in a convoluted search for reality. He lowered the gun and turned away from the van. He dropped to one knee and racked the side of the pistol against his temple, again and again, a desperate effort to still the demons that had taken over.

Then he remembered.

He rose and turned back toward the girl as fresh realities began to take over, a sharp jolt, like grabbing loose electric wires. A tortured past had almost caused him to do an unspeakable thing. He recalled it all now, the girl in the van, where she had come from, why he had followed her here.

And he had no idea what to do next.

He turned away from the girl, his body stretching, arms crossed and wrapped tight behind his head, and he began pacing in a tight circle, searching for guidance. Finally he stopped, facing her, and expelled a huge sigh of relief, one final discharge of all the remaining negative energy that had completely taken him over.

Time to regroup.

He tucked his pistol away. After everything that had gone down he knew she could trust no one, especially a stranger. And he was another stranger. No, worse—a stranger that had pointed a loaded pistol at her head.

As he took inventory of the situation he reminded himself that his coarse appearance was not exactly a vision of good will. The blood stains on his jeans didn't help. He pulled off the bandana and tucked it into his hip pocket, then tried to smooth his tangled hair back with his hands. Not much else he could do for now. He eased over to the van and gingerly sat on the edge of the opening.

She was still in a fetal position, in her underwear, shivering. His first aid was rusty but not forgotten. He looked into the back of the van and retrieved a crumpled green blanket. He recalled the words of the last dead man, and after he cleared his throat twice, he called her by name, softly.

"Julie?"

There was no response.

"Julie, it's over now."

He waited a few seconds and continued. "The bad guys, they're all gone." Pause. "I know I scared you, but it was a mistake."

He knew it was much more than a mistake.

"It's important for you to get warm, to keep from going into shock. I've got to cover you with this blanket." He had no idea if she heard any of it.

A hesitation, then he turned and scooted on his knees toward her with the blanket held in front of her to shield her body. She recoiled. Another whimper escaped her mouth but he had no choice. He gently wrapped the blanket around her, then laid her back gently on the floor and let her gather it tight.

He rummaged through the debris scattered in the back. He

found a hiking pack stained with what looked like blood. A plastic canteen was attached. He opened the canteen and poured some of the contents into his hand and tasted it—water, warm but fresh.

Despite her attempts to resist him he raised her upright and leaned her against the wall of the van. With the blanket as cover only her head and neck were visible and her shivering had slowed. She glanced at him, terrified, self-conscious, then back down to the floor.

"Julie, this is water. You need to drink, as much as you can."

She looked up, wary. He turned his face away and extended the canteen back at her with one arm. Cautiously she reached her hand through the seam in the blanket and took it, then raised it to her lips, first a sip, then several gulps to quench her thirst as droplets trickled down her chin. She set the canteen on the floor.

He took it and screwed on the top. He'd collected his thoughts by now. Waiting wasn't going to make it any easier.

"Julie. My name is Patrick." He waited. "I only know your name because one of those bad men said it."

No reaction. He was miles out of his element.

"I know I don't look like it," he said, dropping his head, his voice as tactful as he could manage, "but I'm . . . I'm one of the good guys."

The emotional depth he had once shared freely with Allison was in short supply, carried away in the smoke when his life took a hopeless dive into despair. Now here he was, stumbling forward, trying to find common ground with a traumatized young girl that had just gone through an experience he could never begin to understand.

He searched for the right thing to say but nothing came, so like any team leader laying out the details of the next mission he began rattling off a clumsy list of bullet points, his head nodding to punctuate each one. "Julie, I promise not to hurt you. I'll get you back to your parents. I won't do anything to make you feel uncomfortable. Once we get you—"

"Did you kill them?" she interrupted. Her eyes no longer avoided him. Ruthless candor, and it caught him off guard. She stared at him, asking for the truth, unseasoned with evasive disclaimers. The truth. Nothing less. After what she had been through he decided she was entitled to that.

"Yes . . . I did."

She glared at him, no trace of judgment. "They're all dead?"

"Yes." He dipped his head slightly, then looked at her, solemn, without apology, "I did what I had to."

She studied him for what seemed like a long time before he saw her eyebrows furrow, an awkward combination of relief and revenge, one that seemed inappropriate for an innocent young girl.

"Good," she said, her voice heavy with conviction. Then she burst into an involuntary, heaving sob. After several seconds she recovered, cut herself off, and wiped her face with the edge of the blanket.

Chapter 11

HE GAVE Julie Oliver time to gather her bearings. They sat without speaking for a while. When he looked up he saw her staring at his hands. A quick glance and he understood—his right forearm and wrist were crusting with blood. Self-consciously he uncapped the canteen, leaned out the doorway, and splashed water over the red-brown stain on his arm and gave it a quick once-over with a rag on the floor of the van. "Sorry."

When he settled back against the door jamb he saw that she had retreated back against the wall of the van. Finally she managed a trembling question. "Are you going to shoot me?"

It jarred him. "Why would I . . . why would you even think that?"

Her eyes darted from his face to the floor behind him. "I saw the gun, in your belt."

He resisted the urge to reach back and check for it. Finally, a twitch and a half-smile. "That was for those guys," he said, tilting his head toward the bodies.

"You pointed it at me." Her statement was soft, more like a question.

He looked away.

"Please, you don't have to," she said.

"I know, I know . . . I mean . . . I'm not," he stammered. He realized how close he had come to that very thing and a chill ran through him. After his prideful resistance to every attempt at PTSD counseling from those know-it-all Army doctors and psychotherapists, *could they have been right after all?*

He debated for a second before he retrieved the Colt from behind his back. Julie's eyes widened. Without comment Grainger held the pistol out in front of him where she could see every move. He released the magazine and slipped it into his pocket. He then pulled the slide back and the single round in the chamber jumped out onto the blanket. He picked it up and placed it in Julie's hand and smiled as he closed her fingers around it.

"Okay? Let's just get you back to your parents. Work with me here."

She looked at the single bullet, then back at him. "OK."

His next question embarrassed him. "Do you know what they did with, uh, your clothes?" The question seemed forward, invasive, but she was already looking around the floor.

"My jeans are over there," she said pointing through the fold in the blanket to the back of the van. "But they tore my shirt."

He retrieved her denim shorts, shook them out, and tossed them onto the blanket in front of her. He emptied the first duffel bag. It had a musty smell, the clothes oversized. The big man wouldn't need them anymore. The second and third bags yielded little more than wrinkled t-shirts and jeans. He finally pulled out one t-shirt that looked unworn, navy blue emblazoned in white with a simple cartoon and a name—Bert's Bar and Grille. He tossed it to her. He zipped open the hiking pack and found a windbreaker bearing the logo for Auburn University. It didn't belong to any of the men lying dead outside the van. It would have to do. There were no shoes to fit her but he dug out a pair of white socks, also too big. At least they would keep her from having to go barefoot on the way back.

He stepped outside the van and slid the door shut. As soon as she was dressed she knocked. When he slid the door back he gave her the once-over and ventured a weak attempt to lighten the mood. "A real fashion plate."

Even after all she had gone through she couldn't stop herself from flashing the universal adolescent squint-and-smirk.

Grainger turned toward the back of the van. He dug a hairbrush out of the pack and handed it to her. As she worked on her tangled hair, he leaned back against the door jamb and looked upward, then closed his eyes and released a palpable sigh of relief. A terrible ordeal was behind her, at least the worst of it. She was safe. The healing would have to come later.

After several seconds of introspection he opened his eyes. She was watching him and it made him uncomfortable.

"You feeling any better?" he asked.

"I guess," she said as she continued to watch him.

"You still scared?"

She looked away. "A little."

"I'm sorry about all this," he said, his right hand flicking toward the barn stalls.

"I know."

He handed her the canteen and a candy bar he had found in the pack. "Drink a little more before we head back. The candy will give you energy."

As she tore open the wrapper he looked away into the barn and tried to scope out how the rest of the day might play out. The State Patrol would be out in force. Her parents would be catatonic with fear. Julie *seemed* to be holding up well, but the grief counselors would know best how to handle that. The trip back could easily produce an encounter with the State Patrol but he'd have to play that by ear.

The intensity of his planning was cut short by Julie's voice. "Do you have any kids?"

His brow furrowed as he glanced back at her. He wondered if he really heard the question right. Coming from her, given the circumstances, it seemed innocent. Still it was out of the blue and it disarmed him. Today's tragedy had been a traumatic experience but it was all about her. Only her. *His* life had no place in the discussion. Then again, as he studied it, the ordeal had introduced them, made each of them an unexpected part of the other's life, a circumstance neither had chosen. She had asked. Maybe she *was* entitled to know something about him since they were now connected by fate in an unplanned relationship borne from disaster and response. He braced himself for the answer, one that would give him equal ownership in the struggle.

"I used to."

Her eyes requested more information, but nothing came.

"How many?" she said.

"A daughter," he breathed gently, "just one."

After several seconds, "How old is she?"

He wasn't seeing Julie now. Only Aimee, laughing, spitting as she kicked in her crib, reaching with pudgy, outstretched arms for the brightly colored rings draped between the rails. He saw her in Allison's arms, the eyes of mother and child locked, exchanging a rare moment of unconditional love. He used to find them both in his dreams as he tossed on a creaky, uncomfortable cot on a far-away desert outpost, sand and heat filling up space where air belonged. Now he was having trouble finding the words. There was no way to explain it and give it justice. Not here. Maybe not in a lifetime. Still, she had asked. Finally he looked at her and gave in with an honest answer of surrender.

"She died. When she was a baby."

She started to speak, then held her words. Too many questions, at least for now. Finally, she said the only thing that made sense to her.

"I'm sorry."

The exchange was unexpected, an awkward, symbiotic connection that neither understood but both seemed to welcome, an unspoken helping of sympathy and respect. A faint smile passed between them.

"Ready to go home?" he asked.

The keys were in the ignition. While he slid the side door shut she climbed in the passenger seat. As he slipped in behind the steering wheel he caught her staring out the side window at the giant face-down in a pool of blood. Both her hands were shaking, gripped in tight fists of rage. She didn't take her eyes off the body when she spoke, her voice hard and unforgiving, "He deserved to die." Then she turned to him with conviction. "You didn't do a bad thing."

He nodded. As he backed the van out of the barn they passed the second body face-down in the grass, swimming in its own pool of crimson. She winced while they turned around in the lane and she started to ask the obvious question but decided against it. The reality of too much death had finally settled in.

The van crawled through the rocky field past the pond and found the opening in the woods. It was a trip she had already traveled but had never seen. She took it all in, putting the pieces together in reverse. Once they emerged into the overgrown front yard the questions finally came.

"How did you get here?"

He stopped the van next to his motorcycle parked in the bushes and pointed.

"You saw them take me?"

He nodded.

"And you followed me?"

"Yes."

"Will my parents still be there?"

"I expect so."

She stared at the motorcycle and pondered for a moment.

"The police will be looking for this truck. They're going to think you're the one that took me."

"I know but we'll work through that. It's the only way back." She pointed to the Harley Davidson.

He winced. "Probably not a good idea."

Her shoulders sagged and she twisted around in her seat, glaring into the back of the van, eyes darting at the blankets, duffle bags, random trash, all reminders of the torturous experience from an hour earlier. She shifted nervously in her seat. "I don't want to ride back in this." She glanced again out the window at the Harley Davidson, then at him. "Please don't make me."

She bored a hole in him, refusing to turn away. He couldn't tell if she was honestly struggling with having to ride in the van but after what she had been through it seemed like a minor concession.

"If we do this you have to hold on tight. You promise?"

She nodded.

When they approached the cycle he pulled his dog tags out of the saddlebag and slipped them back over his neck. The pistol and half-used magazine went back into the bottom of the saddlebag. His denim shirt was stained with blood so he stuffed it into the other saddlebag and fished a clean white t-shirt out of a duffel bag. He pulled the purple bandana out of his back pocket and fitted it back around his head, then straddled the motorcycle and walked it back out onto a flat spot in the yard. The packed gear that was secured to the seats with bungee cords left no room for a rider so he unstrapped them and buried them in the brushy tangle at the base of the tree.

He explained the foot pegs, where to sit, how to hold on, how to keep her legs away from the hot pipes, and then he swung his leg over the bike and seated himself. He held his hand out to her. She took it and stepped onto the peg and swung her leg over too, settling onto the seat behind him wedged snugly between him and the back rest.

"It's gonna be loud," he said, looking back at her.

She gave him the thumbs up.

When he pressed the electronic ignition the motor roared alive and he pulled out onto the county highway accelerating smoothly through five gears.

Chapter 12

THEY BACKTRACKED from the deserted farmhouse to the interstate and glided down the southbound ramp heading toward the rest area. The 5-foot concrete barrier wall that ran continuously for miles down the I-75 median prevented them from crossing over.

When they reached the rest area, isolated on the opposite side the interstate he recognized the blue patrol lights flashing in the rear parking lot. A telescoping satellite antenna jutting up through the pines and water oaks like a metallic giraffe told him a local news station had already arrived. He pointed it out to Julie as they cruised by and she threw an excited wave that no one would see. He smiled and continued on to the nearest exit a mile south.

They crossed back over and re-entered the northbound lane. In less than a minute he was decelerating into the rest area—the scene of the crime. The Georgia State Patrol's response team was gathered in the rear parking lot to avoid the gawking public that continued to drift in unaware of the unfolding tragedy.

He sounded several staccato blasts on his horn and the uniforms turned toward the sound, one by one recalling Julie's description from the incident report. Two officers with shotguns raised their weapons. The rest stared, slack-jawed, pistols holstered, trying to put the pieces together.

Patrick and Julie coasted in at a crawl as the shapeless crowd parted, morphing into a neat circle like a raindrop in a pool, and closed back around them. He came to a stop surrounded by a ring of armed police, the rhythmic reverberation of his Harley punctuating their grand entrance. Finally pistols leaped out of their holsters. He hit the kill switch and the engine went silent, the only sound the distinctive click of cooling tailpipes.

Before anyone could act he dropped his kickstand. Without looking back he held out his right hand over his shoulder to the young girl behind him. Julie Oliver took his hand and stood up on the side pegs. She moved her hands to his shoulders and searched the crowd. Finally she saw her parents leaning against their Suburban, arms locked, praying for a miracle they never expected would come.

"Mom! Dad!" She bounded off the bike and made a record-setting dash for them, both socks flying off, breaking through the police line into her parents' outstretched arms. The smiles and tears were instantly devoured by the news cameras.

A small arsenal was still aimed at Patrick Grainger. No one was sure how to reconcile his coarse biker appearance against the curious fact that he had safely returned a kidnapped girl. The blood on his jeans amped up their concern. He sat on his Harley, calm and conspicuously unaffected by the sudden attention, before he finally surveyed the crowd and a wry smile crept onto his face, "Man, I'd give anything for a Diet Pepsi."

Unamused, two uniforms approached him, pistols drawn. Without prompting he calmly clasped his hands behind his head. While one trooper kept his weapon aimed the second patted him down, unsnapping the leather sheath and sliding out the hunting knife. When he examined it in the sunlight, the bloodstains drew a predictable reaction from the crowd. The patrolmen pulled Patrick's arms behind him and secured them with handcuffs.

A lanky GSP Lieutenant in his 40s moved toward him. The officer made a mental note of the full-color tattoo on the biker's left shoulder: a gold sword and three lightning bolts on a blue shield—*Special Forces, Airborne*. Finally he offered the predictable first question.

"Got a name?"

"Billfold, left hip pocket." The search officer fished it out and withdrew a driver's license and handed it to the Lieutenant.

"Alright, Patrick Grainger, you want to give me your version of what happened here?"

"The girl's name is Julie. Don't know her last. She was walking her dog back there," he indicated with a tilt of his head, "when three low-life's grabbed her. Their intentions were less than honorable."

"And you just happened to be there? Minding your own business?"

"Pretty much. Nobody else saw it. So I followed them. I was hoping to raise backup with my cell phone but I lost it during pursuit."

The Lieutenant recalled the details of the 9-1-1 report. . . . *an un-named male . . . presumably on a motorcycle . . . claims of a kidnapping . . . call ended abruptly . . .*

Patrick continued. "I had no choice. It came down to me doing what I had to, to intervene." He rattled off the sketchy details—the roads, the barn, basic analytics like so many debriefings before.

"So what are we gonna find if we go out there to this farm near Lake Baxter?" the Lieutenant asked.

"Three scum-of-the-earth degenerates disguised as human beings. At least they used to be."

"You killed these three, did you?"

Grainger gave the Lieutenant a steely look. "They terrorized her. Getting ready to rape her. No doubt kill her when they were done." He recalled the look in the eyes of the third man—the giant—mocking, unrepentant. He flinched and his gaze snapped back to the Lieutenant. He was calm now. "I couldn't let them do that."

"That's it?"

"You'll see when you check out the barn." He shot a sly grin at the officer. "I'm betting the girl will give me a good reference."

The Lieutenant considered his response. "Assuming things happened the way you say, you may get a pass. But dammit man, you can't go around killing bad guys because you think they deserve it."

"You think I chose this?"

"Maybe not. But vigilante's not the way to go. You should've called the State Patrol, let the law handle it. There's standard procedure for everything."

"Standard procedure," Patrick replied, nodding thoughtfully, his chin jutting out. "So, if I had followed 'standard procedure' then you probably would've been interviewing me an hour ago about what I saw—van color, plates, physical descriptions, stuff like that?"

"That's the way it works."

"And right about now the third piece of scum would be finishing up his turn at that little girl, or what was left of her, out in that abandoned barn. None of us here would be hearing any of her screams. Or they would have already killed her, tied a rock to her body, thrown it in the pond next to the barn. I guess, all things considered, following standard procedure didn't seem like such a good idea at the time." He paused. "'Course I could be wrong."

A long silence passed between them and the Lieutenant paced while he surveyed his options.

"OK, Patrick Grainger, here's the deal. We're gonna put you in the back of a cruiser and you can direct us to this supposed crime scene. If things are like you say we'd like you to join us for a more in-depth conversation, if you don't mind, in the comfort of the Georgia Highway Patrol Post? Diet Pepsi's all around. That'd give us time to get the girl's version of the events and do a little background check on you."

"Standard procedure," Patrick said.

On the way to the cruiser Patrick made a request. "I'd be grateful it if you'd pick an experienced rider to bring my bike."

Then he remembered. "Oh, there's a 45-caliber Colt in the left saddlebag and a partial magazine. I fired four rounds. You'll find all four of 'em in creep number three, or more likely swimming with his dick on the dirt floor underneath him."

Chapter 13

SIX GEORGIA STATE PATROLMEN surveyed the kill zone in stunned silence. The entourage listened as a handcuffed Patrick Grainger narrated a detailed replay, each body an individual snapshot of the final resolution. The troopers would brag later that the kills had been professional, and that night some of them gave their own sons and daughters an extra hug, privately convinced that vigilante justice might have been just the ticket.

Once the GSP forensics team arrived the Lieutenant ferried Grainger back to the police post outside of Macon. In a secure conference room he removed Grainger's handcuffs and pointed him to a chair. He dropped a file folder onto the table and took a seat across from Grainger while another armed officer stood guard at the door. A secretary brought in a Diet Pepsi for each of them.

"Looks like you've had an exceptional career, *Sergeant*," the Lieutenant said, reading through pages he'd just received. "Some of it Classified." He glanced up. "There's a curious information gap in your service record during the mid nineties?" He waited for a response but got none.

He nodded toward the Special Forces tattoo on Grainger's arm. "Does that explain how you managed to take out those three punks by yourself?"

"Not punks. Psychopaths."

The Lieutenant nodded in agreement. "So, the right place at the right time? Pure coincidence?"

"That's right."

"The 9-1-1 recording does match your story. By the way, we managed to find what's left of your cell phone on the interstate. The SIM card actually survived."

"Any chance I can get it back? There's a few important numbers on it. I'd like to let my employer know why I'm running late," he said as he took a drink.

"Later. We've already called your boss. He actually spoke highly of you. Said a new phone was on him, by the way."

"How long you plan on holding me?"

The Lieutenant ignored the question. "You have a passport?"

"Look, Lieutenant, the only place I'm going is Knoxville. If you talked to my boss you already know that."

"May be. But you killed three men, Grainger. On the surface it appears to be justified. But your, uh . . . methods were, let's just say, extreme." Then his eyebrows raised and a smile sneaked onto his face. "Especially that big'un." His lips pursed and he released a sigh of resignation. "Did that just come to you all of a sudden-like?"

"Everything happened so fast, Lieutenant," he said. "Heat of the moment and all."

The officer's head nodded in mock agreement. "Yeah, yeah, it's just that it may come down to a grand jury's decision on whether to indict you. I'm guessing most of 'em will be parents with no particular soft spot for sex predators. Still, I need to make sure you'll be available, just in case. I don't want to have to explain how you suddenly took off for the south of France."

"They've got great fries. And toast. But I can get those at any Waffle House. Besides, I have family in Kentucky."

His comment triggered a thought and the Lieutenant pulled a page to the top of the pile. His nose scrunched as his head tilted back behind a pair of reading glasses. "Says here your mother's deceased. Father's in a VA assisted care facility in Maryland. One brother in Indiana. Your . . ."

He abruptly stopped. Then he glanced at Grainger with a mixture of sympathy and suspicion, before continuing. ". . . your wife and daughter, also deceased."

He waited for Grainger to react but got only a stone face. "Are your wife and daughter your family?"

Grainger dropped his gaze to the table, silent.

The Lieutenant returned to the report, searching for details, when Grainger spoke up. "You still think I should have followed protocol, Lieutenant?"

The officer's focus on the pages in front of him went empty. Finally he let his pencil fall to the table and rubbed his eyes with tired fingers, then looked Grainger in the eye.

"You and I both know what would have happened to that girl if you had. Can we leave it at that?"

"Fair enough."

A female officer entered the room and laid another page next to the open folder. The Lieutenant read the handwritten information, then placed his elbows on the table and rested his chin on clasped hands. For an uncomfortable time he evaluated the hard man across the table from him.

"I'm probably making a mistake, Grainger, but . . ." He pushed his chair back. "I'll be right back."

When he returned a civilian man and woman followed him into the room. They approached Grainger's side of the table.

"Patrick Grainger," the Lieutenant said, "meet Karen and Randy Oliver—Julie's parents."

Chapter 14

GRAINGER AWKWARDLY shoved his chair back, nearly a stumble, and stood up to face them, then threw a cautious glance at the Lieutenant.

"You were right," the Lieutenant said, "Julie gave you a good reference. She didn't see *all* the grisly details, thank God, but she pretty much confirmed your version of what took place." He glanced at the Olivers. "A meeting like this is a little unusual but these folks were pretty insistent and under the circumstances . . ."

Grainger's mouth was agape as he faced the couple standing in front of him. He did a rapid self-appraisal of his appearance: a t-shirt discolored with sweat from the late afternoon walk-thru at the barn; dirt and blood stains on his jeans; a purple doo-rag on his head that screamed 'renegade biker.' Finally Julie's father broke the ice.

"We didn't get a chance to thank you, Mr. Grainger," Randy Oliver said, his hand extended. Grainger searched for a clean spot on his jeans and wiped his right hand before he accepted Randy's firm handshake, one that didn't seem to want to end.

"*Patrick*," Grainger said, a slight bow of deference. He ventured a tentative smile behind his beard stubble.

"We don't know what to say," Randy said, his emotions firmly planted on his sleeve. "If we'd lost her . . ." He shook his head as he struggled with the thought.

Pat Grainger's right hand was still trapped in Randy Oliver's grip so he touched his left hand to Randy's arm. "Mr. Oliver, I didn't have any choice."

Randy Oliver straightened up. "*Randy*," he said, "Please. Just Randy."

Karen Oliver had waited long enough. She reached across the brace of arms and slipped between the two men and placed both hands on Patrick's upper arms.

"Mr. Grainger—Patrick—I don't know what happened out there," she said, "but they told me, without you our daughter wouldn't be alive." With that her strong front broke down. She slipped her arms under his, laid her head on his chest and embraced him, sweat and blood and all.

Pat's initial discomfort evaporated when he felt the first silent sob and with some hesitation he raised his arms and gently returned the embrace while Randy nodded his approval. It was a long hug. Once it ended Karen stepped back. Her cheeks were streaked with tears. Pat slipped the purple bandana off his head and offered it to her.

"It's clean on the outside . . . kinda," he said, an attempt at a faint smile. Karen couldn't hold back a tiny gasp of laughter before she took it and dabbed at her face and eyes.

"Could I ask how Julie's doing?" Pat said while she finished up.

Randy and Karen gave each other a knowing look. Randy pulled two chairs from under the table and set them directly across from Pat's. The three of them sat down while the Lieutenant eased away and joined the trooper standing against the wall.

"She's actually holding up pretty well," Karen said. "I have no idea how the next few weeks will go, but for now . . ." Her voice picked up some confidence. "We're a close family."

"She was a trouper," Pat said. "She sure as hell didn't hold back how she felt about those . . ." He searched for a sensitive word.

"Rapists?" she said firmly. "Killers? We know what they were. It's OK to say it."

A thoughtful pause passed while Karen looked at her husband. They were here for more than one reason.

"Actually," Karen said, "once we got some hot chocolate in our daughter and she was able to calm down she couldn't stop rambling on about what you did."

"And about some things you two talked about," Randy added.

Pat felt a touch of apprehension.

"She said you told her you're a father too," Karen said.

Pat hesitated before he corrected her. "I was, once."

"Julie said your daughter passed away?" Karen continued, the statement disguised as a question. Her tone was rushed, dispassionate, much like her delivery when she grilled a witness on the stand.

"She died at 14 months," Pat said, expelling an involuntary sigh that filled the room.

"We're really sorry, Patrick," Karen said, before pressing on. "Could I ask how?"

Pat wasn't picking up on the abruptness of her pointed inquiry. He was busy wandering in the past. He'd lived that night over and over for the last twelve years, unable to find solace from all the counselors and pastors that offered hope when there was none. Yet here in the interrogation room of the Georgia State Patrol, knowing that his actions had returned someone else's daughter to them, for the first time it almost seemed easier.

"An accident, a long time ago."

Karen accepted his answer with a detached nod. Her mouth opened again, ready to probe deeper when Pat cut her off and volunteered the rest. "Our house caught on fire back in '02." He turned away from her and his voice broke. "While I was away in Kuwait."

The answer stopped her cold. She shot a mortified look at the Lieutenant who had been quietly reading through Pat's file. He held up the folder and acknowledged Pat's statement with a subtle nod.

Any suspicions Karen and Randy Oliver had about Patrick Grainger's possible involvement in his own daughter's death evaporated in that moment. Their rush to judgment, pegging Grainger as little more than a coarse outlaw biker with killing skills, changed. Randy's apprehensions disappeared as he found himself looking at a man apparently weighed down by a personal torment that rendered him vulnerable.

Karen saw it too. Still, she couldn't help blurting out the next question.

"Your wife . . . ?"

He shook his head.

"Oh, God! Oh, God! I'm so sorry, Patrick." Karen said.

They'd had concerns. How else to find out but to dig for answers? Now she had them.

Pat mercifully changed the subject. "Is there any way you'd consider letting me see Julie, just for a minute? That is, if she's up to it." He glanced over at the Lieutenant for his reaction.

Randy was already stammering through his answer. "Actually, she's been asking if she could see you too. It's just that . . . Well, hell, we just needed to know a little more about you. And about how your daughter . . ." He didn't know how to finish.

Karen saved him with a glance. After eighteen years of marriage and two children they had mastered the art of subtle communication. Her unspoken decision was an easy call. She scooted her chair back. "I'll get her."

The Lieutenant opened the door for her and within seconds Karen returned with Julie, her hands firmly planted on her daughter's shoulders. Brad Oliver trailed behind, making no attempt to hide his curiosity about the man who had killed three men singlehandedly.

Ten feet away Pat Grainger stood up, unprepared for the personal dynamics that could be in play for Julie, even in the safety of the present. He waited for her to say something. She waited for him. Finally, he grinned and made the first move.

"Busy day, huh?"

A tentative smile broke across her face. "Yeah."

She ventured a slow first step toward him, slipping out of her mother's grasp, and closed the gap. Pat leaned down and exchanged a long hug with Julie Oliver, survivor.

"You'll be fine," he whispered in her ear. "Give it time."

When they pulled apart, she looked to her Dad for reassurance, then back at her Mom, and settled in one of the empty chairs. Pat got a visual 'OK' from Randy before he sat down across from her. The Lieutenant had rounded up two more folding chairs from the next room and arranged them in a loose circle with the rest. Before they all sat down, Brad stepped forward and boldly offered Pat his hand. Although he was grateful to the man who saved his sister's life he secretly found it surprising that, other than a little dried blood, the handshake from a triple killer didn't feel all that much different from that of his school counselor.

While the Lieutenant and the second officer observed, Patrick Grainger and the Oliver family spent a while maneuvering through a minefield of fragile feelings. They shifted from the predictable flow of gratitude to a light-hearted introduction between strangers brought together by fate and circumstance. The interaction was natural and unforced, a personal connection that none of them had anticipated. Karen would wonder later if the banter simply made it easier to take the hard edge off what had been an emotional Armageddon. No one mentioned a word about the terrible ordeal itself.

During one interlude Randy's eyes met Patrick's and they exchanged discreet nods, his a measure of thanks for saving his daughter's life, Patrick's a humble response of recognition, no words spoken, both understanding the personal investment in that one mutual gesture.

As they talked Julie's confidence picked up. The positive vibes seemed to be her way of diluting the aftermath. Still she couldn't get them out of her mind, the lingering questions about Pat's daughter. She didn't know how or why, not yet. As the conversation played out she began to sense a subliminal bonding, some connective tissue between her and Pat's daughter that wasn't yet defined. When it was revealed that Pat's daughter would have been about Julie's age, the reason finally became obvious.

Without considering the potential fallout Julie opened a door. "Patrick, your daughter would have been really proud of you today."

Pat dipped his head, and for a split second he teetered on the edge, a precarious place from which he often leaped into grief. Today though, unlike times past, he stepped back. "I think maybe she would."

Randy knew nothing about the death of Pat's wife and daughter but from the subtle underpinnings of their conversation he wanted to know more. Not simply because he was editor of a small town newspaper, or because of his early beginnings as an investigative reporter. He sensed there was something more to the man.

"Patrick, if there's anything…" said Randy.

"It's OK," Pat said, wrapping his head around a greater truth, one that seemed to dilute the pain for the first time in a long while. "Maybe today was meant to be, you know? Karma?" He studied it in space. "You, getting a daughter back. We don't all get that chance."

Before anyone could decide whether to continue the discussion or end it, before a stilted silence had a chance to appear, Julie jumped in again and made it personal the way she did with him back in the barn.

"What was her name?" she asked softly.

He cocked his head and threw an exasperated look at her. "You don't shy away from direct questions do you?"

She cowed slightly, afraid she might have crossed some imaginary line but his smile eased her concern.

"Aimee," Pat finally offered. "Her name was Aimee."

Randy intervened. "Maybe being the daughter of a newspaperman gives her a pass."

Julie forged ahead, emboldened. "Tell me about her."

Karen watched it all unfold, Julie pulling invisible strings, out of nowhere drawing personal emotions from a man that had killed three murderous psychopaths, while her husband worked both of them like the professional he had been in a younger day. At Julie's urging, Patrick relented and spent the next half hour telling it. Some details of his wife and daughter's deaths and the loose ends that still haunted him, even after twelve years.

Finally during a lull in the discussion the Lieutenant interrupted.

"I hate to break it up, guys, but we need to spend some time with Mr. Grainger. We've still got some ground to cover. Official stuff. Sorry."

Reluctantly Pat Grainger and the Oliver family exchanged hugs, phone numbers, email addresses, and promised to stay in contact, even though they wondered if they would. After they left the Georgia State Patrol sat down with Pat armed with the growing results from an impressive background check and spent the next two hours questioning and recording specific details of the kill-fest at the old barn near Lake Baxter.

As the Oliver family swung their Suburban out of the parking lot, without looking at him Karen asked Randy a question she already knew the answer to. "You're going to dig into this a little aren't you?"

"I might," said Randy.

Chapter 15

RANDY OLIVER pressed the speaker button on his desk phone. "Mike, how's business these days?"

"Dead," said Mike Turner, Commonwealth of Kentucky's Chief Medical Examiner.

"You need some new jokes."

Turner brushed it off with a laugh. "What can I do for you, Randy?"

Randy Oliver leaned forward. "I met a fellow last week. He went through a family tragedy a few years back, and in the course of our conversation he expressed some doubts he had about conclusions out of the ME's office. Claims he has personal insight, details that weren't available during the original investigation."

"We don't miss much, Randy, but if there's a chance something slipped through the cracks I guess we could take a look. That is, assuming it's important."

"It might be. I just put today's edition to bed. Any chance I could run over?"

"Maybe later." Turner checked his calendar. "How about around 3:30? You got a name and approximate date? I'll see if Janice can pull the file."

"Allison Grainger. Sometime around December, 2002."

* * * * *

A smiling Mike Turner greeted Randy and they chatted a few minutes about Julie, how she was getting along following her ordeal. Finally Turner pointed to a small round table in the corner of his office and a lone manila file folder.

"I took a couple minutes to scan the reports," Turner said as he opened the file. "Coroner, State Fire Marshall, Arson Team, our office. Nothing unusual jumped out." He turned the file toward Randy and continued from memory.

"An old farmhouse burned down right before Christmas in '02 down in Campbellsville. Mother and daughter were killed, husband away overseas with his National Guard unit. Point of origin was the nursery. Space heater under a window with curtains. Fire Marshall ruled 'accidental.' Arson boys found no accelerants, no hot spots except the heater."

He droned on like a report. "Family records and modest insurance turned up no financial reasons to torch it. No family disagreements. No apparent enemies. So they ruled out arson."

He continued as Randy paged through the file. "The Coroner, Charlie Reed, was a casual friend from high school of the adult victim and the husband. Charlie's a small town coroner but he knows his stuff. Determined cause of death was smoke inhalation, as expected."

Randy interrupted. "What'd the autopsy find?"

Turner took the file back and paged through the documents, talking as he read. "The mother was badly burned. Even so, the damage to her internal organs was moderate. We confirmed a high concentration of smoke in her lungs. CO level nearly 85% which means she was alive when the fire started. Died from smoke and carbon monoxide."

"Nothing suspicious?"

Mike shook his head. "No foul play—bullet holes, knife wounds, the usual suspects, although the body was so charred it would have been difficult to detect those unless we were looking for them." He flipped to another page. "No alcohol, narcotics, barbiturates showed up in the pre-emptive drug screen."

"How about the child?"

"Damn near incinerated. Not as bad as a cremation but the fire started next to the crib so the heat was intense. It didn't destroy all internal tissue but it did enough damage to invalidate tests for smoke and CO in the child's lungs. Got so hot the metal slide rods on the crib were melted into the baby's tissue."

Randy cringed. "DNA tests?"

"No reason to. We normally do a pre-emptive first-tier drug screen. Only when something suspicious shows up do we pursue second-tier and get into more detailed confirmatory screens. With the budget cuts these days unless we have a good reason to go there we don't. The report indicated we actually did extract tissue from both bodies but the degree of burn for the child would have invalidated her DNA."

Mike turned the questioning back on Randy. "So what's your new information?"

"My source is the husband and father of the victims, Patrick Grainger."

Turner flipped through the file. "His name was mentioned briefly. He was, I believe, stationed in Kuwait at the time of the fire?"

"Yep. He was driving a Humvee that ran over an IED less than a day before the fire at his home. Killed two soldiers with him, put him in a semi-coma for nearly two months. By the time he came out of it his wife and daughter had already been buried. Devastated him. For twelve years now he's been analyzing, agonizing over little disparities. After hearing his story last week I can see why he might question some things."

"Like what?" Turner said as he slid a legal pad over and began taking notes.

"For one, the space heater. Pat said he and his wife had discussed them and she had emphatically ruled them out. He said there's no way she would have allowed one in the baby's room."

"That's hardly conclusive evidence. More like a guess."

"Maybe, but you're a family man, Mike. Dead of winter; an 80-year-old farmhouse out in the country; old, original wiring. Would you leave your year-old baby unattended in the next room with an electric heater running when there's a spare crib right beside your bed?"

"Another crib?" Turner said, thinking before he made notes on the pad.

"Second, Pat says his wife tested the smoke detectors every week. So why didn't they go off, give her a chance to get the baby out?"

"Sometimes a fire like that gets going so fast there's no way to get to anybody. Happens all the time."

"You've seen those NFPA videos, how a fire builds. If the curtains had caught fire like the report said, smoke would have filled that room in seconds. Pat claims the smoke alarm was less than ten feet away. It would have gone off maybe a full minute before flashover. Even if the baby *had been* in the nursery, which he refuses to believe, the wife in the next room twenty feet away, she would have been up like a shot. Do you really think she would have only gotten five feet to her bedroom door before the fire had time to cause that explosion?"

"Maybe carbon monoxide got her first?"

"They installed CO detectors before he left for Kuwait."

"Didn't know that." Turner wrote it down. He studied his notes. "I see his concern, Randy, but we had no reason to know about any of this. Besides, there's still no hard evidence here to contradict our findings. Just your man's suspicions."

"There's one more thing that never made it into the report."

Turner looked up. "Go on."

"The neighbors told Pat and the Coroner they saw another vehicle driving away from the scene right after the fire started. That never made it into the final report."

"Might be hearsay."

"Actually I drove out and talked with them. McCormick. They still live there. They gave me the same story."

Turner scratched his head.

"That seems kinda important, don't you think?" Randy said.

"It would have raised questions," Turner confessed.

"If you'd had all of this information at the time of your investigation what would you have done differently?"

"We probably would have run second-tier confirmatory screens. As far as DNA, maybe, maybe not, but that's a moot point. The mother-daughter connection is cut and dried."

"Well?"

"Well, what?" Turner asked.

"Can you re-open the file, finish the testing?"

Mike recoiled a bit. "Second tier testing's pretty expensive. Pulling this file back out as a cold case on a bereaved father's hunch?"

"You told me this morning you were here to dig out the truth."

"Well, we are," he stammered, "but I'd need a good reason, something I can justify to the commissioner. Why is this so important to you? Is he a close friend of yours?"

"He is now, Mike. He's the fellow who pulled Julie out of that van last week."

Mike Turner thought back to the grisly details from the newspaper story and released a visible sigh. "I guess I could go out on a limb and open the file. Even if I pushed it'll take a few weeks, and unless the rest of the tests show something new it's not likely to lead to anything. Tell him not to get his hopes up."

Chapter 16

RANDY SPREAD A NAPKIN on his lap ready to dive into the tomato-basil bisque, the first half of a soup and salad lunch special, when his phone beeped a text message from Mike Turner: "Call me." He excused himself and slipped out the front door away from the noisy lunch crowd and dialed.

Mike Turner recognized the caller ID and dispensed with a formal greeting. "Randy, I'm getting ready to walk into a meeting with my Commissioner so I can't talk right now but this Grainger thing has taken an interesting twist. Thought you at least deserved a heads-up."

"What's wrong?"

"Don't have time to explain right now. I really shouldn't be talking to you but since you brought it to me in the first place . . . You want to run by my office? Maybe an hour or so?"

"Sure, but why?"

"That information you gave me a couple weeks ago? We got the tests back. Let's just say things aren't what they seem. Gotta go."

The line went dead.

* * * * *

"What's such a big secret you couldn't tell me on the phone?" Karen said as she slid into her chair on the outdoor patio at Casa Fiesta and dipped a tortilla chip into a bowl of salsa.

Before Randy could answer, the waiter appeared with a pitcher of margaritas.

"A pitcher on a weeknight?" Karen asked. "I've got some case files to go over tonight."

"You'll need more than one." He poured two mugs and began regurgitating the information that had overwhelmed him a few hours earlier at Mike Turner's office. As he told it he watched her face change from end-of-day-weary to personal shock. She struggled to speak as she sorted through the options and downed the last of her second mug.

"Randy . . . how?" she asked. "What's he gonna think?" She lost focus, searching for explanations. "And reopening the case? He's lived with his grief for twelve years and out of the blue part of it turns out to be a lie?" As expected, her next question was the same as his had been. "Who's going to break this to Pat?"

"There's one more thing," he said. "Mike posed another theory."

As soon as she heard it Karen began shaking her head. "No, I can't believe that . . . No." She stared at her empty mug, idly rotating it on the table. "You heard his story. There's no way he could be part of that . . . is there? " She pushed her mug over next to his empty one so he could drain the pitcher.

After he poured the last two drinks Randy reached across the table and laid his hand over hers. "I don't believe it either, hon, but do we take a chance? I mean, we've known him a month and a half."

She looked away past stucco archways, out into the parking lot, and reflected on the last several weeks. Following Julie's ordeal in Georgia, Pat had re-joined his crew in Knoxville. It took them less than two weeks to complete the steel erection for a small retail wing at Willowgate Mall. It was his next project, the Eastern State Mental Hospital in Lexington that turned out to be an unexpected opportunity.

Only twenty-two miles from the Olivers' residence in Frankfort, ESMH had given them a chance to reconnect. Reluctantly, Pat accepted an unexpected invitation to join them for a weekend cookout. Two weeks later he brought his tools and helped Randy finish framing the backyard gazebo that had stalled out during the summer. Over steaks and corn-on-the-cob in their backyard they'd re-acquainted and shared personal moments, including Pat's mental slog through the aftermath of his wife and daughter's death.

On the surface it had appeared to be a relationship that had little chance of being. A well-intentioned exchange of gratitude and good will. Instead, even as mismatched personalities emerged, it had turned positive, flourishing while they encouraged him to open emotional boxes that had been shut for so long. It surprised no one when he confessed the association he had made between his own daughter and Julie, a cosmic link in which saving Julie's life had somehow softened the burden of losing his own daughter and helped him silence his demons.

During that time of bonding the ME's re-examination had ground on. No one expected anything to show up, especially not this startling twist.

She leaned her forehead into her hands and deliberated before she rose and shook a wisp of hair out of her face. "We owe him, Randy, for Julie. We have to tell him."

"OK," he said as he raised his glass. "We'll give it a shot. Let's just be cautious."

Chapter 17

THE LAPTOP under the plywood work table fielded the email's arrival. The faint ding was lost in the non-stop grind and roar of the Eastern State Mental Hospital under construction.

Patrick Grainger removed an oil-stained hard hat and with the back of his arm wiped sweat from his forehead. Planted in the bowels of a dimly-lit, oversized erector set of steel beams and columns he was a study in concentration as he methodically paged through Brannon Steel's erection drawings unrolled on his plan table. He muttered while his eyes darted back and forth between tabular beam numbers and their corresponding location on the floor plans.

His comments to himself were drowned out by the constant, raucous concert of the jobsite: the grinding whirr of a concrete truck, steel drum churning, emptying another load of wet concrete; the repetitious, monotone beep of an all-terrain forklift backing up; arc welding machines chugging to feed current so that torches could produce the static crackle that would magically transform steel into molten glue; the heavy mechanical drone of the diesel engine on the 200-ton crane forty feet from where he stood.

He tore a hand-written list from a spiral note pad and strode to the 'bone-yard' where a dwindling pile of structural steel I-beams, in shades of charcoal and rust, patiently awaited their turn for a ride into the steel framework. The massive crane swiveled around, the motor in a high-pitched grind, and a steel hook slithered down, effortlessly lifting the next 6-ton steel beam like a 2x4, then swinging back toward the building where ironworkers on the raising crew waited. On it went, hour after hour, piece by piece, the tedious repetition offset by the satisfying sweat of hard labor and the instant gratification from seeing their handiwork bolted into place.

Two minutes before 5:00 he drew his finger across his throat, a signal to the crane operator, and the mammoth diesel engine whined to a halt. On cue the crew began to dislodge themselves from the steel framework, one by one laddering themselves down to ground floor. They headed across the gravel parking lot, tool belts slung over their shoulders, slogging past blue portable johns standing guard like fragrant, mute sentinels.

He rolled up the plans and powered up his laptop from sleep mode and made a final check for emails. There were three. Two from a familiar daily source, the structural engineer, delivered from a comfortable air conditioned office outside of Nashville, most likely routine field orders or answers to his RFIs—Requests for Information. The third one was from Randy Oliver.

The engineer's messages could wait until tonight in his hotel room after a shower and a couple of burgers. It was the alert flag on Randy's email that caught his attention: *high importance*. Over the last several weeks an unexpected rapport had grown between him and the Oliver family, positive feelings he had not experienced in years. He was probably overreacting but *high importance* played with his insecurities and he didn't want to wait until tonight to find out. A beer would help, only not in the rowdy, smoke-filled Blue Buffalo where he and his crew usually gathered after work.

He slipped the laptop into his motorcycle's saddlebag and

cruised over to the Hilton a few blocks away where the happy hour atmosphere in the upscale bar was distinctly more subdued. His dusty jeans and sweat-stained work shirt didn't blend with the suits and briefcases of the business crowd so he found a small table off in the corner, ordered a Corona, and allowed the elevator music and the first long drink from the long-neck bottle to settle him while he powered his laptop on. He ignored the sideways glances from two businessmen sipping their Manhattans with disdain while they silently questioned why he had invaded their territory. He opened the message.

Pat:

I hope you don't mind but after you told us your story a few weeks ago about the fire at your farmhouse, and the questions you raised, the investigative reporter in me kicked in. Through some sources in the business I took it upon myself to do a little checking. Turns out there actually were a couple of things you may have been right about. And some things you need to know. I'll share them with you but they're probably better discussed in person. Is there any way Karen and I could meet you after work tomorrow?

Randy

Pat stared at the email. *What kind of things?* Even though there was no indication of good news or bad he detected a sense of urgency in the message. *Things I need to know?* He connected to the Hilton wireless and typed in a terse reply. *"Sure. Tomorrow after work. Where and what time?"*

After another long drink from the Corona he re-read Randy's email and tried to dissect its meaning. *What things had he been right about?* He thought back, his mind wandering, lost in the sparkle and brass of the Hilton lobby trying to recall the details he had shared with them. He was mildly curious why Randy had taken a special interest in his story. Probably some sense of moral obligation because of Julie. Still it was personal and unexpected.

His concentration was interrupted by the waitress. "Sir, is everything OK? Can I get you an appetizer?"

She was young, barely old enough to serve drinks. Probably a college student but different from so many of the phony skirts that spouted cavalier phrases to her customers and showed some leg to bump the tips.

"No thanks," he said, waggling the nearly empty beer bottle "but I'll have another one of these."

She nodded politely and turned back toward the bar when he called out to her. "Miss, excuse me." Then in a low voice, "Would you also bring another round for my two friends at that table over there?" He nodded his head toward the two businessmen who had been making no effort to conceal their not-so-subtle expressions of condescension. She looked at them and then back at him, a question mark over her head. He winked. "Another drink might lighten 'em up, not be so stuffy having to share space with us common folk."

A mischievous grin crept across her face. "You want me to spit in their drinks?" she whispered and winked back, then smiled. "Just kidding."

He drained his Corona and re-read the message a third time. The waitress brought the drinks and the suits listened in surprise as she explained who had ordered them. When they looked over he exaggerated an effeminate wave and blew them a kiss. Messing with idiots was always an effective coping mechanism.

Chapter 18

THE OUTDOOR PATIO at Buddy's Bar and Grille was crowded for a Thursday night. Couples from the surrounding Chevy Chase neighborhood—most of them straight, some gay, a few versatile and indifferent—strolled by on their evening walks. Randy and Karen recognized the purr of a motorcycle a half block away and they waited at their street-side table while Patrick's Harley Davidson turned into the parking lot and found an empty spot in the back corner. In less than a minute Pat appeared around the corner of the restaurant.

Over the past few weeks they had seen another side of him, more than the rough-around-the-edges drifter who had single-handedly executed three drug-fueled gang-bangers that gambled with Julie's life and lost. A revitalized Pat Grainger had surfaced and was walking confidently toward them, clean shaven, no bandana, jeans with no traces of blood or body parts, well-developed arms and shoulders filling out a teal blue golf shirt. And, thankfully, no weapons. Wind-blown, salt-and-pepper hair grazed the top of his ears and neck. His rugged features and amber-colored eyes displayed a hometown charisma not evident during those tense moments following Julie's ordeal. As he approached their table they mustered a smile even though they knew the next hour was going to be difficult.

They ordered three beers and after some small talk Pat cut to the chase. "Your email said you found something?"

Randy and Karen had debated how they might ease into the conversation and break the news. In the end they had decided to plow straight through, see what direction the conversation took.

"After we got home a few weeks ago," Randy said, "I took the liberty of calling the State Medical Examiner's office. The Chief ME is a professional acquaintance. As a favor he pulled the old files from '02 and reviewed them. Not much to find fault with. It was ruled an accidental fire, no foul play. First-tier drug screens found nothing suspicious."

The beer arrived and Randy continued. "I relayed the information you shared with us—the space heater, the smoke detectors, the car driving away, all that stuff that never made it into the reports."

"What'd he think?"

"Those additional facts had no bearing on the original tests. However they did raise questions, and he agreed to run second-tier confirmatory drug screens as well as DNA tests."

"And?"

"Nothing new in the confirmatory screens."

"So they don't think those things sound even a little suspicious?"

"The ME agrees your points were valid, yes, but you weren't around. Without your input or some other proof, there's nothing they would have done differently."

Pat sagged a little. Randy's email had offered hope that something might have surfaced to explain the loose ends he had battled with for so long. At least now the investigation finally had all the information. Maybe this would let him find some closure after so many years of second-guessing.

"However," Randy said, staring nervously at the beer bottle in front of him, then back up at Pat, "the DNA was another matter."

Pat shook out of his reverie. Karen pulled out copies of the DNA reports they picked up that afternoon at the Medical Examiner's office. She laid the first one in front of Pat and he scanned the first few pages before he commented in mild frustration, "Just a lot of tables, graphs, technical terms. Is this supposed to mean something?"

"Go to the Summary," Karen told him, and she turned to the last page for him. When she pointed to the last line he read it out loud. "DNA profile of Subject at fire scene, reported to be ALLISON THERESE GRAINGER, obtained from autopsy samples, matches DNA profile obtained from blood tests on file, also reported to belong to ALLISON THERESE GRAINGER." He re-read it and looked up at her. "So, this confirms what we already knew, that Allison died in the fire?"

"Yes it does," Karen replied. Then she placed the second report in front of him, gently, as if it might self-destruct. Without being cued by Karen he fast-forwarded to the Summary: "mtDNA profile of Subject at fire scene, reported to be AIMEE LYNN GRAINGER, obtained from autopsy samples, does not match mtDNA profile, reported to belong to ALLISON THERESE GRAINGER, obtained from autopsy samples." He digested the sentence a second time, then looked at her matter-of-factly and shrugged. "So? This says that Allison and Aimee's DNA doesn't match. It's not supposed to. Last I heard everybody's DNA is unique."

Karen and Randy traded nervous looks. Randy picked up the thread, and began reciting a distilled version of the science lesson that Mike Turner had given him earlier. "The DNA used to match individuals to known samples is *nuclear* DNA. That's what they used to identify Allison." He tapped the first folder. "It's complicated, but you're right, everybody's *nuclear* DNA *is* unique. Unfortunately the baby's body was too badly burned to extract any reliable *nuclear* DNA."

Pat looked back at the page. "But this second report . . ."

Randy interrupted him. "The second report refers to *mitochondrial* DNA." He pointed to the terminology: 'mtDNA'. "It's different from *nuclear* DNA. It's hardier, it's 1,000-times more abundant in every cell, and it's easier to recover from a burned corpse. They were able to get plenty of mitochondrial DNA from the baby."

Pat stared at the report, waiting for more explanation, and Randy continued.

"*Mitochondrial* DNA—'mito'—has limitations, but it does have one unique characteristic. 'Mito' is passed from generation to generation only from mother to child," Randy said, raising his eyebrows for effect, "and only through the *maternal* lineage. In simple terms, the 'mito' of every female will match the 'mito' of her mother, which will match the 'mito' of her grandmother, great-grandmother, and so on. In theory this maternal link remains unchanged for thousands of years."

Pat read the summary statement in the second report again. As he neared the end of the sentence he felt a nervous pang, and his brow furrowed. "I don't get it. What does this mean?"

"They expected the *mitochondrial* DNA from both bodies to match. Passed from mother to child, Allison to Aimee," Randy said. He pointed again to second report. "But they don't."

Randy took a deep breath and looked to his wife, then back at Pat.

"I don't know how to make this easy for you, Pat. The child who died in the fire . . . wasn't Aimee."

Chapter 19

PAT GRAINGER stopped breathing. His body came to a halt, like an old celluloid film reel stopped mid-frame. As he processed the words his head began to move, slowly at first, a gentle shake of denial, then more animated.

My daughter, Aimee, she died that night, December 20, 2002 with Allison.

He opened his mouth to speak. His lips parted and closed, once, then again, but nothing came out, his face a blank canvas, the empty stare drifting away to the climbing trumpet vine that covered the patio fence. He turned to Karen, begging for an interpretation.

Her limpid expression tried to hold him upright, protect him from the shock of an inconceivable revelation, but she was losing ground. She laid her hand on his forearm. "Pat, the DNA tests are solid."

Pat's eyebrows scrunched in disbelief. In slow motion he raised his elbows to the edge of the table and leaned his forehead into his hands as he tried to grasp something that couldn't be. His brain thrashed hopelessly between polar opposites—the weight of Aimee's death that he had carried around for the last twelve years, and now this impossible mistake.

His mind staggered, tripping over itself, trying to cover too much ground. He picked up the report and read the summary again word for word, then once more to make sure there was no way to misinterpret the conclusion. He looked at them both. "They're obviously mistaken. They need to run it again."

"They ran it twice, Pat."

He continued to stare at them. "But . . ."

Their expression didn't change.

"This mtDNA thing, it's reliable?"

"Yes."

"But it can't be . . . How *can* it be? . . . They're positive?"

They both nodded, half-smile, half-apology.

Pat felt his stomach surge, an involuntary convulsion, changing places with his heart, and a chill flooded his body, perhaps a reflex to cool nerve endings that burned like the fire that took his family. He struggled not to break down again. Another deep breath before his eyes pleaded for relief. "What in God's name, Randy? How?"

"Nobody knows yet," Randy said quietly. "All the ME knows at this point is what's in this report. How? That's the real question."

"But if that child wasn't Aimee," Pat finally said, desperate to claw his way back, "then what happened to her?"

Then the next logical thread caused his heart to skip a beat. "Is it possible that she might be alive?"

"Anything's possible."

Pat pushed his chair back, scraping brick pavers. He stood up and began a slow, deliberate, circular pace, his body tense, eyes half shut, hands clasped tightly on top of his head to keep his thoughts from exploding. He dodged shadows as he ran the gauntlet through an alternate realm of disbelief. The discipline he had brought to bear during so many crisis situations failed him now.

The more he paced the less he understood any of it. His

hands still on his head, he shuffled away, his expression blank, past dinner tables that gave him looks he would never see, into the parking lot, ignoring cars entering and leaving, wandering blindly toward the familiar comfort of his motorcycle in the far corner. Then an about-face back toward the restaurant, his brain searching for some clear spot in the fog, all rational thought suppressed by an emotional upheaval that gored him from within.

Then he stopped in the middle of the parking lot, as still as a breathing human could be, and closed his eyes. Allison joined him in his deliberations, as if she had never left him and the living world behind. *You cannot stop, Patrick, until you find the truth.* And like the sudden ending to a torrential rainstorm, clouds parted and his options crystallized, leaving only one. This absolute fact that had been irrevocably decided twelve years ago—might now be undecided. And it came to him that his life had a purpose again. Only one.

He dropped his hands down to his side and tried to gather himself and exhaled loudly, a signal for the beginning of some unknown process.

When he returned to the table he recognized the helpless looks of concern on Randy and Karen's faces. He slipped into the empty chair, his calm exterior a drastic turn-around from minutes earlier. Neither believed his conversion was anything more than a charade, a desperate coping mechanism that papered over the turmoil boiling inside him.

"Has the Medical Examiner told you what will happen next?" he asked.

"Are you OK?"

"I'm fine," he said curtly. "The Medical Examiner?"

Randy looked cautiously at Karen, then relented. "There'll be a new investigation of course. This is a shock to them, too."

"Randy," Pat asked, his thoughts running free now, "if the child that died in the fire wasn't Aimee, who was she? Where did she come from?"

Incrementally his training was kicking in as he fished through layers of possibilities, speaking to his inner self as much as to them.

"How could somebody switch another child for my daughter? Allison would have never let that . . ."

The first realization—that Aimee might be alive—had been a jolt of visceral shock. But this new thought was a bludgeon, freezing him mid-sentence. His expression emptied into space while he tried to fight back the dread. His hands jerked to his forehead while he searched for any answer other than the obvious one.

"No!" he gasped, and sank back into his chair, his hands sliding down to cover his face. Karen had already scooted her chair over to him and put her arm around him.

Through his fingers Pat asked the question he already knew the answer to, his voice a slow, empty monotone. "Does the ME think Allison's death may not have been an accident?"

"He considers that's a possibility, yes," Randy said, as Karen continued to hold onto him.

His breath nearly left him. "Dear God . . ."

How much more could he take before he imploded and sank to the bottom, his torment covered over by the soothing residue left behind while the river of life flowed on? The current pulled at him, a powerful vortex swirling, dragging him under.

But before he could slip beneath the surface her familiar voice hauled him back in with the same whispered instructions she had delivered in the parking lot moments ago: *You cannot stop, Patrick, until you find the truth.* She was there beside him. He marveled at the power in her determined stance, remembered her delicious scent as her face closed on his, felt her delicate hands grab hold of his shoulders with a strength she never had in life, pulling him back in the boat.

He opened his eyes and leaned past two worried faces sitting beside him and poured a short handful of ice water out of his water glass, splashed it onto his face, then dried it with his napkin.

After a moment of reflection, his voice barely above a whisper, "Randy, do they know anything? Suspects? Anything to go on?" He fidgeted in his chair, his nerves on fire, as he examined possibilities, hesitant to ask questions for fear only bad answers would come.

"I have no idea, Pat. I know *we* went through hell when Julie was kidnapped. I can't imagine what you're feeling."

Julie. The mention of her name steadied him for a moment. He had watched her back in that chamber of horror after her ordeal was over as she summoned an incredible, unexpected well of strength. She was thirteen. Was it possible that by her example he could follow her lead? Her way of returning the favor, even if she didn't know it?

"Maybe we need to let you get home so you can calm down, rest a little," Karen said, as she stood up. "Sharing all this with you in a public place might not have been a good idea after all."

"I can't," he said calmly as he looked directly at her. "I promised Allison."

Karen dropped back into her chair.

"You guys go on," Pat said. "I'll be OK. I'm gonna stay a little longer, have another beer, try to think this thing through."

Randy and Karen gave each other the same look. "I don't think that's a good idea," said Karen.

Pat smiled without looking at either of them. "If you're worried I might go postal, don't be. I just need time to sort things out."

"If you don't mind we'll hang with you for awhile," Karen said.

Chapter 20

THEY SAT WITHOUT TALKING for a bit while Pat stared across the table at the empty fourth chair. Forgotten scenes from a previous life flashed by, quick in and out, not stopping long enough for him to get a good look, jabbing at him, rubbing sandpaper on raw wounds. In the background he heard Karen ordering appetizers, then her sympathetic, veiled voice when she placed a hand on his arm and tried to change the subject. "Tell us more about your time in Kuwait?"

He knew they were making an effort, anything to divert his thoughts from mind-numbing revelations. The more he wallowed in distant memories, the more it would hurt. He knew that too. But if he was going to survive he had to find some way, any way, to distance himself from the pain. When the time was right he would dive into the fray, organize his analytical skills, come up with a plan of action on how to move forward. More to the point, how to right a terrible wrong.

Randy was right, they didn't know enough yet. He'd have to wait until more information surfaced before he could go proactive. For now, even if all he could muster was small talk maybe it would help him get through it until useful details surfaced. He leaned back and looked up at a dusky sky, his hands intertwined, before he gave in, took another sip of beer, and in a defeated voice he gamely began to tell it.

"Operation Iraqi Freedom," he started slowly. "The President and Secretary of Defense were hell-bent on the second Gulf War, despite weak intel," As his mind dug in, the sharp edge of his despair became dulled enough to carry on and bit by bit he lost himself in the story.

"My Guard unit was part of a Logistics Battalion in Bardstown—a supply group. Weekend warriors putting in our time, building a little retirement. Then 9/11 hit."

Pat's expression turned cold as he recalled that day: a staff member from the hotel interrupting their conference, then his rising and standing in shock with four dozen strangers, their mouths open in abject disbelief, when the class leader switched on the TV in the corner of the hotel's meeting room and they watched the twin towers fall.

"Goddamn those cowards," he said as his fist slammed against the table, drawing startled glares from nearby diners. He took a sharp pull on his beer and let his anger subside.

"Four months later we got called up. Hell, I was a simple accountant."

Karen wrinkled her brow. "I thought you were a steelworker."

He feigned an offended squint. "What can I say? I'm versatile. Got my accounting degree courtesy of the Army Tuition Program. I was always good with numbers."

Randy didn't smile, his focus zeroed in on Pat. "There's no way a simple accountant could pull off what you did to those psychos."

Pat calmly surrendered more information. "Before the Guard, I pulled sixteen years active duty, most of it Airborne."

"Airborne?" Randy said. "So that would mean . . ."

Pat filled in the blanks. "Special Forces, Green Beret."

Randy and Karen looked at each other.

Pat reached for his beer. "Spent the last few years in Iraq, after Desert Storm."

"I thought that first Gulf war only lasted a few months?" Karen said.

"Thirty-eight days, officially. 'Shock-and-Awe' they called it. But it was all for show," he said, his disgust mounting. "Despite the cease fire Saddam never let up. He continued attacks on the Shiites in the south, the Kurds in the north, and we did nothing to stop 'em. Wholesale massacres. Entire villages wiped out. We finally sent in humanitarian forces, set up no-fly zones, but it was all a sham. When the air combat between us and Iraq picked up, they sent some of us in and we spent the next four years fighting the Republican Guard, training the Kurds against Saddam."

"Fighting? Like with weapons?" Karen asked, almost wishing she hadn't.

Pat wondered how to put it gently. "Not conventional warfare. Strictly covert. Small groups. Engaging the enemy one-on-one. Only some of the brass knew we existed."

Karen grabbed her beer and took a gulp.

"That explains those three in the barn," said Randy.

"We were young, full of ourselves," Pat continued. "We lived for the danger. But after a while it weighs on a man. My conscience finally caught up with me and I had to get out. By a huge stroke of luck I found Allison. We fell in love and had Aimee. We just wanted a normal life." He looked away. "We came close."

"The authorities will find out what happened," said Randy.

"I want to be involved," Pat said.

"Better let them do their job."

Pat didn't turn away from Randy. "What would you do if it was Julie?"

Randy was tempted to offer up a mature, responsible answer but he knew this wasn't the time for a lecture. Or a lie.

"I'll keep my word to Allison," Pat continued, "Find out what happened. Whoever's responsible I'll find them, too. If you think less of me I'm sorry."

Karen returned his gaze. "And then?"

"I don't know about 'then' yet."

When the appetizers arrived they ordered another round. Randy dipped a fried jalapeno in some white sauce. "So were you in Iraq when the fire at your house broke out?"

"Kuwait," he said, shaking his head. "Camp Ahmadi, gearing up for the war. A new logistics strategy some think tank wizard dreamed up. Everything for the second war went through us. I was an NCO chasing invoices and contracts in the Resource Office."

He made a half-hearted bite at a potato skin. "Pretty intense, three shifts, 24/7, running billions of dollars in materials and supplies out to the LSAs every day to stock the war machine in case Saddam didn't hand over the infamous WMDs and the President decided to drop the green flag."

"LSAs?"

"Logistics Support Areas. Bases located across Iraq near active war zones. Four of 'em. Basically small towns we built from scratch in the middle of the desert. Anaconda was the biggest, maybe 35,000."

"People?" asked Karen, wide-eyed.

"Yeah, people," Pat grinned. "Had its own newspaper, movie theater, storage warehouses. Anaconda was the busiest airport in Europe. All four LSAs were hubs, distributing weapons, vehicles, equipment, food to the Forward Operating Bases so our troops could fight the war."

Randy was intrigued. "If Ahmadi was feeding the LSAs it must have been pretty big, too."

"That was part of the problem. In the first war in '91 the US operated out a smaller base on the Gulf, Camp Doha, but it had limited capacity and strategic shortcomings. Ahmadi was better located, but in the beginning it didn't have the capacity to supply the upcoming war, just a few buildings the Kuwaiti's had built and given to us. So our job was to gear up and complete massive additions and development at Ahmadi before the new war started—utilities, infrastructure, housing, storage yards—as well as being the ongoing distribution center for the entire conflict."

Pat took another sip of beer. "So we built up a new town at Ahmadi—operations centers, admin buildings, motor pools, gigantic warehouses, three gyms, three mess halls, a dozen barracks. I can't remember all of it."

Pat wasn't surprised at the flabbergasted looks in Randy and Karen's faces. He'd seen it before.

"Even while we were building we were shipping goods out to the LSA's every day. The gravel lay-down yard for mobile equipment alone covered 50-60 acres. At any one time we might have three, four thousand trucks and track vehicles ready to be shipped forward. From the air it looked like a freaking car lot the size of a small town. It was a madhouse, building and shipping like crazy. Hell, I had just run across . . . a big . . ."

Pat's voice trailed off as his forehead furrowed and his face went blank. He closed his eyes while a missing piece, lodged for twelve years in the folds and recesses of his brain, shook free and began rattling around in his head, calling for attention.

"What's the matter?" asked Karen.

Pat was lost, deep in thought, transported to another time and place. Fifteen awkward seconds passed before Karen shook his arm. Her touch brought him out of it. "Sorry, I just . . . something I hadn't thought about for awhile."

"You zoned out."

"Yeah, I know," he said as he raised his eyebrows and cocked his head. He studied it, examined it from another angle, a hustle of mental activity churning as he reached deep for recall.

"What?" Randy asked.

Pat returned to the conversation, his expression contorted, as he began to remember pieces, proud discoveries, as if he had just found a missing cell phone behind the cushions of the living room couch. "I stumbled onto something."

"Like what?"

"Our largest defense contractor, Wyndham-Lynch. Big-time international player," Pat said, the details rushing back. "They had a well-organized team set up in Resource. They even recruited collaborators from inside our own Army staff. That's the only way they could have pulled it off."

"Pulled what off?"

Pat shook his head, unable to hide his loathing, as he recalled it. "A freaking license to steal. Huge, well organized. Illegal invoicing, overpayments, bogus contracts. Over time it added up to a pretty sizeable amount."

"How sizeable?"

"Don't remember exactly. But as I recall, just the part I found, a little over a billion dollars."

Randy and Karen's jaws went slack.

"You can't be serious?" Karen asked.

"I turned them in, made an official complaint to the Inspector General."

"You were a whistleblower?" said Randy.

Pat nodded.

"What the hell did you find?"

Pat took another drink and shook his head. "Too much to go into. We'd run out of beer before I could tell you all of it."

Randy flagged the waitress.

Chapter 21

"HOW DID WYNDHAM-LYNCH pull it off?" asked Karen. "Surely the Army had safeguards."

Pat smirked derisively and stared at the center of the table, shaking his head. "It was a massive operation. The logistics were overwhelming. So much material, moving so fast, God Almighty couldn't have gotten a handle on it. Department of Defense had no choice but to rely on the down-line command structure to track it."

"So?"

"So when a defense contractor targets a key officer or non-com making $40-50,000 a year and offers him ten, maybe twenty times that much to work from the inside, the temptation's overpowering. It was easy to justify, some of them, especially when they considered a million here and there was a drop in the bucket in an unlimited defense budget. In our case that was Major George Fowler, contract officer in our Resource Office."

"Weren't those guys afraid of getting caught?"

"Sure, but there was a lot at stake. And Wyndham played for keeps. It was a dangerous time."

"Wyndham-Lynch had a reputation for being ruthless," Randy added. "They operated another subsidiary—Aurora—nothing but private mercenaries. Mostly ex-soldiers."

"Big players like Wyndham," Pat said, "it's their mindset. No matter how much they make, it's never enough. It's the little guys like Fowler that get in over their heads. Hell, George Fowler wasn't a bad egg. A big Texas Longhorn fan from Fort Worth. I think he saw an opportunity to retire rich, got greedy, and left his moral compass at the door."

"What finally happened to Wyndham-Lynch and Fowler?" Randy asked.

"No idea. I turned it over to my Command Sergeant Major. He took it to the Inspector General."

"So you spent a lot of time with the IG?"

"Nope," Pat answered, his face cocked slightly as recollection continued to kick in. "It wasn't a couple of weeks after that meeting with Sergeant Major when that IED kicked my ass. No idea what happened during those weeks I was out. When I came back to life and they told me Allison and Aimee were gone, I lost it. Everything from then on was a blur." Pat's shoulders sagged at the painful recollection. "They discharged me a month later."

Randy shot Karen a look of alarm. His investigative antennae were vibrating at all the red flags. "But if you never testified, how could they prove anything?"

"All the evidence against Wyndham was on the server. Contracts, invoices, emails, memos. Sergeant Major had all the proof and my office staff could retrieve all the documents. Hell, I even wrote a narrative describing how they did it and gave it to him along with hard copies of the documents. He kept them in his office safe. It was ironclad."

"You never heard what happened?" Randy asked.

Pat stared into his plate, his voice barely a whisper. "It didn't matter anymore."

They continued their discussion for awhile and Randy made a few notes. Once they finished their last beers and Pat reassured them he had calmed down, they said goodnight. In the car Karen confronted Randy before they made it out of the parking lot.

"Well?"

"If you were corrupt enough to embezzle a billion dollars, probably more," he said, "and suddenly you were in danger of losing it all and going to jail all because of what one National Guard accountant found, wouldn't that make a couple of murders look justifiable?"

"If they're so ruthless why didn't they just kill Pat?"

"Could be they tried. Pretty convenient, that IED exploding the same time his house caught fire. Maybe they believed Allison was a threat too. They had no idea how much documentation he might have sent her."

"Honey, I want justice for Pat but I don't want to lose a husband in the process."

He didn't answer as he pulled out of the parking lot.

* * * * *

Tracey was squinting into her monitor, two fingers poised over the mouse, when Randy's head popped up over the top edge of her office cubicle. She lurched backward. "Jeez, you scared the holy crap outta me!" she panted, her right hand patting her heart.

"Sorry. You in the middle of something?"

She took a deep breath, "Background for the courthouse story. Shouldn't take more than an hour."

"Put it on hold. I've got something I want you to check out."

An hour and a half later he was staring blankly at his paneled wall, nursing his second cup of coffee, when Tracey popped in the doorway.

"Find anything?" he asked.

She handed him a stack of papers. "It's amazing how much information on the war is out there available to the public. DoD white papers are dime a dozen. It reads like a thriller. Pretty hairy stuff—blackmail, rigged bids, fraud, congressional hearings, bribery of government officials by Kuwaiti companies, three suicides, a couple of 'accidental' electrocutions. I'm sure I could find more."

"Anything on Wyndham-Lynch?"

"Other than a few minor billing violations, not much. A lot of accusations, reams of media criticism on the wires about shady deals. Even several well-documented news stories with big numbers. But no prosecution. I called a buddy out at the National Guard Armory but haven't heard back from him yet."

None of this surprised Randy. Pat's ironclad evidence probably never saw the light of day. "Is your friend out at the Armory any good at research?"

"He has access to military databases and search engines that I don't. Why?"

"Come in here when you get finished with that stuff on the courthouse. I've got a few more things I'd like you and him to try to chase down. It may take awhile."

* * * * *

Friday afternoon, end of the day and the work week, as his crew broke ranks and headed off to the Blue Buffalo, Pat made one final check on his laptop. Another email from Randy, again flagged *high importance.*

Pat:
Any chance you could run over to our house in Frankfort tomorrow morning. I did a little more checking and turned up a few things we'd like to go over with you. We'll have breakfast ready. Maybe around 9:00?
Randy

Chapter 22

SHE STARED at the phone, the receiver still warm, and backed away from the desk. How had he found her? All these years, nothing—no phone calls, no letters, no emails, no contact at all from any of them. Now this.

She made a hasty retreat to a familiar spot, pulled a proven remedy down from the glass shelf, and poured into a clean glass. In her disconcerted state of mind she realized she'd rushed the order of things. She opened the mini-fridge and grabbed a few ice cubes and carelessly dropped them into the glass. No time to worry about splashing onto the counter. She took a steady sip and the bourbon sent a wave of healing fire down her throat. Then another.

She shuffled back to the desk and slouched into the burgundy, leather-bound swivel chair, its arm rests and side wings outlined with antique brass dots, and tried to sweep away the confusion. Another sip, this time not such a long one. Again she examined it, how he'd found her, but she knew she was out of her element. She'd watched too many police shows. These guys were professionals. They had unlimited resources at their disposal—databases, contacts, private detectives. She was just Brenda. And George was not here to help her.

The caller had identified himself but the name didn't ring a bell. Maybe it would be in the journal buried somewhere in the damning text. She didn't recall the name Randy Oliver. He said he was a newspaperman? Not good. Those guys never let facts get in the way of a good story, no matter whose reputations fell under the weight of journalistic excellence.

The bourbon was working its magic now, slowing her down, allowing her to piece together the gist of the conversation. Bits of this and that started to fall into place. He'd asked about George, whether George ever told her about a conspiracy during that ridiculous war? Had George ever mentioned anything about large sums of money? Of course George mentioned money. That's all they talked about back then. How they would spend it. How they could hide it. How he had figured out a way to send it back. That must be how he had gotten in so much trouble, why he wanted out. Why he was killed. They said it was suicide? She knew that couldn't be. George was too much of a coward. He would never have done that. Besides, he loved the kids too much.

She was almost through the first glass. Maybe she should slow down. If she got smashed she'd never be able to piece it together. Take it easy, Brenda. Use your head. Stay clear, focused while it's fresh in your mind. Tomorrow you won't remember half of the conversation. She made a calculated decision and pushed the glass to the back edge of the blotter and retrieved the note pad, the one on which she had made a few notes during the conversation.

Thank God she had the foresight to ask the right questions. She had lost track of these two, and her ability to locate people was severely limited. Oh, *their* resources were top of the line, they could find anybody, but all she had was Google or maybe some simple White Pages search. Useless if they really wanted to remain out of sight.

But the caller, this Randy Oliver, he'd been a big help even if he didn't realize it. He was polite, not nearly as pushy as she assumed a newspaperman might be. She stared at the two names on the pad in front of her. Two names that were listed regularly in most of George's emails. Names that were the prime topic of the journal. That's what made the journal so valuable for her. And so dangerous for them. And maybe now so profitable. Names that may have been responsible for George not making it back home.

Even though George wasn't a schemer at heart he had done well with the plan. It had made her life comfortable, especially since he wasn't around anymore. But she suspected these two names had done even better. They were the ones that had planned it all. George had just gone along for the ride. In the right place at the right time. He would never have been smart enough to figure something this complicated out by himself. And until he explained it to her she never dreamed he would have been greedy enough to go for it.

It was too late to start feeling guilty now. The damage was done. Anyway, the government had plenty to spare. That made it easy to lose the guilt. Even though her windfall was significant when spread out over 100 million taxpaying Americans it wound up being a pittance for each of them. They'd never miss it.

She always wondered how much the other two reaped from the deal. If her share was substantial theirs must have been enormous. That wasn't fair either. George was the one who took the biggest risk, the one most likely to be exposed if it ever came to light. And considering he never made it home to spend any of it, even more unfair.

Now she had a way to contact them. Finally. Maybe now it was time for a more equitable distribution. Especially since she held the key to their grand lifestyle. She had no doubts they would recognize the logic in peeling away a small portion of their share and shuttling it back to her. They'd never miss it. Even if they did, her proposal would be much better than the alternative.

She held the power over whether they could continue in their grand lifestyle. She was certain they'd never let their greed cloud their judgment.

She took a longing glance at the near-empty glass, just out of reach, calling to her. In her renewed state of mind she gave in, arms outstretched, and took another sip. Sure she had to keep her wits about her but no reason not to celebrate a little in advance. Now she had an address attached to these names. Now, a treasured item that had seemed like nothing but a poorly-written history of a clever deed gone bad, suddenly was priceless.

She swiveled the chair around and stood up and removed the framed portrait from the bookcase nook behind her. A few clicks and the safe clanked open. She had to dig under a stack of documents but there it was, just like she left it, waiting for her, wondering why she hadn't visited for so long. Her ticket to a comfortable retirement.

She withdrew the red leather journal and sat back down, thumbing through the pages. It had been a few years since she had looked at it. But she had no trouble finding the appropriate sections and she smiled as she read the passages that meant so much. George had never been much of a writer but his words here were golden. In her mind, a best-seller.

She laid the journal down on the desk and slid it back next to the reading lamp, at the same time retrieving the glass, and she drained it, savoring the last swallow. She opened the laptop to her left and Googled the company name that Mr. Nice Guy, Randy Oliver, had given her. She wasn't tech savvy but it wasn't difficult, even for her, to search the company website until she found the names she was looking for, the same ones she had written on the pad. Randy Oliver had been correct. Perfect, in fact.

In the morning, after a good breakfast at the club she'd run a few copies, some sample pages, to let them know. Those pages along with the appropriate letter of instructions, terms of their contract actually, would be enough. She should be able to whip up a document in a couple of hours tonight. Given the delicate nature of the situation no signature would be required. Her signature would be the journal itself, wrapped and delivered as agreed, once the proper transfer was made. No sense in getting greedy. Overnight mail would get her message to them bright and early Monday morning. A great way to start a week. Just another routine business decision for them.

She closed the laptop and switched off the lamp. Satisfied, she rose and visited the wet bar again, one more toast to her good fortune. And this time a toast to a total stranger, the deliverer of this wonderful, fortuitous, totally unexpected news that would make her retirement so pleasant.

Chapter 23

PAT'S HARLEY pulled into the Olivers' driveway five minutes early and Julie met him on the front walk. In the kitchen Julie poured him a cup of coffee while Karen dumped a bowl of pre-scrambled eggs into a hot pan layered with onions and peppers.

"You look beat," Randy said.

Pat stirred in some sweetener. "You said you found some things?"

Randy glanced at Julie and Brad. "You guys sure you want to be part of this discussion."

"Sorry, Dad, we decided all that last night," Brad said, as he planted himself in a chair at the dinette table and pulled a warm muffin out from a cloth-covered basket and layered it with margarine.

Randy sipped his coffee and began. "You're pretty confident you had Wyndham-Lynch dead to rights?"

"Sure, why?"

"What would you say if I told you Wyndham never got prosecuted for that fraud? Or any other for that matter."

Pat threw him a skeptical look. "There's no way the government would let something that big get away, not with all the evidence we gave 'em. Those JAG lawyers would've had wet dreams over it." He caught himself, too late, and winced when he saw Julie shaking her head at his crude remark.

"You're assuming the Inspector General got the evidence."

"Damn right. I gave it all to my Command Sergeant Major, Eddie Wainscott. I don't doubt Wyndham tried to put the squeeze on the brass but if it flowed downhill to Wainscott he would have fried them. Even their stable of big-time lawyers couldn't have gotten 'em out of it."

"Maybe your Sergeant Major had a motive for not following up."

"Like what?"

"Like maybe he already knew about it."

"How could he?" Pat's brow furrowed, then he finally made the connection. "You mean involved?" He shook his head. "No freaking way. Eddie Wainscott was straight arrow. Career Army."

"But you never got called back in to talk to the IG?"

"No."

"And the only person you gave your information to was Wainscott."

He nodded as Karen placed a plate of eggs and bacon in front of him.

Randy waited for Pat to make the connection. "Don't you think it's a little suspicious, you getting hit by a roadside bomb and your house burning to the ground, both on nearly the same day, two weeks after you turned over your evidence?"

Pat picked a muffin out of the basket and studied the question before he answered. "I never gave it any thought. I was out of it. When I woke up and realized my wife and daughter were gone, things went straight to hell for me."

"Give it some thought now. Look, by all rights you shouldn't have survived that explosion. Even after you regained consciousness, for all practical purposes that fire took you out of the picture. On the other hand it turned out to be great timing for Wyndham."

Pat scowled. "That's a stretch. How would they even know I was on to them?"

"If Wainscott was in on it they'd know."

"I'm telling you Wainscott's solid," Pat said.

When Randy failed to return fire Pat shrugged and played along. "OK, let's say he was tempted and gave in. If they wanted to shut me up why didn't they just buy me off? They had hundreds of millions to play with."

"I'm guessing you're not bribable and we've only known you for a couple months."

"All right then, if they're such bad-asses," he said, another apologetic nod toward Julie, "why not kill me? It wouldn't have been hard. Accidents," he said, his fingers making air quotes, "happen all the time in a war zone."

"Maybe that's what the IED was. Besides, even if you'd died in that blast there could have been loose ends."

"Like what?"

"Who else besides Wainscott knew about what you found?"

"Nobody, I told you. I found it on my own. Didn't tell a soul. No buddies. Not even my staff."

"Nobody?"

"How many times do I have to say it," he said, irritated, "the only person I told was Sergeant Major." As he took another sip of coffee Randy and Karen remained silent, staring back at him, challenging him to see it.

Randy confronted him. "You told one other person."

Pat cocked his head searching for an explanation. Then a frightened recognition appeared and his shoulders sagged as he placed the cup down and looked into the plate of untouched eggs and filled in the missing piece. "Allison. I talked to Allison about it," he said under his breath. "But that doesn't mean . . ."

Randy didn't ease up. "Wainscott knew you talked to Allison about it, didn't he?"

Pat buried his face in his hands and rubbed his eyes as he struggled to pack all the pieces into the puzzle. *Of course I told Eddie Wainscott. The only one I trusted.*

Randy and Karen sat silently, waiting for him to come to grips with it. Finally, Pat looked up. "Are you guessing or did you find something?"

"Yesterday I had my research tech get on the internet and search a little, see what she could find. She has a contact out at the National Guard and he poked around some in their military databases. All that digging turned up some interesting stuff. Which in turn led to a very interesting phone call at the end of the day."

"Well?"

"Understand, what we found doesn't prove anything. But it does establish some curious connections. Enough to take it to the authorities."

Pat waited.

"Command Sergeant Major Eddie Wainscott retired early from the Army in 2007. He is currently vice president for a construction and development company in Richmond, Virginia. You care to guess what company?"

"Just tell me."

"Wyndham- Lynch Enterprises."

Pat slumped back in his chair.

"Your former Brigade Commander, Colonel Brent Masters, the man that co-signed every invoice paid at Ahmadi, he also retired, four months after Wainscott. He's currently vice president for a construction and development company, also in Richmond, Virginia."

"Wyndham," Pat said.

"Yes."

Patrick turned in his chair and looked out the dinette window toward the gazebo in the back yard, searching for explanations that weren't there. He absentmindedly played with his coffee cup.

"You said there's not enough to establish proof," Pat finally asked. "Is there enough to investigate?"

"We'll give what we have to the authorities. But if Wainscott *was* in on it, unless he was really stupid, he's already destroyed all of the evidence, paper and electronic. No evidence—no motive. They'll simply deny it ever took place."

"And Allison and Aimee?"

"Even weaker. They'll claim they learned about the deaths through regular channels."

"How about Fowler?" Pat asked. "He was the key player. Did he go to work for Wyndham too?

"Unfortunately Major George Fowler committed suicide about a year after you were discharged."

"What the hell . . ."

"Yeah. Now why would a man running a billion-dollar scheme, kill himself before he could enjoy the fruits of his labors? Turns out his wife still lives in Fort Worth," Randy continued. "We tracked down her number and I called her late yesterday afternoon to see if she could shed any light on the story. She was a little nervous at first about the call but she agreed to chat with me for awhile. Acted totally shocked that her husband might have been involved in any scheme or conspiracy. No surprise there. But then a strange thing."

"What?"

"She asked me what ever happened to Colonel Brent Masters and CSM Eddie Wainscott. Now why would those two names come to mind?"

"I'd say she knows more than she told you," said Pat. "If the three of those guys were running this thing, Fowler probably communicated details to his wife in emails, letters, something."

"Exactly. When I finally told her where they worked she

thanked me, said she had to go. I didn't get to finish the conversation."

"The woman knows something, Randy."

"Probably, but without some hard evidence it's still all circumstantial for now."

Pat leaned back in his chair. "Randy, I trusted them."

Karen spoke up. "Yes, but by your own admission you were a mess. Even if you had been on your game it would have been hard to believe people you trusted could do this. How could you have known?"

Pat pushed his plate back from the edge of the table, the food untouched. His face took on a hardened look of resolve. "I know about it now."

"Actually you don't *know* anything."

"That may be, but there are ways to get to the truth."

Karen admonished him. "Patrick Grainger, this is not the time to go rogue. We've got a lot of work to do, dig up enough evidence. But we will." She caught herself. "I mean, the authorities will. You're not back in Iraq going stealth. You can't start your own war."

"If I knew they were responsible for Allison's death—or Aimee's—there wouldn't be anywhere they could hide."

"Then I guess we need to find some proof, don't we?" said Randy. "And until we find it, we need to keep cool heads. On one hand there's always the remote possibility this is all a coincidence, that they weren't involved in the fraud, the IED, or the fire. However . . ."

Pat looked at him curiously.

"If Wainscott and Masters *were* involved in what happened to Allison and Aimee do you really think they were capable of pulling off something this well-coordinated without an organized, well-funded team?"

"Wyndham." Pat said, under his breath.

"We want to find out what happened to Allison and Aimee but we need to get to the right people," Karen said. "*All* the right people."

Pat sighed as he remembered the marching orders that Allison had given him. Whatever happened to Aimee would drive him first, above revenge, above anything.

"You've done a lot of homework," Pat said. "Do we wait for the authorities to investigate or do you have another plan?"

"I might," said Randy. "I've got a few calls to make Monday."

Chapter 24

A SATURDAY NIGHT and Pat's Harley glided into the crowded parking lot of the Blue Buffalo. In the front row he recognized Axle's red 4x4 pickup truck, its multi-colored custom detailing streaming across the hood and down both sides to the tailgate. Boldly displayed in the back window was a rack with the badges of honor for a true outdoorsman—a .30-30 lever-action Winchester rifle and a fiberglass hunting bow with a quiver of tri-blade, razor-tipped deer arrows.

Pat eased his bike into a landlocked corner at the far end of the lot. He dropped the kickstand and ambled toward the front door. Halfway across the aisle, a horn blared and a well-traveled pickup truck bore down on him from out of nowhere. It screeched to a halt less than three feet from his hip. A hulk of a man in a denim shirt and jeans slid out of the cab and waded toward him, a scraggly, unkempt gray beard grazing his chest, his muscled arms smothered in faded blue tattoos.

The man's menacing expression gave way to a wide-eyed laugh. "Where the hell you been, Pitty Pat. We missed you the last couple nights, boy," Mongo said with a growl, wrapping him in a bear hug. "Got anything to do with a female?"

"You might say that," Pat said, reflecting on the irony. He

forced a grin. "Nothing I can tell you about."

"Why the hell not, boy? We ain't no Dear Abby here."

"A few things on my mind," Pat said, dropping the conversation down to Mongo's level. "You know how it is with us James Bond types. If I told you I'd have to kill you."

Mongo bellowed his gravelly country laugh at the tired joke, then parked his truck on the sidewalk and the two of them entered the Buffalo together. As soon as they pulled open the second door of the tiny vestibule the raucous sound of a long week finally at an end hit them square in the face, a dam giving way to the flood of humanity behind it.

Boisterous men and women, laughing, flirting, some looking for action, others for respite; the clack of billiard balls and the ensuing groans or cheers over shots missed or made; beer bottles and cheap glasses clinking in dissonant aggression; rowdy voices shouting, singing, competing for attention with the pulsing bass from the Buffalo's pre-programmed honky-tonk soundtracks. In its own crude way it could have been a classic Norman Rockwell moment, poignant and predictable, none of it subtle.

Many in the crowd worked together every day in their calloused, sweat-stained world of construction and trade labor, then dropped their guard after hours and played together here and other places like it, in a high-key, low-down environment that held few expectations other than camaraderie and simple pleasures.

After learning about Aimee, Pat's two-day hiatus from this after-work socializing to recover and find his way had been the opposite, deep and complex, an emotional karmic drama filled with soul-searching, unanswered questions, and hope. But tonight he had another reason to rejoin the uncomplicated company of friends, life travelers who offered a comforting haven and demanded little in return. He needed to make arrangements for a short vacation.

The Buffalo's barn-wood-paneled main room, spacious and uncomplicated, was drenched in the musky smell of cigarettes and cheap cologne, and accented by the crisp aroma of grease-drenched appetizers peeking out from under wax paper in plastic baskets. Waitresses, young and old, hustled the tables, sweeping tips and replacing empty beer bottles and mugs with full ones.

Pat peered through the stale, smoky haze softened by the neon glow from the Buffalo's vast collection of beer signs, over toward the busy game room where darts flew like wayward missiles and pool cues rocked and shot forward, more power than finesse, or served as spindly leaning posts for the next shooter.

As he and Mongo weaved their way toward the bar a welding foreman sitting at a table with his wife and another couple raised a long-neck bottle in salute and tossed him a whole peanut from the bucket on their table. Pat caught it in mid-air and acknowledged him with a nod before cracking open the shell and popping both nuggets in his mouth.

As usual Granville Mullins and Hanley Pike sat at the bar on adjacent stools. As he approached them from behind Granville spotted Pat in the back-bar mirror through the jumbled choir of liquor bottles and swiveled around, his gray pony-tail giving a lively flip.

"Well, look who's here. Buddy, we was beginning to think you didn't love us anymore."

Pat exchanged power grips with them both and Caleb, the bartender, set a Bud Light on the bar for him and was already pouring a Jack Daniels on the rocks for Mongo. Pat took a long draw and then toasted with them all.

"Needed a couple days to think, Granny."

"Everything OK?"

"Not really," Pat said, "but it has promise." This was not the time to open doors. He needed an escape from the drama for one evening. He turned the conversation.

"Pike, I gotta be off a few days. You've got the controls while I'm gone."

Hanley Pike was his assistant superintendent, approaching 60 now. He'd worked the steel erection business for almost forty years and his gray hair, thinning to little more than a comb-over, showed it. Despite his age he could still outwork younger men and his experience made him invaluable.

"No problem. Take your time," Pike said.

"I'll keep my cell phone on," Pat said.

A twangy voice behind Pat interrupted them. "Word's going around that Pike might be a little sweet on that skinny dude on the concrete crew, the one with the earring."

"Kiss my ass, pretty boy," Pike said, dismissively, as Pat turned around to see Axle grinning at them, his hand outstretched.

"I didn't see you when I came in. You too good for your own kind?" Pat prodded.

Axle stepped back and bowed gently toward a table across the room where a young parchment-blonde woman waved demurely back at him.

"Priorities," said Axle, under his breath.

"How old's this one?"

"Old enough to know better," scoffed Mongo, as he took another swallow of Black Jack.

Pat playfully threw his arm over Axle's shoulder. "You gonna take her out to your truck, show her all your weapons?"

"She's already seen those. I've got one weapon she's not seen yet. After a few drinks," he winked.

"You got a permit for that thing?" Granny asked, pointing.

"Concealed carry."

"Maybe I ought to go over there," said Pat, "and tell her what a degenerate you are. That she'd better head home before she gets her heart broken."

"I'm the one should worry about getting his heart broke," said Axle.

"You ain't got a heart," said Granny. "All you've got's a perpetual hard-on."

"There you go, Granny. Reading that dictionary again? Bet you can't even spell perpetual," Axle said with a fake sneer.

"No," said Granny, "but I can spell 'man-whore.' You need business cards," he said, using his hands to form a fake frame around imaginary words: "Axle Morgan, Man-Whore."

Axle gave up under the wave of laughter. "Guilty as charged."

"You party all you want, stud-boy. Just make sure you show up in good shape," said Pike. "Pat's gonna be out a few days. I can't afford to have you hanging iron with a hangover."

"You don't worry about me, old man. Have I ever let you down? You read the plans, Granny'll crane us the iron, and Mongo and me'll run both settin' crews. We'll have that erector set bolted together before Pat gets back."

* * * * *

An hour later back in his hotel room Pat opened the GPS app on his phone and programmed his route. It would take a little over 8 hours to make the trip from Lexington, Kentucky to Richmond, Virginia.

Maybe it's time to see what's going on in the new lives of Eddie Wainscott and Brent Masters. For old times' sake.

Chapter 25

"YOU HAVEN'T OPENED your mail yet?" he screamed, as he slammed an opened FedEx package on the walnut executive desk. The impact sent loose pages flying onto the floor.

The man seated behind the desk, dressed in a polo shirt and casual slacks, delayed his remarks with a casual sip of coffee and coolly picked up the package, examining the address on the routing label. "Is there a problem?"

"Yeah. A big one. I checked your inbox on the way in. You got a package same as me," he said, pointing at the envelope.

Brent Masters showed no expression until the name and address of the sender finally registered. He looked back up at Eddie Wainscott. "Is this who I think it is?"

Without waiting for an answer he pulled out the two page letter along with several photocopies and began to read. Once he examined the documents he laid them on the desk and stared out his picture window, screwing his swivel executive chair back and forth as he studied their options.

"She's in over her goddamn head," he finally said. "Thinks she's making some kind of business proposition."

"I don't know about you," said Wainscott, "but I only see one option."

"Garth?"

"Yeah. How soon can you mobilize him?"

"He and the boys are puttin' up hay this morning but his cell phone's always on. He can be in here ready to go in a couple hours. Shouldn't take more than 20 minutes to brief him. I'll have Marge set up a flight."

"This is not a negotiation you know."

"No," said Masters. "It's gone too far for that."

"We going to let Garth do it his own way?"

"You know him as well as I do. We'll let him pick the time and place and how he wants to handle it."

"He stands to lose here, too."

"I'll remind him."

Chapter 26

PAT STUFFED an empty sausage and biscuit wrapper into the paper sack and tossed it into the passenger-side floorboard. He removed a plastic lid and took a sip of lukewarm coffee and resumed his vigil.

Across the road the corporate sign for Wyndham-Lynch International sat proudly, recessed into a waist-high wall of hand-laid sandstone and surrounded by a landscaped display of ornamental trees and grasses. Fifty feet beyond it a small gatehouse clad in the same chamois-colored stone guarded the property. The uniformed guard checked every vehicle that entered and left. Each time a car slowed to log out Pat raised his high-powered binoculars and checked out the driver. It had been nearly twelve years but he knew he would still recognize them both.

He'd arrived in Richmond Sunday evening after a tortuous nine-hour motorcycle ride across the Allegheny Mountains, alone with haunting memories, fighting to keep his loathing in check. The passing landscape had been a visual feast, the lush, verdant foliage of summer still ripe, every sweeping curve offering a new vista of mountain and valley, sunlight and fog. But he remembered none of it. Other than the bright green interstate road signs that showed the way he was fully engaged as he struggled to fend off the demons that had returned, knives bared. In Richmond he found a cheap motel. With his laptop and a wireless connection he pulled up the corporate website of Wyndham-Lynch and, as he had done several times already, he clicked to the appropriate Staff pages to confirm the subjects of his mission. He couldn't conceal his bitterness at the two smug faces that glared back at him, hiding safely behind their devious pasts—Brent Masters and Edward Wainscott, Vice Presidents in charge of new accounts.

The gray mid-sized SUV he selected early morning from a local rental car company was a safe, nondescript stand-in for his motorcycle. By 9:00 he had found an unobtrusive vantage point with a clear view of the entrance.

Finally at 11:45 his binoculars picked up his first target in a navy blue Cadillac Escalade. The burr haircut and pebble-textured, square-jawed face had not changed much since Kuwait. The only thing different now was Pat's slow burning hatred for a man he now believed may have been involved in the death of his wife and daughter.

As Eddie Wainscott pulled out, Pat slid down in his seat and let the Cadillac glide past the front of his SUV. He rolled out behind him. In less than 10 minutes Wainscott turned into the unassuming entrance to a private country club and wound his way along the tree-lined main drive past lush fairways and greens, arriving at an expensive but understated clubhouse nestled in the heart of the golf course.

At the parking lot Pat found the nearest vacant space and observed from a safe distance as Wainscott changed from his sport coat into a lime green sweater-vest and golf visor and began lugging his out-of-shape body toward the locker room at the left end of the building. The slight limp that had followed Wainscott most of his army career had grown more noticeable with age.

Playing the role of a regular member, Pat ambled to the front entrance that was highlighted by a pair of tall glass-and-mahogany-stained pine doors set back under a timber-framed porte-cochere. There was no plan, no rational reason to put himself this close to his quarry, just an irresistible pull by some unknown force, a deep-seated loathing that he hadn't been able to shake since he left Lexington. As soon as he stepped into the expansive foyer the voice of an older woman called to him from the front office.

"Can I help you?"

He turned toward her and smiled, the ad-lib rolling out as if it had been scripted. "Yes ma'am. My wife and I are new to the area and I was wondering if your membership was exclusively by referral or not."

She returned his smile, politely but with apology. "I'm afraid you must have someone sponsor you unless you happen to own one of the homes around the golf course. Of course if you're a rock star or happen to own some internet start-up that'd get your foot in the door," she said, a mild attempt at humor.

"Hardly," Pat said, prolonging the charade. He gestured toward the pro shop. "Would you mind if I took a quick look around as long as I'm here? If it's what I'm looking for I'm sure I can get one of my partners to put in a good word."

Without waiting for permission he wheeled and turned left, easing down the wide central hallway past the bar and a half-empty dining area. He nodded silent greetings at the two members he passed in the hall. At the end of the corridor, as he neared the pro shop he heard a door from the locker room open behind him and in the reflection of the glass door ahead he saw a brief flash of lime green. He reacted and bent down over the water cooler on the wall while Eddie Wainscott brushed past him in the hallway lugging his golf bag, his plastic golf spikes crunching on the indoor-outdoor carpet.

Pat's hands clenched in an unexpected rage, or maybe

something more visceral. He felt an immediate impulse to pull a pitching wedge from the bag as it passed and take several carefully-aimed whacks at the degenerate head of the man that carried it, enough that the man would never recover from a vegetative state. The vicarious rush from his past that used to take him over in the dark as he crept up behind his next victim, a blade glinting in the moonlight, grabbed him now, familiar and comfortable as if he had never left it.

In that split second the burst of vengeance flared, provoking him with one inarguable reason: what chances had Wainscott given Allison? But his inner voice reined him in. There were others, and they all had to pay. First, he'd find them. There would be time later for justice. As Wainscott moved out of reach the muscles in Pat's forearms relaxed. He had too many things to come to terms with before he could justify a final reckoning.

Pat pulled back from the fountain and wiped his mouth with his sleeve, then retreated back to the vestibule and out to his car. As he strode briskly away from the clubhouse he felt the rush ebbing away. It surprised him, the exhilaration. He'd abandoned it long ago, buried in the blood-soaked sands of Mosul, Kirkuk, Tal'Afar. Yet here it was front and center again, transporting him back to the familiar edge of bloodlust.

As he sat in his car and allowed it all to drain out he took stock of what had happened. He had nearly allowed his emotions to jeopardize a not-so-carefully-crafted plan. 'Out-of-control' was a condition that they always reserved for the enemy. He couldn't forget again.

He recorded the license plate of the Cadillac as he left the parking lot and returned to his station across from the entrance to Wyndham-Lynch.

Chapter 27

AT 4:38 HE WATCHED his second mark slow down and log out at Wyndham's gate house. When the white Mercedes S-Class 550 sedan turned right onto the state highway Pat pulled out behind Colonel Brent Masters. Twelve minutes later the Mercedes turned into a suburban parking lot buffered from the road by light woods, and parked in front of a modern one-story glass-front brick building occupied by a routine lineup of commercial establishments. The sign above the wide storefront: Raise the Bar Gymnastics Academy.

Pat deliberately eased past the Mercedes, just another inconspicuous shopper, and found a parking space in the adjacent lot. His binoculars had a clear line of sight on the Mercedes' license plate. A couple of minutes after five o'clock the Academy's door opened and a string of girls rolled out, loaded with gym bags and teenage chatter. Two of them located Masters' car and hopped in the back. Pat felt a rush of hatred at the unjust irony. Then he let it go, shoving the ghosts aside, and re-focused on his quarry.

Back on the road Pat followed at a safe distance. Within minutes they left the suburbs behind and wound their way through the Virginia countryside past expanses of pasture and fields lined with black plank fences.

Finally Masters' brake lights glared in the distance and he turned right down a straight tree-lined lane flanked by pastures on both sides. Horses grazed in the field to the left. As Pat passed the entrance he reduced his speed and watched Masters' car fork left at the far end of the lane. Two seconds later Pat got his first glimpse of the residential compound maybe eighty yards off the road: a modern white farmhouse—brick, stone, and horizontal siding—with a covered porch that swept around the front and left side. There were two prominent outbuildings—a large white metal pole barn in front and, nestled behind it, an older, smaller traditional barn with oak siding stained black. Both were emblazoned with the distinctive black silhouette of the Tennessee Walking Horse Association. Paddocks and riding rings filled in spaces between and around them.

A half mile down the road Pat turned around in a driveway. As he retreated toward town and passed the entrance he made a note of the lane number on the fence and the small, non-descript sign—Four Chimneys Farm.

* * * * *

That afternoon the Property Valuation Administrator was cordial. She directed Pat to the central catalog file and the metal cabinets that held the plat maps. Within a few minutes he had located the catalog cards with all the pertinent information on Brent and Betty Masters. Their mini-farm encompassed nearly 40 acres and from the latest appraisal it was evident that Masters had accrued some significant wealth in amounts not normally associated with Army take-home pay, even for a decorated full-bird Colonel.

A brief study of the aerial plat map revealed unobtrusive gravel farm roads on both sides of the property, branching away from the county road. A mature forest bordered most of the land at the rear, sweeping like a foliated carpet up into the low mountains, and a sinuous creek skirted the property to the northeast, winding in and out of the farm from forest to pasture.

From the map he made a list of parcel numbers for the properties that adjoined Masters'. When he looked up the names of those landowners in the card file he got his first surprise. The private lane to Masters' house was shared by a familiar name, Eddie and Helen Wainscott.

* * * * *

Back in his hotel room, as he wolfed down the last of his carry-out tacos, Pat powered up his laptop and typed in a detailed summary of all that he had gathered today. He pulled up Randy's home email address and attached the summary.

In the body of the email he typed a half-hearted apology for taking off on his own. He felt sure Randy would not be pleased with his decision to journey into enemy territory. But fifteen years in covert operations had taught him that any mission involved risk. If his presence here in Richmond, and any intelligence he could gather, could lead to discovering what happened to Aimee it was the most important mission he would ever undertake.

Chapter 28

SHE'D BEEN READING since 9:00, hoping the combination of her Xanax and the over-hyped mystery novel propped up in her lap would work their magic but sleep wasn't coming yet. She reached for the glass on the side table. The ice had melted, diluting the last swirls of bourbon and ginger ale in the expensive crystal tumbler. She kicked aside the knitted afghan covering her feet and laid the book open face down on the white leather ottoman and shuffled on unsteady legs to the wet bar where the open bottle of Makers Mark awaited her. The quiet of her walnut-paneled library was jarred awake by the glass scooping through the ice bin. She refilled, this time more bourbon, less mixer.

On her way back to the cushioned armchair she glanced with approval at the red leather journal resting on the library desk. Its contents were powerful. And in her case, lifesaving. Thankfully George's guilty conscience wouldn't go to waste. He always wanted the kids to get good educations, especially in their prestigious private colleges. Unfortunately he didn't stay alive long enough to get them past their sophomore and junior years. But her backup plan would kick in soon so there would be no need to discuss it with them over fall break. She'd mailed her contract proposals to the two parties Friday. If she didn't hear from them soon she'd have to make a call.

George would have wanted her to enjoy a good life even if he couldn't be around to share it with her. The country club and her well-appointed two-story Colonial overlooking the seventh green in the Estate section weren't unreasonable although this extravagance had eaten into the college fund. All in all, her fresh investment strategy seemed logical now. Fortunately, George had planned well enough to keep the journal and send it to her a few weeks before she got the call that he had ended his life. Timing really was everything.

She fell back in the recliner, spilling a little bourbon on the oversized Persian rug George had shipped back from Kuwait. It was convenient that the carpet had a busy pattern with lots of dark colors. This fresh liquid simply blended in with the other spills this section of rug had suffered lately. She took a long sip and picked up her book again and began to read.

* * * * *

Nearly three hours later the door to the study eased open. Lights were on. He saw her slumped in the chair, as planned, the novel half open in her lap. The tumbler was empty. He set his bag down and moved quickly to the window and pulled the curtains shut, then turned out all the lights except the one by her chair. His fingers checked her pulse. It was steady.

He didn't waste time. At the wet bar his gloved hands emptied the contents of the open bottle of bourbon into the sink, then placed it in his bag and withdrew another one, identical to the first. He folded her limp hand around the neck of the new bottle, then carried it and her fingerprints back to the wet bar. He removed the distinctive cap dipped in red wax and poured enough into the sink to match the original bottle and set it on the counter.

As he picked up his bag and surveyed the room he saw it

lying there on the desk next to the lamp, out in the open. He would not need his tools tonight. He calmly picked up the journal and thumbed through it, making sure all the pages were intact. Satisfied, he placed it in the bag. He crossed the room to the brick fireplace and reached up inside the hearth opening and closed the damper. A brass key protruded from the face of the brick a few feet from the ottoman and the unconscious woman. He gave the key a full turn and the sinister hissing of natural gas from the fireplace logs began to fill the room.

He took one last look at her before he closed the door behind him.

* * * * *

The flashing yellow button caught his attention, right before his secretary's voice on the intercom, "You have a call, sir."

"Who is it, Grace?"

"He wouldn't identify himself but said to tell you 'the price of gas is outrageous.' Does that mean something to you?"

"Thanks, I'll take it." He cleared his throat and picked up the receiver. "Yes?"

"It's done."

"Any problems?"

"None."

"You find it?"

"Lying right on her desk. Didn't even need to search."

"Good. Your flight gets here tomorrow afternoon. Bring it over as soon as you arrive."

"Right."

He hung up the phone and dialed another number. After four rings an answering machine came on and he left a brief message.

He limped to the liquor cabinet in the mahogany sideboard and stared past the drink glasses into the back mirror. A blocky face and crew-cut smiled victoriously back at him. He poured some blended scotch over a few cubes of ice and began to pace. He nervously cast his line of sight out the huge windows overlooking the expanse of groomed lawn that led away from the building, falling away down a wooded hillside toward the hustle of downtown Richmond.

Their offices here felt secure, a fortress almost. Perched high above the city, it was accessible by a single private road that wound a half-mile from the guard gate to the main building through a mature forest of pine, walnut, and hickory. Similar to any Virginia college campus, he once said, but without the hundreds of eager, hormone-fueled kids waiting to fix the planet. Children, really, who didn't have a clue how the real world worked. Most of them planned their careers, picking some dedicated profession where they could work their 8 to 5 lives, pop out their kids, build a retirement, and hope social security was still around when they needed it.

He had chosen another path, a non-traditional one. His choice had taken a surprising turn for the better and now it had made him wealthy beyond anything he could have imagined during those early days in basic training.

He turned and proudly surveyed his luxurious office, splaying his arms outward in grand silence. It was something for which he'd planned well, saw a golden opportunity, and seized it. And nobody was going to take it away. Especially not some desperate, alcoholic bitch who couldn't manage her money and had no clue what the stakes really were.

He took a healthy drink of his scotch, swirling the ice around the glass, and continued to pace, confident, although not totally at ease yet about this latest hitch. The customized ring tone from his smart phone broke his concentration. He tapped the green icon and answered. "You get my message?"

"I did. Everything go as planned?" the voice asked.

"That's what he said. I didn't ask details over the phone."

"The item?"

"He's on the way with it. His plane gets in tomorrow. Give me tomorrow evening to analyze it, then come down the next morning and we'll go over it together, make sure there aren't any other loose ends hiding somewhere in the pages. If things go as planned we'll have a good old fashioned book burning in the fire pit next to my pool."

"Unless we find something new, is this our last connection to the whole mess?"

"If the Major hadn't gotten a conscience he and his greedy wife would be sitting pretty for life. But he made his bed. Hers, too, as it turns out. At least now we don't have to worry about the past jumping up and biting us in the ass."

"It still makes me nervous."

Eddie Wainscott took another sip of scotch. "You remember what it was like back then—organized chaos. None of those fancy-ass military lawyers had a clue what to look for, even when was fresh, right under their freaking noses. You think anybody gives a crap this many years later? Not a chance."

"You believe that?"

"By my way of thinking this last little episode is the final connection between us and what made us rich. I'm gonna sleep easy tonight. I suggest you do the same."

Chapter 29

MIKE TURNER was the last of four men to sit down at the conference table.

"Thanks for coming on short notice," Randy said, plopping his pen onto a legal pad cluttered with scribbled notes.

Major Jack Huddleston, Staff Liaison for Public Affairs at the Kentucky National Guard, doctored a cup of coffee with sweetener. "Mike briefed me a little on his discovery. All very interesting but I'm not sure why we're here."

"Right now all we know for sure," said Randy, "the Medical Examiner is re-opening an old case. As soon as the paperwork catches up an official investigation will follow, probably under the jurisdiction of the State Police."

"So how come you know before we do?" asked Sergeant Phil Damron, lead detective at the Kentucky State Police.

Mike Turner interrupted. "I gave Randy a heads up, off the record." Mike set his diet cola down and briefed Huddleston and Damron on the crime scene investigation twelve years earlier, and the latest revelations. "Somebody went to a lot of trouble to disguise what appears to be kidnapping. Possibly murder."

"The only reason any of this new information came to light," Randy said, "is I did a little research as a favor to a friend. What I assumed would be a little fact-gathering has turned up some pretty powerful stuff. Details that have been buried for years. I've gone as far as I can and I need a little help from you guys. You've got more resources and sophisticated methods for gathering information."

"Why are you getting involved?" said Huddleston. "You're a newspaper guy. You report the news, not investigate it."

"That friend I'm trying to help? He's the one that pulled my daughter out of that van this summer."

"Still you can't go out on a limb and play detective," said Damron. "And in our official capacity we can't help you do that. There's an ethical and professional line somewhere in here we can't cross."

"I understand. All I want is a little research, nothing more."

"Whatever we might find, won't it eventually show up in the investigation anyway?"

Randy clasped his hands on the table. "If we wait for official channels this case may never see the light of day."

Huddleston and Damron looked at each other.

"Why?" Damron asked.

Randy slid two identical packets of information over to them. "We're not just dealing with two army buddies that got rich off the war." Randy re-played the short version—Kuwait, the conspiracy, no investigation, the fire, and Wyndham-Lynch's likely involvement in all of it.

"Wyndham-Lynch International," Huddleston said, whistling as he scanned the packet. "Kinda out of our league isn't it? Even more reason to let the authorities do their thing."

"That's why I can't wait," said Randy. "Wyndham's got connections at the highest levels. Especially since their former General Counsel is part of the President's staff. As soon as an official investigation opens and people start asking questions and taking depositions, one well-placed call to one of our indebted Senators, followed by a call to our Governor, and we're looking at an open records nightmare that could take years to wade through. With Wyndham's contacts inside the military they could try to classify records from Kuwait, maybe make them disappear. Even if we managed to get around all that, they've got so much money and influence they'll lay down a trail of legal maneuvers a mile long that'll delay the investigation for years. They can spend and stall and wear down the authorities over multiple administrations until somebody gives up or gets tired and decides it's too big a mountain to climb. You know how it works."

"And you expect to accomplish something by doing a little research?"

"Who knows. But if there's anything there, I want to have enough information out in the open that they can't sweep it away. Until then it's just research. Off the record."

Huddleston piped up. "Your research assistant—what's her name, Tracey?—has already *borrowed* one of my techs for an hour or so for some simple stuff," he grinned. "That's no big deal. We share information all the time. But there's a limit to how much manpower I can commit. Not to mention some of what you are looking for may already be classified."

"Understood," said Randy.

"Just so you'll know," said Damron, "nothing happens like you see on those big-city CSI shows. Our budget's tight, staff's as low as it's been in years." He paused as he thought about it. "Although that's not to say we don't have some resources. I've got one gal—a real techno-nerd. She likes a challenge."

"I guess I'd be willing to do a little digging too, within limits," said Huddleston. "Maybe build a few files before it hits the fan."

"I need to add," Randy said, "that my friend, the husband and father of the victims, is taking this pretty seriously."

"Tell him to chill out," said Damron.

"You don't know Patrick Grainger," Randy said. He looked

at Huddleston. "You'll find this out anyway, Jack, but he's not your standard weekend warrior."

Damron's eyes lit up. "He took on those three psychos by himself didn't he?"

All eyes turned toward the derisive laugh coming from Mike Turner. His head was nodding in obvious satisfaction as he stared at his hands bundled together on the legal pad in front of him. "I read the GSP incident report, guys. He took the first two out with a survival knife, 8" blade. Very efficient, almost surgical. The third guy . . ." he hesitated before he finally looked up. "Hell, he shot the bastard's dick off with a 45." He smiled his approval.

"Sonofabitch!" said the Major, coughing as coffee went down the wrong pipe.

"That little detail didn't make it into the paper," Damron grinned. He gave Randy a concerned look. "Anything else we need to know?"

"There is some urgency here. I didn't know about it until last night but Patrick took off on his own to Richmond, Virginia."

"And that's a problem . . . why?" asked Damron.

"That's where Wyndham's corporate office is. And Wainscott and Masters."

"Dammit, Randy," cursed Damron, "Tell the guy to stay out of it. He'll compromise the investigation."

"Phil, if I could control him I would. He called me after he'd already gotten there. He promised me he was only there for surveillance to pick up any information we might be able to use. I'd say, given his background, that's not such a bad thing."

"And his background is what?"

Randy gave them a quick rundown on Patrick's Special Forces training.

"Randy," Damron asked, "is this guy out of control?"

"Not yet."

Chapter 30

FRIDAY MORNING AT 9:00 Jack Huddleston and Phil Damron arrived at Randy's office with their internet research technicians. Sgt. Danny Blake, the National Guard tech, passed around copies of the information he had assembled and began narrating a methodical summary.

"Colonel Brent Masters. West Point graduate. No social or disciplinary issues. Like most of them he started as a Second Lieutenant in a minor post. Received various assignments stateside, always in Logistics. No combat experience."

The group followed the written information while he spoke. "Quietly moved up the ranks. Headed up a support battalion in the Granada fiasco. When we invaded Iraq during Desert Storm in '91 he was assigned one of several battalion commands, performed admirably during what was a massive fast-tracked transfer of equipment and supplies. Of course, a month later the towel-heads surrendered."

"Blake!" the Major curtly reprimanded him.

"Sorry," Blake said, no trace of apology, and continued. "He was a career officer. Stayed overseas during the Iraq and Afghanistan conflicts. In 2001 while the US was gearing up to invade Iraq the second time—Operation Iraqi Freedom—he received a prestigious brigade post, Commander for Camp

Ahmadi, the new distribution facility for the entire campaign. Stayed until 2007 when he retired."

Blake flipped to the second page and resumed his commentary. "Command Sergeant Major Edward Wainscott. Volunteered during Vietnam, served two tours. Came back home after taking shrapnel from a mortar on a supply run. The injury wasn't bad enough to prevent him from staying career Army. MOS was Logistics, served at Ft. Bragg as a Supply Sergeant. Must have made connections with Masters during Granada because after that, every time Masters moved to a new post he took Wainscott with him, the first time as his First Sergeant. When Masters took over his first battalion in Iraq in '91 Wainscott was promoted to Command Sergeant Major and went along. That's the rank he held when he went with Masters to Ahmadi. He also retired in 2007, four months before Masters."

He laid his papers down and waited for questions.

"Find anything irregular during their tour at Ahmadi?" Randy asked.

"Tons of it," he said, thumbing through his stack. "A bunch of mid-level purchasing or contracting officers got caught skimming or accepting bribes. Lots of outright embezzlement at all levels. Most of them went to prison although it appears they were lone wolves. And way too many unexplained non-combat deaths. But no direct connection to Masters, Wainscott, or Wyndham that I could find.

"Of course, it's common knowledge that Wyndham-Lynch, and dozens of other contractors to a lesser degree, milked billions out of our war budget. The media was on 'em like wolves on red meat. I found two dozen articles and official DoD white papers with accusations and documented numbers to back 'em up but DoD and Congress wound up burying most of it."

Blake looked around the table, accusingly. "I'm sure the fact that a trusted member of the White House staff was formerly

General Counsel at Wyndham had no bearing on that," he said, spitting the words onto the table.

"Were any charges ever officially brought against Wyndham, through the Inspector General or otherwise?"

"We didn't find anything," said Major Huddleston. "It's possible those records were classified. At our clearance level there's no sure way to know. That'd take more digging and some serious authorization."

Randy shook his head, before Blake added more.

"There was one officer in Ahmadi's Resource Office, a Major George Fowler. He was the cat apparently responsible for writing contracts at Ahmadi."

Randy nodded. "We already know a little about him. Committed suicide."

"I'll get to that. It looks like he had a hand in about all the contracts to Wyndham. Whatever he did, it must have been pretty blatant because DoD brought official charges—bribery, conspiracy to defraud the government. But the wire stories hinted at unusual circumstances. Not only did he have a spotless career record prior to that point, after he was charged he requested a meeting with the IG and asked for military counsel. He was scheduled to be interrogated through the military courts but before they could get to him, like you said, he offed himself."

"Seems like an awful lot of guilty consciences." Randy said.

"Yeah, only this one was weird. The official report said they found him dead at his desk with an open bottle of pills and an empty pint container of antifreeze. Autopsy verified it. That's not a pleasant way to die. Why would anybody intentionally turn the can up and drink that corrosive shit? An official investigation challenged the suicide but they couldn't prove different."

During Blake's report Alice Warner, the KSP technician from Phil Damron's office, quietly pulled one of her documents to the top of her stack. When Blake paused his narrative she jumped in. "About your Major George Fowler? After you sent me copies of your search results I dug a little more. Ran across an article in the Fort Worth Star-Telegram on a Mrs. George Fowler. His wife."

Randy perked up. "What about her?"

"Her obituary," she replied sheepishly. "She turned on the gas in her fireplace two days ago."

"Holy crap," said Randy, "I talked to the woman on the phone last week."

While Randy wrestled with the coincidence of husband and wife suicides, Alice Warner addressed Danny Blake. "I sent you some files, too. You have a chance to go through them?"

"Took a look," said Blake, "but didn't see anything that jumped out at me." As he replied he detected a knowing smile. "Don't suppose you happened to find something else?"

She returned a smug grin. "I ran a search on all the key officers in Wyndham-Lynch. Several had prior military service, all honorably discharged. Seven divorces, some more than once. One bankruptcy. One sexual harassment suit, settled out of court. But no apparent criminal activity as far as I could tell. Disappointing. I was hoping for a little more dirt.

"Then I did a personal search on Wainscott and Masters. Command Sergeant Major Eddie Wainscott's wife, the former Helen Young, died a few years back—pancreatic cancer. Colonel Brent Masters, on the other hand, provided an interesting twist. His wife, Betty Masters, was formerly Betty Pentecost." She looked across the table at Blake. "That's an unusual name, don't you think?"

Blake's eyes flicked back and forth, searching his pre-frontal lobe before something registered. He fished a page from the stack in front of him and ran down the list until he found it. He flashed an approving smile. "Franklin Pentecost, Chief Executive Officer, Wyndham-Lynch International." He looked straight at

Warner with a tight squint. "I don't suppose you could tell if they were related?"

She smiled. "Brother and sister. The CEO of Wyndham-Lynch International happens to be our Colonel Masters' brother-in-law."

"Bingo!" Randy said as he leaned back in his chair and digested the connection. The table was quiet for several seconds. "Anything else?" he asked.

Warner looked down her page and shook her head. "Mostly routine family lineage. Wainscott has one son. Masters had a daughter but she died."

"Died?" Randy flinched. An uncomfortable thought, not fully formed, jarred his subconscious.

"Yeah, barely a year old. A rare blood disease."

Randy recalled Pat's surveillance at Raise the Bar Gymnastics Academy. "So, I assume they have other children?"

"Uh, no," she said, checking her notes. "Just the one daughter that passed away. An only child."

Chapter 31

RANDY AND KAREN were on their second iced tea refill when Pat's Harley Davidson swung into a parking space at the Huddle House in Beckley, West Virginia.

As Pat strode down the sidewalk toward the door he caught their casual wave from the window booth inside. Karen welcomed him with a nervous hug and sat down beside her husband while Pat shucked his leather jacket and slid into the empty seat across from them.

"Didn't expect you both. So are you guys out on a date?" He made no effort to conceal a condescending smile.

"After eighteen years," Randy said, "our expectations have gotten less demanding."

"I have to admit it is a cozy little getaway." Pat's sarcasm was as thick as the waffle syrup in the condiment caddy. He swung his arm backward toward the restaurant's 50s decor and the half-dozen diners. "A little nostalgia, grease on the grill, burgers and hash browns, Hank Jr. on the jukebox . . . ambiance," he said, no apology for his poorly executed French accent.

"I tried to get you to meet us back home," Randy said.

"And I told you I'm not knocking off my surveillance yet. I'm losing time today meeting you halfway."

Pat waived off the waitress approaching their table. "Look,

guys, I know something's up or you wouldn't both be here." He let out a breath. "If you've got some bad news spit it out. It's not your fault." He didn't avert his eyes.

Randy glanced out the front window at the nearly empty parking lot and tried to remember how he and Karen had decided to begin. "First of all we do not know anything for sure about Aimee."

Pat released an inaudible sigh. At least the worst was off the table.

"But," Randy continued, "we do have some suspicions . . . about what *might* have happened to her."

Pat's eyes widened and the worst crawled back onto the table.

"Things aren't always black and white," Randy said.

Pat didn't answer, impatient.

"Whatever we discuss here," Randy said, "you've got to promise me you'll keep your cool no matter how crazy it may seem."

"For God's sake, Randy, get to the fucking point!" Pat exploded, his frustration boiling over. "Tell me what the hell you think happened to Aimee. Is she alive or not?" His frightened words flew across the restaurant, drawing uncomfortable looks from startled diners.

Randy ducked his head to avoid the glare of the customers and cleared his throat and started over.

"You said you saw Masters picking up his daughters at a gymnastics club."

"Correct."

"The Virginia State Police checked with that gym club. According to the owners Brent Masters only has one daughter— Emily. The manager verified that the second girl was a friend who sometimes goes home with Emily, to ride horses with her."

"OK, so?"

"We have reason to believe Emily may not be his daughter either."

Pat winced. "Why not?"

Randy answered slowly to let it sink in. "Brent and Betty Masters' daughter died as an infant. Our sources confirmed it."

"Then who the hell is this Emily girl?" Patrick asked. He looked back and forth between Randy and Karen. He got only muted stares. He asked again, "Well?"

Karen reached over and took hold of Pat's hand. "Pat, we think it's possible that this girl, Emily . . ." She stopped, struggling to find impossible words, ". . . might really be your daughter."

It hit him broadside like a speeding car from cross traffic running a red light, the sound and force of the sudden impact on him before he had a chance to brace for it. In an instant he took on inanimate characteristics, his body rigid, eyes ghostly vacant, breathing halted. His heart fell away as he tried to process what she had said and he felt his hand beneath Karen's turning colder.

Behind a deep shiver he closed his eyes and tried to visualize the two young girls getting into the white Mercedes while dozens of other budding gymnasts scurried to their own parents' cars. He'd paid no attention to their faces, hair color, clothes. He only remembered resenting them.

"Pat?"

Karen's voice called to him from somewhere in the void but he couldn't sort out her words. His eyes remained shut. In increments he began to feel the pressure from her hand, squeezing his, shaking his arm, trying to revive him while he struggled with the cruel concept, distorted and unconscionable. As he tried to dig through the confusion his eyelids parted, first a slit, then more, and as they grew wider the voices across the table slowly began to reassemble into complete sentences. A man and woman finally appeared, familiar friends waiting for him, just the way they were before he took a vicious detour into a nightmare world.

He shifted in the booth seat while his heart floated back into place trying to seat itself. His lips began moving and vocal chords made an effort to function again. Finally he managed an agonizing whisper, each word measured in individual bites, "How could you know this?"

"It's not a hundred percent," Randy said. "There's a chance it isn't her. But too many things point to the possibility."

Pat began to regain his bearings. When he cleared his throat his reasoning followed. "You're positive this girl, Emily, isn't his daughter."

"They had one daughter," said Randy. "Only one. She died from a blood disease."

"Maybe they adopted?"

"We checked. No adoption."

"How about family."

Pat, we looked at everything. Cousins, aunts, uncles. There are a couple of nieces in Masters' extended family but the ages aren't right. We even checked Wainscott's family tree. One son, two grandsons."

"On the other hand," Karen said, "Emily is the same age as Aimee would have been."

Pat racked his brain for options. He leaned back on the seat and steadied himself, both hands on the edge of the table. "My God . . ." he said, softly, looking for something to sustain him. "Is it possible that my daughter is still alive?"

"It's possible."

Pat looked at them and shuddered. Then abruptly, like a slide show advancing from a sunny beach shot to one in a snow storm, his expression turned grim as he acknowledged the agonizing reality. "If that's true then the bastard *stole* my daughter?"

He looked skyward, the heels of his hands tight against his

temples. Karen moved over to his side of the table and put her arms around him trying to absorb the force of his trembling body until it finally began to subside. The waitress came over offering help and Randy asked for some water.

As soon as Pat settled down they slid a glass of water in front of him. After a few sips he stared at the table for a long time trying to come to grips with it all. He finally looked up at Randy. "You said you don't know for sure?"

"That's correct, we don't . . . for sure."

Pat's expression hardened. "I think you do."

"Let's say it looks that way."

A steely look came onto Pat's face. They both recognized it at the same time. He calmly looked at Karen. "Scoot over."

The storm began all at once, out of control in an instant. Karen put her hand on Pat's arm. "No, Pat . . ."

Before she could finish Pat wrapped one arm around her and his body forced her out of the booth. Randy slid out to intervene but Pat was already holding Karen upright as he exited the seat. Randy was no match as Pat bulled past him, pulling on his jacket, and stormed out the front door. Every eye in the restaurant was glued to the scene unfolding in front of them. Randy and Karen ran behind calling out for him to stop but he heard nothing.

He mounted his motorcycle and inserted the key and the engine roared to life. As he walked the bike back out of the parking space Randy grabbed at his left arm, but against Pat's strength and the momentum of the 700-pound motorcycle it did nothing. From the other side Karen threw her arms around him but he was in a blind fury now. With a powerful sweep of his right arm he sent her sprawling to the pavement. She rolled twice before coming to rest, face down in the parking lot. Randy ran to her, lying motionless on the asphalt, and Pat revved his motor, oblivious to the aftermath of his rage. Randy gently turned her over and she looked up at him, more stunned than hurt as blood began a slow trickle from the scrape on her right elbow.

Then the sound of the motorcycle went silent. They turned and looked up at Pat, twelve years of anguish weighing on him, his hands pressed tightly against the sides of his head trying to battle the demons that had turned him against the people who meant the most to him.

As Randy helped Karen up, Pat slowly dismounted and stared at the pavement with empty eyes before he turned back toward them. His breathing was labored, his face a contorted picture of torment, trying to find words that wouldn't come.

Finally Karen made it easier. "I guess we had to get rough with you," she said, a smile creasing her face.

Pat mouthed a silent apology. Randy placed his hand on Pat's shoulder. "Let's see if they'll let us back in the restaurant. We've got things to talk about."

"After all that?" Pat asked quietly, his voice finally coming.

"We didn't drive all this way for the hash browns," said Randy. "We have a plan. Unfortunately you're part of it. You think you can listen for a minute without killing anybody?"

"Another freaking plan?"

Randy nodded.

"Is Aimee alive, Randy?"

"I hope so. You willing to find out?"

Chapter 32

HER STROKE was steady, monotonous, the stiff-bristled brush sweeping soap suds down across the flanks of the gelding tethered outside the open barn door. At 15 hands tall the bay's withers were higher than the girl's head and she pushed up on tiptoes each time the brush reached for his back. Every few minutes she grabbed the running garden hose draped in the metal tub behind her and doused the horse with another rinse before she dipped back into the bucket of soapy water and returned for another round.

Pat watched from his leafy cover in a sparse stand of trees less than 100 yards away. At that distance his high-powered binoculars couldn't pick up enough detail. Still he noted the girl's prominent features, ones he had ignored four days earlier at Raise the Bar Gymnastics: slim build, tall and rangy, medium blonde hair down below her shoulders, jeans and sweatshirt. Perhaps it was wishful thinking, the pensive admiration he held for her, but he sensed a calm confidence as she worked through her labors. He had seen her thousands of times in fitful dreams, imagined her growing from infant to child, finally to young woman. For years it had been the only thing he had left, a vaporous image of a daughter he would never know.

He tried to temper his hopes that the girl washing and

grooming a sculptured walking horse that outweighed her twelve to one might really be his daughter. It was still a calculated guess, Randy had emphasized that. But once Pat reviewed the evidence turned up by Randy's team, even as he tried to distance himself from his feelings, he had to agree that things pointed to the girl in the binoculars.

He watched her rinse the gelding one last time before she led the horse in a brief circle around the ring and disappeared into the shadows of the barn. A few minutes later she left the barn by a side door and jogged toward the house. The sun had already started sinking below the forested hills beyond.

This was Pat's third day watching her from this vantage point. He'd spent most of this time observing, plotting how to execute the plan. Until an official investigation finally unfolded, assuming one made it past Wyndham's legal roadblocks, their loose-knit scheme to gather evidence, in particular her DNA if the opportunity presented itself, had to be executed without Masters' knowledge. Trolling their garbage had been his first choice. The family dog that roamed the compound at night made that unworkable.

As he watched the screen door to the house close behind her a new idea materialized, a riskier one, pulling at him. A different plan altogether, one with a personal, vicarious edge. He felt the same pinch of anxious anticipation that fueled the rush twenty years earlier on the other side of the world. As he weaved through the undergrowth back to his car he finalized his strategy, how he would approach them.

Preparation was crucial. Google provided a cursory history of Tennessee Walking Horses: the industry, the terminology, the breeds, training techniques, famous horses. Further inquiry with the local chapter of the National Walking Horse Association turned up information about prominent owners in the region and active farms. His charade depended on him delivering a credible performance.

Through the week he had watched her as she followed a predictable schedule with her horse every day after school. Usually alone, sometimes with her friend. A staged call to Masters' office feigning an appointment request had unveiled an opportunity.

Now he just had to pull off one of the most convincing acting jobs of his life.

Chapter 33

WHEN HIS RENTED SUV turned down the private lane to the
white farmhouse Pat's stomach tightened. He didn't anticipate
that. He'd always been master of the nervous preparation that
hijacked some of his comrades, an uneasy stage fright, especially
the edgy apprehension that preceded a kill. Even though no one's
life would end today the stakes seemed higher. The game had
taken on new meaning, no longer the dispassionate slash of a
blade turning crimson in the dark, or the tension of a garrote
pulled tight while the victim kicked violently in the sand until it
was over. Today he was preparing to face the demons of a life
gone to ruin.

He couldn't flinch. The scene in front of him was unscripted
but if things unfolded in the right way, the one particular
moment, foolhardy or not, when he looked directly into her eyes
was full of potential.

When he angled left at the end of the lane and approached
Masters' house he saw her there in the first paddock by herself,
her brush moving rhythmically across the horse's flanks in easy
cadence. As he entered the wide parking area between the house
and barns his willpower dissolved and he found himself adrift as
the surreal notion of a daughter reborn took him over. He
recovered, just in time, as he bore down on a car parked next to

the porch. He slammed on the brakes while gravel crunched under skidding tires.

The sound drew the girl's attention and Pat gulped when the storm door from the kitchen opened and a 50-ish woman rushed out onto the porch. Not the entrance he had planned. Even before he had gotten started he was already off-script.

He gathered himself, put the car in park, and stepped out with one leg. He looked over the roof of the car and offered a sheepish apology to the agitated woman on the porch, obviously uncomfortable with the uninvited visitor.

"I'm so sorry. I was looking at the horse in the paddock instead of where I was going."

"Can I help you?" she asked defensively, wiping her hands on a dishtowel.

Without shutting off the engine he slid into his loosely-scripted charade. "I'm not sure. My wife and I are moving to Richmond in a couple of months and I was scouting around. We have a small stable of Tennessee Walkers in Shelbyville, Tennessee. We were hoping to find a place around here where we could set up something similar."

"Well, we aren't interested in selling if that's what you want to know."

"I understand. I was just driving around and saw the logo on your barns, and wondered if you might know of anyone in the area that might be in the market to sell."

"Have you considered finding a good realtor?" Her tone was borderline condescending.

"I'm going to do that tomorrow. I just saw your place and thought I'd ask. Sorry to bother you. By the way, are there any convenience stores out this way? I didn't bring anything to drink and I'm parched."

She measured him before her tone softened. "Nothing nearby. I guess I could spare a soft drink if you'd like."

"That'd be too much trouble."

"It's alright. We've got bottled water, Pepsi, and Mountain Dew. Just diet though, I'm afraid."

He tilted his head in appreciation. "Water'd be great."

As she went back into the house Pat shut the engine off and got out. Finding old news clips of Betty Masters astride a black walking horse, decked out in competition attire, might pay off. It gave him a starting point, something to stimulate a conversation and see where it led him.

Nonchalantly he glanced back toward the paddock where the girl had resumed her grooming. Within a few seconds the woman returned with three bottles of water. She handed him one and extended her hand.

"Betty Masters. My husband is at work. He might know somebody. I can ask when he gets home."

"Pat Cooper," he lied, as he shook her hand, then twisted the cap off the bottle. "Thanks."

She turned toward the paddock "My daughter will probably want one too." As they walked she quizzed him, "How big a stable do you have back home?"

"Small. Two young colts in training. Nowhere near being ready to show. Actually I'm a novice but my wife and daughter are both into it. Do you ride?"

"I used to. Lost my taste for it."

As they continued across the parking lot, Pat cast a furtive glance past her toward the second barn where a workman in jeans and a red-and-black work shirt was loading hay into a dark green extended-cab pickup truck. The man rose up in the back of the truck bed and his eyes followed them as they crossed the gravel lot.

When they reached the black paddock fence the girl stopped brushing and walked over. Betty Masters handed her a bottle of water. "Emily, this is Mr. Cooper. He and his wife are moving to

Richmond. They're looking for a place to relocate their stable of Tennessee Walkers."

Emily Masters smiled. "Hi," she said as she offered her hand.

A disquieting fear came over him, a sudden, overwhelming collapse of the steely bravado that had always held up under perilous conditions, and he hesitated. He felt a twinge of panic, an odd wondering if this moment might be an aberration, a bad dream from which he would awaken and find his life still mired in disarray. But as he thought back, all the times he had walked to the edge with fate right behind him and options running out, he couldn't remember ever losing his nerve. Now was no time to start.

He took her hand and twelve years of grief evaporated in the blink of an eye. That was all the time it took to recognize the telltale indicators—Allison's brilliant green eyes, the same upturned nose, a soft symmetry to her cheeks and chin that perfectly framed her, and the delightfully mischievous smile that he recalled in his dreams when he wept for them. Indisputable. Patrick Grainger didn't need DNA to recognize a living, breathing, version of his wife.

The swirl of emotions was hypnotic, a dizzying rush of epic proportions. His first glimpse of a half-grown daughter. He felt his arms tingling with a combination of exhilaration and fear and he summoned every ounce of inner strength to keep the masquerade from breaking down in front of them. As he fought to contain it, to keep up appearances, a voice appeared from behind a veiled curtain, spoiling his reverie, the familiar, constant, imbedded reminder from Allison: *You cannot stop, Patrick, until you find the truth.*

What seemed like an eternity to him was only a second or two and neither Betty nor Emily Masters recognized any hitch in the exchange. He heard himself engaging them both, desperate to maintain the charade and not to let his emotions give away the reason for his visit.

"That's a nice colt you have there," he finally said.

"Actually he's a gelding. They're gentler that way," she said, as he watched her uncap the bottle of water and take a drink. With his eyes only, he scanned the paddock for where she might discard the bottle he could retrieve later.

"Do you ride him?"

"Sure I ride him," she said, as a devilish look crept over her. "We talked about using him to plow the back forty but Dad got a John Deere instead." A deadpan expression filled her face before she finally broke a grin ear to ear, proud of the biting sarcasm.

The comment caught Pat off guard before he realized it had been at his expense and he turned red. "*Very* funny. I *know* he's a walker, I just didn't know *you* rode him," he lied. "Is he mild-mannered?"

"Sure. You saw me brushing him. You want to try?"

Betty Masters gave them both a cautious look. She knew nothing about this stranger. But farm hands were nearby. She nodded her approval and Emily went over to the gate and unlatched it, then closed it behind Pat after he entered the paddock. As he approached the gelding he used every ounce of self-control to juggle the purpose of his mission with his growing elation at the interactive encounter developing with his daughter. He approached the horse cautiously from the left side, talking softly, stroking the side of his neck with his palm.

Emily handed him a brush and he tried several broad strokes before she corrected him. "Too soft. Don't be afraid to use some pressure. They like it better." Pat pressed harder and continued around toward the rear flanks.

"You're not pulling a 'Tom Sawyer' on me, are you?" he grimaced over his shoulder, "convincing me that doing all the work is fun?" He noticed her taking another drink from the bottle of spring water and saw an opportunity. He swung back toward her, awkwardly pretending to hand her the grooming brush, and deftly knocked the bottle from her hand. It landed in a footprint in the paddock dirt and water began to gurgle out. "Oh, crap. I'm so sorry!" he said in mock apology as he reached toward her. "Clumsy." He handed her the brush and stooped to pick up the bottle.

"Don't worry about it," Betty called to them from the other side of the fence. Toss it in the trash can over there," she said, pointing to the barn door.

He distracted them both with more apologies, followed by idle chatter about why people buy water when it's free from the tap. At the trash barrel, with his back to them he tossed his own bottle and capped Emily's before slipping it into the pocket of his leather jacket.

They chatted a few minutes longer while Pat's deceit carved out the simple story of a couple looking for property in Richmond to raise a family and establish a small stable. As they talked he couldn't help but bask in the euphoria of his discovery, this amazing, never foreseen interaction with a daughter reborn from the ashes.

As the conversation wound down, out of the corner of his eye he absently noticed the red-and-black work shirt again, the one that he had seen loading hay earlier. The man was standing quietly near the corner of the barn, taking in the conversation. His demeanor was calculated, not that of a casual observer.

When Pat said goodbye and headed across the parking lot to his car Betty called to him, an afterthought, and pulled out her cell phone as she caught up to him. "Give me your phone number," she said, "and I'll call you if we hear of anything."

Pat had no intention of leaving a phone trail. "Don't worry about that. I'll get with the realtor tomorrow like you suggested."

"Nonsense," she pressed. "We might hear of something that

isn't on the market yet."

Things had gone too smoothly and he needed to avoid raising suspicion. "Tell you what," he said, pulling out his cell phone, "give me your number and I'll call you back later. That way you'll have mine."

She recited ten digits to him and watched as he punched in the number for a call he would never make. When he was done she stepped closer, her eyes fixed on his screen. "Let me see." Her finger traced the number and before he could stop her she shot an impish grin and pressed the Call button. He screamed a silent curse and three seconds later her phone rang.

He resisted the impulse to deck Betty Masters. Nothing to do now but hope her overbearing move and the link it provided wouldn't jeopardize the plan.

He faked a cordial thank you and eased his car back out onto the tree-lined lane to the county highway. Within seconds he found himself engaged in a replay of his magical encounter with his daughter. Even his embedded training wasn't enough to override personal elation, and he failed to notice the red-and-black shirt writing his license number down on a notepad.

Chapter 34

"WHERE ARE YOU?"

Pat lifted his glass off the thin cork coaster and read the name into his cell phone. "Houlihan's Irish Pub. I've got my hand wrapped around a double Jim Beam on the rocks."

"I don't know if that's good or bad. Did you get something we could use?"

"It's her, Randy."

A pause on the other end of the line. "We'll know that for sure after we run the DNA. That's assuming you got something?"

"You don't understand, Randy. It's *her*. I saw it in her eyes."

Randy felt a nervous pang. "You got that close to her?"

"We shook hands. Talked like two ordinary people." Pat breathed a proud sigh. "Randy, she's a wise guy like me."

Randy's pulse quickened. He had expected Pat to be resourceful, find his own way to get a sample, if not from their garbage then some other method, but this pushed the plan to its extremes. "Please tell me you didn't give yourself away."

"Give me some credit. I'm clear."

Randy breathed a sigh of relief. "OK, you saw a girl that *could* be her. You *want* it to be her. Nothing's for sure until—"

"You don't get it," Pat interrupted, "I didn't just see Aimee."

"OK . . . so who else did you see?"

"Allison, Randy. I saw Allison. Her body language, her voice, her face, her smile, everything. It was so freaking real. You know what I'm saying?"

Randy flashed back to the day Pat returned Julie to them at that rest area in Georgia. He did know. But he also knew this was no time to forget why they were here.

"One more time. Did you get something we can use for DNA?"

"A bottle of water," he said dismissively. "She was drinking from it."

Another sigh of relief. "Good. Get it back here."

"I'll leave first thing in the morning."

"Phil Damron wants an informal briefing with you as soon as you get back. We're getting closer."

"Randy, I spent twelve years believing they were gone. I'm not going to slip up now."

"You're doing great. Get a good night's sleep. You've earned it."

"Randy?" he said, as he raised his glass in a toast. His eyes closed.

"Yeah."

"My daughter's alive."

* * * * *

Brent Masters retrieved the vibrating cell phone from his coat pocket. While the gray suit at the front of the conference room shuttled a PowerPoint presentation to the next slide, Masters glanced at the caller ID on his phone's screen. *Garth.* He connected and muttered into the phone, "Hold on." He backed away from the conference table and attempted a graceful exit from the room.

Out in the hallway, he answered, "What's up. I'm in an important meeting."

"You might want to cancel it."

"Why would I want to do that?"

"A stranger stopped by your place today while I was loading hay out of the back barn. He spent some time talking with your wife and daughter."

"Is there a problem?"

"He looked familiar but I couldn't place him. Betty said he was asking around about properties for a new walking horse stable for him and his wife."

"So?"

"So I got his license plate and checked it out. A rental. I drove over here to the rental agency to find out who it was. Flashed my fake police badge. Works every time."

"You want a gold star? Go on."

"You'll get serious when you find out who the guy was. A name from the past. As soon as I saw it, that's when I recognized him."

"Spit it out, Garth. Who the hell's so important you had to interrupt my meeting?"

"Does the name Patrick Grainger ring any bells?"

* * * * *

Pat checked out right before dawn. Despite the brisk chill of a pre-dawn darkness his leather riding jacket and gloves were ideal wind foils and he felt nothing but hope as he aimed his Harley westward while the faint glow of morning sun behind him peeked out from the horizon.

Even though he was backtracking, the trip home took on all the characteristics of a maiden voyage. As he cruised out of Richmond he melted back into the splendor of the Allegheny Mountain range taking in every panorama of fog and valley. He allowed it to come alive this time and the nine-hour trip dissolved into timeless reflection.

As he stirred the stew of circumstance his thoughts caromed out of control. One minute he was analyzing the strategy of Randy's plan, one he had to modify, and how it had allowed good fortune to fall into their laps. The next minute things shifted and he found himself at a private viewing in which he and his daughter were the only players, neither aware of how they might one day reconnect with each other.

The giddy pleasures of his discovery softened hard edges, dulling his instincts and the keen powers of observation that had served him well in the past. Nowhere during the course of the return trip did he notice the dark green extended-cab pickup truck, making the same stops for gas, taking the same lunch break, hanging inconspicuously a mile behind him on the road.

* * * * *

That afternoon, around 4:15 Pat arrived in Frankfort and joined Randy at Mike Turner's office in the state's Medical Laboratory Complex. He dropped off the half-empty bottle of water carrying Aimee's mtDNA, now nested safely in a plastic bag. By the end of the week a forensic technologist would read the results as surely as if they had been written in neon letters, and announce what Pat already knew.

Once they completed their business Pat steered his bike out of the parking lot back toward Lexington. Within a half mile a sense of calm began to wash over him. He felt released from the force field of drama that had taken him over so completely, and he found a gentle pull, a need to re-engage in a setting layered with familiar faces. Tonight seemed like a perfect time to catch up. He glanced at his watch. He would only be a little late for happy hour.

* * * * *

After one ring, Brent Masters answered. He paced in his

study while Garth recounted his itinerary over the past 24 hours, from Richmond to Frankfort, and now in real time as he followed Patrick Grainger to Lexington. It wasn't until Garth mentioned the office complex in Frankfort that Masters stopped him.

"This Laboratory, what agencies were in it?"

Garth pulled the list out of his pocket. As he drove he ran down the names copied off the signboard in the lobby when Masters interrupted.

"State Medical Examiner?"

"Yeah."

"Goddammit!" Masters squalled. "He's digging into the fire."

"What can they find?" Garth said. "We covered every angle. It was perfect."

"Nothing's perfect. We missed something or Grainger wouldn't be snooping around. Why would he visit my house and then drive back to the Kentucky ME's office. Surely he can't know about . . ." Masters stopped.

"Your daughter?"

Masters felt a sharp stab of regret. It had been an ingenious, well-crafted plan twelve years ago, meticulously plotted, one that seemed almost foolproof. Now it looked like a trap, a traceable connection that could take them all down. His instincts back then had told him 'no' but he had done it anyway, for Betty. Now he realized his concession had placed them in one of the most dangerous places known to man . . . between a parent and a child.

"You want me to take him out?" Garth asked.

"Are you crazy? We have no idea who else is involved. Stay on his ass—where he goes, who he talks to. Keep me posted on everything." He thought through his options. "Any chance you could round up some of the old team or have they scattered like rats?"

"Kramer died in prison but some of the others, just living on their pensions, security jobs, bartending. I know a couple of new guys. What're you thinking?"

"I'm thinking when the time's right we've got to close off every loose end before somebody puts two and two together. Round up five or six guys. I'll make it worth their while. We'll move on it when we're sure we can identify all the players."

Chapter 35

DURING PAT'S ABSENCE, Pike had steered Brannon Steel's crew through a seamless completion of the first floor of the hospital's east wing, a portion of the second. On his first day back, Pat got up to speed within an hour and the crew pressed on without missing a beat.

Right before noon Pat signaled lunch break and jockeyed his motorcycle out of the crowded gravel parking lot. His briefing with the Kentucky State Police was scheduled for 1:15. As he eased past the pickup trucks and cars parked on the side of the entrance drive from the main highway, his mind was cluttered with details of his meeting. The driver of a dark green extended-cab pickup truck parked near the end slid down in his seat unnoticed when Pat passed by.

* * * * *

Phil Damron led Pat into the KSP first floor conference room where another detective was rigging up a video recorder. For over an hour Pat recounted the details of his surveillance in Richmond. He provided sheets of printed notes chronicling his actions, times, detailed descriptions, characters and places. As expected, Damron winced when he learned that Pat had approached Emily Masters in a face-to-face encounter.

"You do know," said Damron, "that even if the DNA matches we'll have to gather our own samples as part of an official investigation?"

Pat nodded. "At least you'll just be confirming something we already know."

Damron closed his files and nodded to the other detective. After they turned off the recorder Damron's expression turned somber as he waded through a few unpleasant realities.

"If it turns out she is your daughter you'll get her back but that's not necessarily going to send these guys to jail."

Pat's face turned ashen. "They have her, for God's sake. Isn't that kidnapping?"

"First glance any reasonable person would think so. But a sharp lawyer could concoct a scenario to challenge that theory."

"How?"

"If we could somehow prove they physically abducted her it would probably fall under the Lindbergh Act, kidnapping and transporting across state lines. But they'll argue something different. Since they lost their own child they might claim this was simply a black market or gray market adoption. Bring up some unnamed conspirator, somebody long gone by now. A simple act of desperation by grieving parents."

"That's not illegal?"

"There's a documented history of people selling babies since the early 1900s but it's been going on way before that. Unscrupulous orphanages, profiteering doctors, poor mothers, prostitutes. Even well-meaning obstetricians and midwives that only wanted to find a good home for unwanted babies. These days, now that adoption regulations have gotten so much tighter, babies are big business.

"The penalties for *selling* a child are severe. Not always so much for accepting one. On top of that, states have different penalties, some as little as a simple misdemeanor. Regardless, if these guys make that claim and we can't prove any different it'd be difficult to establish kidnapping."

Pat settled back in his chair, seething. "Those bastards can't get away with this."

Damron added more fuel to the fire. "You're not going to like this either but we still have a way to go to prove they murdered your wife."

Pat stared at Damron.

"In court it always comes down to three things—means, motive, and opportunity," Damron said, counting with his fingers. "Their connection to Wyndham-Lynch gives them the means, and maybe the opportunity, although we'd have to make that case. But motive? We'd have to find some way to tie them to that fraud in Kuwait. Something serious enough to justify murder."

Damron kept talking. "Conspiracy to Defraud the Government is actually a great motive, but we have to prove it even happened. Obviously, we'll request that DoD provide us with computer records for all of Ahmadi's contracts and invoices, but starting from scratch and separating out fraudulent transactions from a sea of legitimate ones would be a herculean task, given how chaotic the war effort was. The proverbial needle in a haystack. Not to mention it all took place twelve years ago. Who knows what might even be available. Could even be Classified. Even if it's not, Wyndham's lawyers will try and suppress it. And all that said, unless Masters and Wainscott were careless I'd be very surprised they didn't erase all of those files."

The comment triggered something in Pat and he clasped his hands on top of his head and closed his eyes as he recalled something from the past. "Besides the paper copies I gave Wainscott, I made a CD of all those records."

Damron perked up. "What'd you do with it?"

Pat leaned over, his elbows on his knees, and buried his face in his hands. He stayed there longer than Damron expected. "Pat, you OK?"

Pat pulled his hands down to his cheeks and stared across the floor at nothing before he spoke, softly, behind his hands. "I sent the CD back to Allison. Tucked it in my hardback copy of a book—*Selected Poems* by Walt Whitman." He forced a laugh at the irony. "I didn't want it to get damaged in the mail." He exhaled, a deep breath and looked at Damron with a helpless expression.

Damron asked the question he already knew the answer to. "The fire take it?"

"The fire took everything."

* * * * *

The next night Pat joined the Olivers over chili and cornbread, a reunion of sorts, recounting the events of the last two weeks. He narrated his daily surveillance in Richmond, a real-life version of a B-grade detective movie. His reckless venture in Wainscott's clubhouse brought predictable grimaces.

His reflection on the encounter with Aimee was an emotionally charged time for them all. He came alive as he shared the details of his meeting and the intensity of his feelings, seeing his daughter, believed lost to him forever. Julie, in particular, felt an odd stirring, her own special connection to a girl she had never met. In a strange way they were already kindred spirits.

"Tomorrow," said Pat, as he got up to leave. "I need to visit somebody." Before anyone could ask he volunteered the answer. "Allison's grandmother. It's time she knew."

"What about Allison's parents?" asked Karen.

"Gone. Cancer got both of 'em. But her grandmother's still hanging on in a retirement home in Louisville, giving the staff hell about the food, no doubt. I don't know how I'm going to break it to her, about Allison. But she deserves to know. Besides, if she thought her great-granddaughter was alive . . ."

A half-hour later, as Pat pulled out of the driveway, he resolved to make another stop tomorrow as well.

* * * * *

"A house in a subdivision?"

"Yeah. Some guy named Oliver. The same one he met at the Medical Examiner's Office. I poked around with the neighbors. He's the editor of the local paper."

"A newspaperman. That's all we need," said Masters.

"This isn't the Washington Post. It's a home town 20-page daily. How sophisticated can they be?"

"This is the new age, Garth. If a hot-shot high-school geek with a computer and enough balls can hack into the New York Times, tracking us down wouldn't be much of a stretch."

"What you want me to do?"

"Your team checked in yet?"

"Three of 'em, so far. In the motel, room next to mine."

"Keep 'em out of sight. We'll re-evaluate tomorrow. In the meantime stay on Grainger. We've got to make sure we have all the players identified before we pull the trigger."

Chapter 36

JUST BEFORE DAWN Brent Masters poured his third cup of coffee and settled in at his breakfast room table, the only light a single bulb from the range hood. For the last hour he'd been staring out across his paddocks, plumbing for possibilities, any explanation for how Patrick Grainger found a way back into his life.

The game plan back in Kuwait was complicated but they had pulled it off, seamlessly it appeared at the time, meticulously planting evidence and leaving no witnesses. Twelve years later, now that his life had turned golden and his future was secure, a nemesis appeared out of the blue threatening everything.

Around 7:30 a dark gray sedan pulled into the driveway. Masters met the driver on the sidewalk next to the wraparound front porch and handed him an envelope.

"That's three grand," he said as the man examined the contents. "Traveling money. No credit cards. Everybody gets a full share when the job's done."

"Me and them," the driver said, tilting his head toward two men in the car, "are hooking up with Garth tonight. The last two can't make it until tomorrow sometime."

"Garth's running the show but I want to make it real fucking clear," he said, tapping a menacing finger at the driver's chest. "You clean up every goddamned loose end. You miss even one and we all go down."

"Who's the target?"

"You remember that farmhouse in Kentucky back in '02?"

"Yeah," the driver said with a laugh. "Torched it after we snatched that baby. Tricky, but one of our finer moments."

"Not so fucking fine," Masters growled. "The husband's back and somehow he's on to us. I don't know how much he knows or how he found out but he's getting too close."

"So that's the job? You're sending six of us to take out one man?"

"He's got help this time. We've got to get him and anybody else that's involved. But *do not* underestimate him. This guy was Special Forces. Not somebody to take lightly."

"Is that supposed to scare me?" the driver said.

Masters' nerves were cut to the quick. Two powerful fists grabbed the driver by the collar of his jacket and slammed him against the car as the two men inside stared wide-eyed. "Don't be goddammed stupid!" he screamed. His face was red with rage. "This is not a dick-measuring contest! He's dangerous!" Then, just as quickly he relaxed his grip and pulled the man back upright and allowed him to regroup. "Just take care of business."

When Masters returned to the kitchen his wife was placing strips of bacon in an oversize frying pan. She watched the gray car pull out of the driveway.

"Who was that?" she asked, tightening her bathrobe.

"Just business." he snapped. His tension level was sky high, and the confrontation with the driver had done nothing to ease it.

She questioned him with a look. "A car with strange men shows up and you hand them an envelope full of money."

He took a sip of lukewarm coffee. "What makes you think it was money?"

"I'm not blind, Brent. I could see out the bedroom window when he opened the envelope. It looked like a lot of money."

"Goddammit, Betty, don't question me," he said, "You take care of the house and your garden club. I'll take care of the money."

"You expect me to ignore something like that," she snapped back, "handing a stranger a package full of money?"

"How about the stranger that stopped by day before yesterday?"

Her confrontational tone relented. "I see you talked to Garth." She turned back to the stove and began turning strips of bacon. "That man and his wife were looking for a farm to start a small stable."

"You're so goddamn naïve," he said, no attempt to hide his condescending tone. "He wasn't looking for property."

"Then who was he?" she said, over her shoulder.

He knew it was a mistake as soon as he'd said it, opening a door to a conversation that had no easy end. "Never mind, just fix goddamned breakfast," he said.

"Who was he, Brent?"

The tension inside Brent Masters was escalating, approaching critical mass. Grainger's unannounced appearance in their lives was a serious threat. His wife's unrelenting questions only pushed it farther up the scale. He felt his blood pressure rising and knew he had to get some air. He lurched out of his chair and headed for the door to the porch when she stepped in front of him. "Who was he, Brent?" she shouted a third time.

Brent Masters' rage had reached a boiling point. He exploded, out of control, and once the gate opened there was no way to stop it half-said.

"Emily's daddy!" he screamed at her, nearly nose to nose. "He was looking for his daughter, Betty! Are you fucking satisfied?"

The words slammed into her without warning, no way to deflect the blow. She caught a sharp breath and stepped back. As her body went slack her knees buckled and the grease-covered spatula in her hand dropped to the floor. The pan of bacon behind her continued to sizzle.

Betty Masters' fragile psyche functioned poorly in the wake of routine disappointments. It had no chance under the weight of this revelation. She staggered toward the bar stool at the kitchen island, groping for support, and he grabbed at her, help for a fallen comrade under fire. He had pushed her into territory she wasn't equipped to visit. Patrick Grainger's invasion into their safe, placid lifestyle, in particular his brazen visit with Emily in the den of the enemy, formed the core of a tense psychological battle and he knew his wife couldn't cope with any of it.

He wrapped his arm around her dreading what he knew he would find—a blank slate, void of emotion, absent all the typical signposts of distress. A return to the empty state of mind he had seen during her first breakdown when she had drifted, helpless for weeks on end.

She made it to the stool, no longer dead weight. With his right hand he gently lifted her chin and moved his face closer to hers, gazing into her eyes, searching for signs of hope. He found only deep, empty pools, her inner child once again crawling back under cover, scrambling for the safety of denial.

As he explored her he noticed an unusual flicker, an almost imperceptible change in her expression. Then an odd glimmer of recognition. He watched her eyes trying to register, looking back at him, except somehow they seemed different. Finally he realized she wasn't looking at him anymore, but past him. Fear gripped him when he realized it was a look of horror, not at something imagined, but at something real. He caught himself, afraid to turn around but the voice told him everything.

"Daddy?"

Chapter 37

THE GRASS was still slippery from the dew. As Pat wound his way down a gentle slope he took baby steps, turning his feet sideways to let his boots bite into the ground. He picked early morning, dawn ready to break through. That meant no interruptions, and he had some things to say today.

He had not been diligent in his visits, partly because his journeys didn't bring him close enough. But he had used that excuse too often, even for those times when a couple of hours and a few miles would have made it possible. The excuse kept him from having important conversations. Mostly the excuse provided a salve for raw emotions, keeping the pain at bay. But something drastic had happened that changed things and he needed to share it with her.

His motorcycle was parked at the top of the slope off the pavement edge. As he continued his descent he passed familiar names: Dixon, Ashcraft, Barnes, Herndon. Some had artificial flowers dropped into simple aluminum vases, fastened at the end of marble bases. A few displayed small American flags jabbed into the ground. Others were bare with no evidence of recent visitors. As he turned into his row his anxiety spiked. He stopped and looked lovingly at the names in front of him:

ALLISON THERESE	AIMEE LYNN
GRAINGER	GRAINGER
BORN APR 28, 1970	BORN OCT 6, 2001
DIED DEC 20, 2002	DIED DEC 20, 2002

Patrick Grainger un-shouldered the backpack and pulled out a rough cotton blanket. He rolled it out on the damp ground and sat cross-legged facing the marble headstone. He wanted to greet them—or at least one of them now that things had taken a surprising turn—and tell her how much he missed her but that would have to wait until he could gather himself. He was tough, rugged, at least those in his blue-collar crowd thought so. Most of them would never understand the repentant spirit that lived inside. That's why he found time alone with them such a comfort.

Today would be easier than most. He had good news. Still, he pulled out a small hand towel in case. He started by telling her how much he missed her and a few tears stubbornly leaked out before he defiantly wiped them away with the towel. But instead of drifting off into the maudlin memories that usually took him down he smiled at her.

"I kept my promise, Sweetheart. I found her."

He recognized her joyous reaction immediately. His imagination was more vivid than most—his English Lit teacher, Mrs. Walters, had warned him many years ago about this gift— and he imagined Allison dancing with buoyant, rhapsodic enthusiasm, swirling, singing in silence, unable and unwilling to repress her happiness at his news. He gave her a chance to settle down and then she listened, composed and wide-eyed, as he relayed the story of Julie's kidnapping, Randy's discovery,

Aimee's survival, and finally the best part—his personal meeting with Aimee, seeing their daughter for the first time as a young adult.

"She looks just like you, Honey," he said, his heart alive with paternal pride.

They talked for awhile together, sharing the excitement of discovery. When it was all out in the open, the trail of facts laid bare, he stopped to take a breath. He slipped a bottle of water from the pack and took a sip. Then he glanced over at the other side of the headstone. "So who *are* you, little one?"

He looked back at Allison, his lips pursed in determination, still smiling. "I've got a lot of work to do to finish this but when I do I'll come back and fill you in. I promise."

He wiped both eyes, and cut off the beginning of a new cry before he took in a huge breath.

"I love you, babe."

He dabbed his face with the towel. The heartache that he always carried away with him was mingled this time with hope and new beginnings. He blew his nose, loud enough to flush a scavenging songbird three graves over, then bravely stood up and exhaled. He threw her a kiss and turned back toward his motorcycle standing guard at the top of the incline.

As he walked away she was cheering him on.

Chapter 38

PAT TOOK the winding, carpeted stairway in the open lobby two at a time and scanned the dining room until he spotted her next to a window with two other white-haired women. Waitresses rolled dessert carts around to the tables with two choices—vanilla pudding or a small bowl of something that resembled apple cobbler, maybe peach, he couldn't tell.

His approach startled her and a wry smirk appeared on her face. A lifetime of well-worn creases moved in harmony with her response. "Well, look who finally decided to pay his grandmother-in-law a visit," she said sarcastically, as the other two women turned toward him and offered a polite smile.

"Hi, Margie. Good to see you, too."

"I 'bout forgot what you looked like, Patrick. How long's it been now . . . two years? Three?"

"You know good and well I stopped by in May, right after Allison's birthday."

"Lost track," she shrugged. "Our schedules are pretty busy around here."

"We're working on a new hospital over in Lexington so I figured it was a good excuse to pay a visit."

"Wouldn't want to put you out any," she said, a faint smile finally appearing, and she pointed to the empty chair.

Once he sat down he looked over at her plate, still half full. "You haven't finished your food."

"You call this food?" she said as she picked up a fork lying on the plate and smashed a few chunks of meat loaf, swirling it into her mashed potatoes. "Look at this. Not fit to eat. I ate my peaches. This gray stuff here, it's supposed to be gravy. They haven't got a clue how to make gravy. Might be fine for patching drywall."

He laughed in spite of himself. He glanced at the other two ladies' empty plates. "Your friends don't seem to have any problem with their lunch," he offered, politely.

"Oh, hell, Marie and Dorothy would eat the box it came in," she said, offering her plate to him. "Here, you try it."

He held his hand up in polite refusal. "No thanks. After dessert how about we talk awhile."

Once she finished her cobbler she backed up her chair and Pat slid her walker over to her. They scooted their way to the elevator and down to the first floor. In her room she fell back exhausted into the lift-chair recliner and he pulled a footstool over next to her.

"All kidding aside, Margie, how're you doing?"

"Not too bad," she said, decided resignation. "It'll never be home, this place. But I couldn't stay at the house any more. Can't be helped," she sighed. She pointed to a growing stack of cheap romance novels on the stand beside the chair. "I read a lot. Never miss Jeopardy. Wheel of Fortune neither. We play bingo in the rec room three days a week." She smiled, a twinkle forcing itself into the corner of her eye. "It beats living under a bridge."

"Making friends?" he asked.

"Waste of time. As soon as you get used to somebody's bad habits they kick the bucket. Have to start all over. It's easier to mind my own business. Besides, these old biddies are meaner than snakes, fightin' over the only three men in the whole place that aren't completely broke down."

Old age made her keen perception about life easy to swallow. Margie Gladman was determined not to go out gracefully. Once the conversation lulled his smile fell away and his gaze drifted toward the floor. He still hadn't figured out how to begin.

"You didn't come over just to visit, did you?" she asked.

"You always could figure me out, Marge."

"I couldn't always," she said. She waited for him to continue and when he didn't she helped him along. "You in some kind of trouble?"

"No, no trouble," he stammered. There was no easy way around it and avoiding the subject only made it harder so he dived in, starting with Julie's kidnapping. He told the story while she followed every word, alert and attentive. When he got to the part at Buddy's Grille, learning the dead child wasn't Aimee, her brow creased and she looked away trying to make some sense out of it. It wasn't until he broke the news that Allison's death may not have been an accident that she became visibly shaken. He held her hand as he told it and she cried while she struggled with the idea of a murder in the family.

He brought her a glass of water from the kitchenette and she drank some to calm herself, then sank back in her recliner, eyes closed, rolling her head side to side, searching for comfort they both knew wouldn't come easily. Despite her cranky demeanor Marjorie Gladman was deeply rooted in her faith. Even with the grace of divine intervention as support this moment was a challenge. It wasn't until his revelation about Aimee that she opened her eyes and leaned forward in her chair.

"You mean she might be alive?"

Pat smiled at her, the only piece of good news he had. "Aimee *is* alive, Margie. I met her. And she's the spitting image of Allison."

Margie Gladman wailed a sustained cry, an uninhibited,

spiritual gesture passed down from mothers and grandmothers, practiced on rickety front porches and small country churches during times of trial, and she reached both arms for him. As she rocked him they embraced for a time, patting him on the back, over and over, a generational display of love for family.

Finally her tremors began to subside and she pulled back. Her weathered face was streaked where drying tears made irregular trails through a landscape of crevasses and wrinkles. She leaned back in her chair, exhausted, and dabbed her face with a tissue. The emotional struggle had taken its toll and he wasn't sure he had done the right thing telling her like this without a doctor present.

"Marge, is there some kind of medicine in the cabinet I can get for you? A tranquilizer or something?" he asked.

She glared at him. "I held up after that awful fire, didn't I." She pushed him away and pointed to the night stand by her bed. "There," she said, wagging her finger. He slipped over to the night stand and opened the drawer and smiled when he withdrew a pint of Wild Turkey bourbon whiskey, two-thirds full. He glanced around at her, a sly accusation, but she was ready.

"Don't even think about lecturing me," she warned. "Bring two glasses."

As soon as he poured a small shot in two juice glasses she killed hers.

"Don't even need a prescription," she said, no hint of a smile.

He followed her lead and downed his. While she waited for the whiskey to calm her and allow her emotions to subside, she leaned back in her recliner, staring across the room into space, before she finally asked, "So, the police know who took Aimee?"

"It looks that way."

"And they're going to jail?"

"I hope so." He reluctantly relayed the loopholes that

Detective Damron had explained.

Margie shook her head. "No, Pat. Hell no. You can't let them get away with it."

She held her juice glass up, wagging it gently, a silent request for a refill. When Pat hesitated she shook it forcefully, this time a demand. He reluctantly poured another shot, smaller than the first, and she killed it again. They sat without speaking for a full minute while she contemplated the situation, deep concentration the way a lifetime of joy and grief had taught her. Her expression went blank, her focus lost in space, when she spoke to him in a calm voice.

"That time you spent in the Army, before you got married?" She slowly turned her eyes toward him. "Allison told me you'd done some dangerous things."

He stared back, surprised at her directness. He was unsure whether to acknowledge it. Finally he dropped his head and gave her an honest answer. "I guess I did, yes."

"Did you ever have to kill a person?"

He grimaced. This truth was difficult, especially trying to express it to his wife's grandmother. But she held her laser stare on him expecting an answer. Margie was invested as much as he was, maybe more so by blood. Too late in the game to lie.

"Yes, I did."

She leaned forward in her recliner and reached out with one gnarled hand, stained with liver spots, tendons standing out in bas-relief, and gently grabbed him by the shirt front and pulled him toward her, close enough to whisper. "If they try to get away with it you kill 'em all."

* * * * *

They visited for another twenty minutes before Pat rose to leave.

"I know you can't come around regular, Patrick, but I'm not

so feeble I can't answer the phone," she said, pointing to the cheap land line telephone with oversized numbers. "No excuses. I want to know what happens. And I don't mean a month later. You hear me?"

"Loud and clear, Marge. I'll keep you up to date, I promise."

He leaned down and gave her a long hug, then turned toward the door, relieved that a difficult encounter was over. On the way out he stopped for a moment at the antique two-tiered mahogany book rack with tarnished brass feet, one of the few pieces Margie had salvaged from the home place. He took one last, admiring look at the crowd of propped up picture frames filled with family photographs, competing for space on the top: Margie and Ellis; Allison as a child; Allison, Pat and Aimee at the hospital; a half dozen others of different sizes and shapes.

His eyes absentmindedly drifted down to the shelves below, filled with the hardback books that Margie stubbornly refused to read—literary classics, current best sellers, mysteries, biographies, all the books that didn't fit her singular, preferred category of cheap romance. That's when he saw the dark green binding, its antique gold lettering as bright as if it were electric: *Selected Poems: Walt Whitman*. His heart skipped a beat as he stared at it.

"What's the matter?" Margie called from the recliner.

"Marge, did Allison ever bring books over for you to read?"

"You bought a couple of those you're looking at—Christmas presents. Wasted your money. She brought me the rest. You both tried to educate me, said I was trashy, reading nothing but romance. But at my age I can decide for myself."

Pat gingerly reached down and with his index finger pried the book out of the lineup. Hesitant, he opened it. There, buried in the center, marking the page to "O Captain! My Captain!" the missing motive glared back at him: the compact disc with every illegal contract and invoice from Camp Ahmadi, 2002.

Chapter 39

"HE'S IN HIS ROOM," Garth said, "settled in for the night. Ran me all over the friggin' state today. First thing this morning he drove to Campbellsville, stopped at a cemetery, spent an hour there talking to a headstone."

"Who's buried there?"

"His ol' lady and the kid he thinks is his. Even with my high-mags I had to get too close. Almost got spotted. Then he hauled ass to a retirement center in Louisville. Spent part of the afternoon there visiting some old broad. Nameplate on her door says Marjorie Gladman. Staff wouldn't tell me anything."

"I'll check it out. That it?"

"On the way back to Lexington he stopped by the Oliver's house. He was carrying something."

"The newspaper guy, he's tied in somehow," Masters said. "That's got to be how Grainger's getting his information."

"Who else could be involved?"

"I don't know but the longer we wait the longer the list gets." He weighed the options. "Look, the rest of your team rolled in this morning. That's all six. Go ahead and take out the ones we know about. Grainger first, then Oliver. "

"Just like that? You make it sound like a honey-do list."

"I know it's not that simple but we can't afford to wait any longer. Just do it. What about the Medical Examiner's office? What's their security like?"

"Rent-a-cop in the lobby. Waves anybody through that can show a drivers license and sign the register."

"Once Grainger and Oliver are dead we won't have much time before somebody connects the dots. Can you find some way to get inside, get the files, maybe locate any DNA samples from the fire that could link Emily to us?"

"Jesus Christ, Colonel. I'm not James Fucking Bond here. That's one huge goddamn place and I don't know shit about their file system. It'd take a computer genius with password access. Even then, DNA samples from twelve years back, that'd be like a needle in a fucking haystack. No way I could find those."

"No, but the Medical Examiner can."

"Oh, so I'm just gonna drop in," Garth said, his voice dripping with sarcasm, "and ask nice for a couple of classified files and then 'oh, by the way, Doc, could you toss in a few DNA samples while you're at it?' Are you out of your fucking mind?"

"Look, Garth, you've got ways. Force the issue if you have to. Once Grainger and Oliver turn up dead you really think the Medical Examiner is going to think that's a coincidence? He'll go straight to the State Police. We can't leave him around to fill in the blanks."

"So you want me to strong arm the ME to pull some files and DNA and then kill him too?"

"You got a better idea?"

"Is there anybody else you want wasted? Why don't you give me a fucking shopping list, all the people you want me to fucking get rid of," Garth screamed into the phone. "You got any in-laws you're not fond of?" He mimicked a conversation with himself. "Oh, here's a couple more things I want you to handle, Garth. Take care of this, Garth. No problem, Garth."

He exploded in frustration. He clicked off and slung the

phone against the stack of pillows at the headboard where it rebounded onto the carpet. As he stormed toward the bathroom he kicked the empty trash-basket hiding under the lavatory sink and slammed his fist down on the faux marble, rattling the shaving cream and deodorant lined up at the backsplash.

The more he thought about the orders he had followed over the years, the risks he had taken, and with so little to show for it, the more his resentment climbed. Masters may have been a planning ace from West Point but, like all of them, his cavalier orders usually rolled out like a list of errands hatched in the comfort of an air-conditioned office.

Garth had watched it all from the front lines his whole career. Now, other than a government pension and a small savings account the only thing his loyalty to Masters had gotten him was a decent salary and an efficiency apartment in a barn loft in Richmond. The Colonel's ego had swelled with his rank. He took for granted all the nuts-and-bolts pieces of their missions where reality called the shots: targets not behaving as planned; situational opportunities; adjustments to avoid detection; risk of exposure. All the things that always fell into the lap of the ones in the field. His lap. And for what?

His hands were shaking. He filled a cheap plastic tumbler with ice and grabbed the bottle of vodka off the dresser and poured. His cell phone on the floor was ringing but he wasn't about to answer it yet. He killed the contents. After eight rings the phone stopped.

He poured another vodka and let it settle him while he stood out on the front walkway, hoping for a breeze. Twice more the phone rang and both times he refused to answer. Finally, the fourth time he gave in. Masters' command voice had turned conciliatory.

"Look, Garth, things are pretty tense around here. Betty already knows it was Grainger that came by. She fell apart again.

And Emily overheard it all. Everything's going to hell. We're under fire. Me, you, Wainscott. All of us."

Fifteen minutes had been enough time for Thomas Garth to distill 20 years of loyal service. It wasn't the first time he had waged this personal battle from within. It was, however, the first time he had options. Two straight vodkas on ice helped him speak.

"Colonel, I've been with you a long time. What you're asking is too much, too fast. You've got to let me handle it. My way."

"All right," Masters conceded, "but time isn't on our side. Whatever you decide, run it by me. There are a lot of factors involved."

"I'm aware of the dangers," Garth said, defensively. "One more thing. I may not be out of the Academy but I'm a professional. Would you agree?"

"You know you are."

"Am I not doing all the heavy lifting here? The one in harm's way?"

"OK," Masters said, uncomfortable now.

"I've earned a bigger piece."

Masters heard it coming before the words were out. "With what's at stake for all of us and it comes down to money?"

"You don't seem to have any problem counting *your* money, Colonel. Nothing happens unless I make it happen. I'm taking all the risks. I've earned a bigger piece," Garth repeated, too far along to stop now. The vodka was making his case.

"How big?"

"I know what you and Wainscott took away from Kuwait. You'd never miss a half-million, especially if you split it two ways."

The phone was silent for a few seconds before Masters spoke. "You know it'd be easy to round up another team. Wyndham's resources are pretty extensive. No telling what might happen to this good arrangement you and I both have right now."

"Not on your timetable, Colonel."

A long silence. Garth could almost feel the tension on the other end of the line while Masters considered his options. The Colonel had shown no mercy on Brenda Fowler when she put blackmail on the table, and Garth was convinced his proposal wasn't going down well now, but his time had come. If nothing else, the Colonel was pragmatic. Garth was betting he would agree the high stakes warranted a little flexibility.

Masters finally broke the silence. "OK, Tom. Deal. Now can we leave all this for our financial planners to work out later and get back to business? There's this tiny little issue with how we're going to eliminate those who can bring us all down."

Garth silently pumped his fist. Colonel Brent Masters had been a golden boy, virtually invincible over a long and storied military career. He had plotted and deceived the United States of America and the Department of the Army, concocting a bold plan, loaded with risk, and had come away with a small fortune for himself and Eddie Wainscott. To Thomas Garth, knowing that he had confronted this powerful man and come away a winner was heady stuff. A personal victory behind him, he slid smoothly back to the task at hand. He was eager to earn his half-million.

"Grainger's a construction guy," Garth began, reciting from a mental notebook. "They'll be on the job tomorrow. They always hang out after work. I'll put three of us on him. Somewhere between work and the motel there'll be an opportunity. We'll make the body disappear. He's got no family to look for him."

"Don't underestimate him. He has a history," Masters warned.

"The newsman, Oliver," Garth continued. "That has to look

like an accident. Anything else would bring too much scrutiny. It's important that these deaths appear totally unrelated. Maybe some tragedy involving his whole family. Like a car wreck."

"Or . . ." said Masters.

"What?"

"A fire got us into this predicament. Wouldn't it be ironic if a fire got us out of it?"

Chapter 40

PAT UNWRAPPED the first of two barbeque sandwiches in his hotel room and mindlessly clicked through TV channels. The bombshell discovery of the Camp Ahmadi CD a few hours earlier had given him renewed hope. A few minutes scanning the disc on Randy's home computer had brought it all back into focus as if he'd never left it, every contract, every invoice, dates, places, pages of summary notes chronicling the conspiracy. The missing piece of the puzzle.

The motive.

Despite the breakthrough he couldn't help drifting back to the intense, personal conversation he had with Margie. Especially her final directive. It surprised him that this older woman, tied into a life of spiritual devotion, could take such a stand, stray from a path he was certain would never meet her rigorous standards for heavenly approval. But on the way to the motel, as he turned it over in his mind he realized it came down to one primal, human need—revenge. It always did.

He switched gears and allowed a smile as he recalled the non-prescription tranquilizer Margie kept in her bedside drawer, and wondered how she had managed to smuggle it into the Center. Special Forces would have been proud. The taste of their shared drink was still on his tongue, enough to stir a subliminal desire for more in honor of his discovery and the possibilities it would bring. He remembered the liquor store in the strip center across the street. Within 20 minutes he was back in the room with a fifth of Knob Creek, a splurge for his private party and a special toast to Margie Gladman.

He grabbed the plastic ice bucket next to the sink and draped the flimsy clear liner into it. On the balcony outside his second floor room he followed the signs to the ice and soda machines on the front side of the motel. Once the bucket was overflowing with ice he bought a single Coke from the machine and slipped it into his hip pocket.

As he walked back along the front balcony a three-quarter-moon grabbed his attention and he stopped and leaned on the metal railing, taking a moment to contemplate the serendipitous circumstances of the day. A sense of calm came over him and he let his mind wander as he absentmindedly surveyed the panoramic blur of lights and color across the way, a busy hustle and stampede of traffic and fast food and gas stations that blinked and swirled and droned out beyond the parking lot below. He sighed and dropped his head, partly in thanks, partly resignation, realizing how little control he ultimately held over these latest events in his life. He'd always been a fan of Walt Whitman but never so much as this moment.

As he took stock of fate he casually let his gaze sweep from one end of the parking lot to the other. A random circus of people and vehicles coming and going: the young couple in a Wildcat blue Jeep Wrangler to his left, pulling under the covered entrance; a dozen service trucks and vans already settled in for the night; the attractive woman, early 50s, with short red hair, emerging with a laptop and valise from her gold Sebring convertible, her thin shapely legs a visual delight; the dark green pickup truck with the extended cab parked below the balcony at the far right end, a broken bale of straw in the bed.

A flicker of recognition flared, although he couldn't place it. He closed his eyes and shook his head to free the thought. Something had made him flinch, something at work under layers of mental cover: an image, a recollection, a quick burst of a visual, a color, then another, rapid fire, nothing he could recognize, although he felt the trigger, a quick jolt of memory, a flash of a picture, then another, a mental slide projector on fast forward.

He blinked and scoured gray matter trying to find it again. Out of habit he forced his eyes to trail across the parking lot a second time, from the blue Jeep to the red-head now walking deliciously across the lot to her room, then to the green truck. A dark green extended-cab truck. Hay. There it was, flashing again, clearer now. That sunny day in Richmond with Betty Masters. Then another, a gas station on the long trip back from Richmond. And another, a line of trucks parked on the entrance drive at the jobsite.

He set the ice and soft drink on the walkway and slipped down the center stairwell to ground level. Out across the front parking lot to the opposite side, turning right, strolling leisurely along the ends of parked cars until he got to the correct point. Another nonchalant move back across the parking lot toward the motel. Out of the corner of his eye, he read the license plate— Virginia. As he skirted alongside the bed of the truck, tinged with the faint aroma of hay, he recognized the distinctive decal on the rear window, in white letters: Four Chimneys Farm.

Chapter 41

THE CALL came to Franklin Pentecost's home in Wellington Estates at 8:15. It interrupted a pleasant evening with three business associates and their wives following a dinner of chateaubriand with shallot butter and roasted asparagus. With the women already strategically dismissed poolside with drinks, Pentecost touched Hold on the screen, took a draw on his cigar, and excused himself from the sitting room, leaving the men to continue their discussion of Wyndham's financing for the Panama Housing Project.

In the privacy of his personal library he re-engaged the call and leaned back in his leather executive chair, his feet propped up on the desk. Rolling the cigar in his fingers he listened as the narrative unfolded. Occasionally a scowl appeared. As each point broke the surface he processed its implications. He could feel the tension in Brent Masters' voice and waited until it was over before he involved himself.

"You believe you have a good team in place?"

"Basically the same one we used back in Kuwait," Masters answered.

"That's not what I asked. Is it a good team?"

"Yes."

"I don't want to interfere but you know we've developed

other resources since then."

"Actually, that's what I want to talk to you about."

Pentecost drew on his cigar and waited.

"Garth can take care of things on our end," Masters went on. "We're dealing with one ex-soldier and a small-town family. A team of six trained killers is more than enough. The problem is Garth himself."

"Explain."

"He threatened to cut and run if he didn't get more money."

"How much?"

"Five hundred thousand. It's not the money that bothers me. We'd never miss it. It's him getting in over his head, going rogue. I'm not sure he's trustworthy any longer."

"What are you suggesting?"

"As soon as he and his team eliminate the threats in Kentucky and we're sure we've gotten rid of all the evidence, we need to consider erasing any traces of the affair."

Pentecost knocked the ashes off his cigar. "I assume you mean Garth?"

"He's too big a risk."

"And you want me to involve Aurora?"

"When the time is right."

Pentecost squirmed in his chair. "I'm not sure Aurora's the answer. Richard runs a tight ship but most of his guys are mercenaries, plain and simple. Our group of renegades last month in Afghanistan got careless and the press still hasn't let it go. Can you imagine trying to explain their presence in a backwoods state like Kentucky, elbow to elbow with hillbillies and rednecks? Although that's probably not politically correct," he grinned. "Appalachian Americans, maybe?"

"I was thinking about not getting them involved until after my team gets back to Richmond. Let a little time pass before we move. There'd be no connections to Kentucky."

"And the other men on his team?"

"They're just followers but they know too much. They need to go. It's Garth that really worries me. A half-million could lead to more. Eliminating bad elements is good business."

"Maybe so, but it's risky," Pentecost said. "You'd better be on your game, Brent."

"Look, Kuwait was your grand scheme but I'm the one who made it happen. You know how complicated that was. I'll handle this one in the field if you can clean it up at the end."

The two men spent a few more minutes discussing strategy and timing before they ended the call. Franklin Pentecost squinted across the room at the floor-to-ceiling wall of books, none of which he had any intention of reading. He took another long draw on the cigar. He'd amassed a small fortune and he wasn't about to relinquish any of it because certain individuals were getting away from the game plan.

He lit up his cell phone and checked the time—9:35. Not too late. He pulled up a number from his Contacts list. When it answered, party music was playing in the background and he allowed the voice to find a quieter location before he relayed a briefer version of the story just told him by Brent Masters. Once the narrative ended Richard Charles, head of operations for Aurora International, finally spoke. "So you want us to take out Garth and his team?"

"That'd be the first order of business."

"I take it there's a second?"

"Our Colonel and Sergeant Major are getting sloppy. They may be liabilities as well. A threat to our job security. I'm thinking it might be better if they weren't part of our group anymore." Then he remembered something.

"A smart man just told me that eliminating bad elements is good business."

Chapter 42

BRENT MASTERS carried two glasses of iced tea out to the covered porch where his wife sat quietly on the edge of a wicker sofa. Her blank stare was focused on their daughter sixty feet away, perched on the black four-board fence grasping for her own set of answers.

For several minutes he said nothing. His careless outburst a few hours earlier, laid bare in a gush of frustration, had opened the door to a personal drama and the timing couldn't be worse. On top of having to overcome an enemy that threatened everything he had worked for, now he found himself in the middle of an intense, emotional upheaval, unfamiliar territory compared to the hard-line decisions that had served him so well in a successful military career. He'd never questioned how important they both were to him. Yet he had always treated them as accessories in a life of professional accomplishments. Now things were in turmoil and he felt ill equipped to handle it.

He held a glass out to her. She glanced at the object that invaded her space. Finally she took it and rested it in her lap, no interest in the contents, and returned to her vigil.

* * * * *

Betty Masters was hopelessly lost. As she watched her daughter she felt no anger, only a mother's unconditional love and a precarious foreboding that a contented life once thought to be untouchable was now in jeopardy. She had let him plan their journey, the hopeful beginnings, his climbing the ladder of opportunity, the inevitability of a rootless military career that would take them to parts of the world she'd only read about. She'd always been fine with her simple, uncomplicated role as wife and mother, no interest in professional accomplishments or the rush of upward mobility and status that drove her husband. It was a satisfying, comfortable life. Now it was unraveling.

She always accepted her weaknesses, her inability to work under pressure. She only wanted a return to normal, some way to make these newest threats go away, for the world to leave them alone the way he had promised.

It had been a long time since she had visited those early days, how they had stumbled on to a solution that turned heartbreak into promise. Time had helped, plying its magic, easing the one personal tragedy that had cut the deepest. But these latest developments were forcing her to confront the fact that she had conveniently ignored things she knew were wrong. She couldn't stop herself from thinking back, turning over in her mind how everything had evolved twelve years earlier.

Mired in despair and unable to cope, even after a year had passed since the death she had given up hope. Their last chance, taken away by a cruel turn of fate. Her first overdose with sleeping pills failed. Then when things seemed hopeless Brent came to her with another option, one that took her by surprise, one that she could have never imagined in her wildest dreams. At their age, one last chance. Looking back maybe she had been delusional, even morally wrong in going along with it. But the joys had seemed worth the risk. Now everything was coming apart. A perfect life torn apart by ghosts from the past.

* * * * *

Finally she spoke. "How are we going to explain it to her?"

He took her hand and squeezed it. "We'll find a way."

"What does he want, Brent?"

Telling her the truth was out of the question. A calculated lie back then had been believable. A lie now, even laid down in bits and pieces, seemed the only way to hold things together until he could fix it. He just needed to buy enough time while Garth's team dissolved the threat. There was still time to right the ship but for now he had to keep up the charade.

"I don't know yet," he said. "I'm guessing he's here to blackmail us. Get more money. He's a dangerous man. When I buy him off this will all go away."

"What if he wants Emily?"

"He doesn't," he said, crafting the deception as he went along. "He's exposed. Selling a baby means prison time. He didn't care about her then, and he doesn't care about her now. It was always about money."

"Those men today," she asked, "Is that what the money was for?"

He recognized another chance to reinforce the deceit. "Yes. I just don't know how much he wants. They're going to make him an offer."

She looked down at the glass of tea in her hands, the ice melted now. "We have more money than we need, Brent. Whatever it takes to keep her we have to do it. You know that don't you?"

He nodded.

With her right hand she took his chin and turned his head toward her, staring into a craggy face stained by years of sun and heat and war. "You do know that don't you?"

"Yes. I know that."

"I can't go through losing another daughter. I can't."

He put his arm around her and pulled her close. "You won't have to. I promise. I'll take care of everything," he said as his mind automatically drifted into comfortable territory, wondering if the last of the hit team had arrived in Lexington.

Chapter 43

THE FRIDAY HAPPY HOUR crowd at the Blue Buffalo was in full swing, music blaring, liquor flowing like spring water, the inevitable sea of rowdy, pent-up tension letting loose.

Pat polished off a greasy fried shrimp basket at the bar with Granny and Pike while Mongo and Axle sparred at the dart boards. Both players gave up and packed it in early, around 7:00. Twenty minutes later Pike killed the last of his beer, delivered a satisfied belch, and wandered out the door, stopping at one table on the way to trade friendly barbs with an electrician from the project. Another ten minutes and Granny slid off his stool and headed to the house, leaving Pat alone bar-side, sorting out life's circumstances.

A few minutes before 8:00, like a Texas Hold-em finalist checking for a pocket pair, he peeked at his tab before he slid some cash over to Caleb and headed out the door to his motorcycle waiting at the end of the sidewalk. Dusk had already settled in.

Instead of his normal route back to the motel Pat turned right out of the parking lot. Within fifteen minutes his tires were crunching on gravel. The Eastern State Hospital construction site was vacant, blanketed in darkness other than the harsh glare of one lonely halogen pole light by the office trailer. He pulled into the far corner of the parking lot, in front of the murky east wing where Brannon's crew was halfway through erecting the third and final floor.

He dismounted and waded into the shadowy structural steel framework. The darkened grays and browns were faintly illuminated by incandescent safety lights strung from column to column with temporary wire. At the waist-high plywood plan table he switched on a cheap desk lamp and unrolled the plans he'd left there earlier. He began paging through them, an isolated island of light in a sea of near darkness.

The clash of construction activity was conspicuously absent, the lonely quiet interrupted only by the swoosh of an occasional car passing on the highway 300 feet away. He lingered there, occupied with the drawings in front of him when he recognized the sound of footsteps on gravel, then on the concrete slab. He looked up to see three men approaching him. Dark clothing, short leather jackets, spreading out left to right, establishing positions, their faces indistinguishable in the diffused shadows.

Pat leaned heavy on the plywood table. "Something I can do for you?"

The men on both flanks were tall and rangy, younger than 30. They said nothing and stopped, expressionless, legs planted. Compact Glock G19 semi-automatic pistols with silencers hung loose by their sides. The one in the center, apparently the leader, had no weapon. He stood with his arms crossed, grinning. He was no more than 5'-6", stocky build, thinning hair combed over. The grin grew into a self-satisfied smirk. His head nodded imperceptibly in anticipation of this moment.

"Working late on a Friday night?" the smirk said.

Pat didn't take his eyes off the man. "It seemed like the best way."

A puzzled look. "For what?"

"I've been waiting," Pat said, glancing at his watch, mildly annoyed, "more than twenty minutes. What took you so long?"

The man flinched at the curt response. He'd been looking forward to the cheap thrill of a brief debate with a war hero caught in a vulnerable position. The tone of the conversation had taken an odd turn.

Pat continued. "Seems like your good fortune, finding me at an empty construction site after dark."

The smirk shifted uncomfortably. He swiveled his head, popping bones in his neck to release his growing tension. He sensed an urgency to finish it and reached inside his jacket.

"Not a good idea," Pat said, calmly.

His sidekicks raised their pistols while the leader withdrew his own Glock, a larger G17 model, and unconsciously checked the tightness of the sound suppression device.

"You don't appear to be in a good position to negotiate," the smirk said.

Pat smiled. In unison, almost as if they had rehearsed it, the three men swung their line of sight upward to the crisp, ratcheted sounds of three lever action hunting rifles simultaneously engaging their first rounds. Each assassin found himself staring into the business end of a gun barrel. On the edge of the concrete slab mezzanine 14 feet above them, Granny, Mongo, and Axle were lying in prone marksman positions, fingers on the triggers.

"These boys are crack shots," Pat said. "If they can pick off a squirrel at twenty yards, they can damn sure nail you between the eyes from twenty feet. Weapons down, gentlemen."

Once the pistols lowered, Pat slipped around the table and took them from the short leader and the one on the left while Pike appeared from behind a stack of concrete form panels and collected the gun from the third. Using the leader's Glock, Pat motioned them around behind the plan table and forced them down on the concrete slab, face down, their arms stretched out in front of them. The riflemen on the mezzanine descended a ladder while Pike slipped over to the front of the building and stood watch in case there were others.

Granny extracted the men's wallets and placed them on the plywood table where Pat flipped through each one. Within two minutes the men's hands were bound behind their backs. The crew rousted them into a sitting position while Axle rifled their shirt and jacket pockets. Pat squatted in front of them, balancing on the balls of his feet. He stared at them, letting the circumstances sink in. Finally, he addressed them, pointing one at a time. "Larry . . . Curly . . . and . . ." he hooked the short man under the chin and lifted his face, "Mo!"

"You boys really do need practice in soft surveillance," Pat said, shaking his head like a condescending teacher scolding students. "Following me to work today from the motel. Tsk, tsk, tsk. Very clumsy. Then at the Buffalo, which one of you was nursing the beer at the corner table? You know, those outfits don't exactly blend." He continued to shake his head. "I know you were waiting for the right spot but we practically had to draw you a map."

The leader reacted with a sneer. "Fuck you."

"You've got anger issues," Pat said. He allowed another condescending sigh before his expression and tone hardened.

"I expect there's more than you three. Who's driving the green truck?"

They glared back, no response. Axle was unfolding a piece of motel stationary he retrieved from Mo's jacket and made an offhand comment to the crew in general.

"It's some street address in Frankfort."

The remark grabbed Pat's attention. He snatched the paper away from Axle and his face flushed when he recognized Randy Oliver's address. A shot of terror coursed through him. He let the page drop and grabbed Mo by the collar of his jacket, shaking him, the eruption spontaneous and violent.

"Why do you have this address?"

The man sneered again. Pat jerked him to his feet and slammed him against the hard face of a steel column. The impact knocked the breath out of the man and notched a gash in the back of his head. With a firm grip on the man's jacket Pat again demanded an answer. Even dazed and in pain the man was defiant.

In a loose rage Pat slung him down to the concrete slab, on him like a ring fighter, sharp punches to the head, his arm a high-impact piston. He paused after each blow, repeating his question, waiting for an answer. Each time an answer failed to come he delivered another punch. The piston engaged again and again—question, punch, question, punch. He continued to batter the man's face.

One of Mongo's heavily tattooed arms finally intervened. He pulled Pat away from the withering body below him. He got in Pat's face, nose to nose, his long gray beard bobbing over Pat's heaving chest. "Easy buddy. He's no good to you unconscious. There's a better way."

Pat backed off, his breathing labored from the relentless assault. His fist was covered in the man's blood. Following Mongo's cue, the rest of them pulled the three men to their feet and herded them, stumbling, through the structural framework to the back of the building. They stepped off the slab and crossed a short expanse of gravel to Brannon Steel's storage trailer, isolated against the back property fence and a vacant field.

When they raised the rolling door they boosted the three men into the trailer and climbed in with them. Someone switched on a battery-powered emergency pack and the inside of the trailer was instantly awash in a stark white light. They dropped the trailer door, sealing themselves from the night, and shoved the men down onto a row of cardboard boxes of bolts and fasteners that lined the side wall. Axle and Granny pulled three fresh cotton cleaning rags from another box and stuffed them into the mouths of their captives and tied them in place with more rags.

Mongo gestured toward the sitting men with an open hand.

"Ask him nicely, one more time."

Pat had recovered from his rage but wasn't sure where this tactic was heading. Still, he followed the big man's lead. He stooped down in front of them and repeated his question. The ringleader was bloody, reeling from the beating, but the same two-word curse, even muffled behind the gag, was unmistakable.

Without comment Mongo slowly crossed behind Pat into the deep end of the trailer and wrestled briefly with a tall, bulky object, hidden behind his own shadow. He backed out and rolled it on two wheels toward the gathering.

As soon as Pat saw it he shot a glance at Axle and Granny. Their eyes returned a guarded panic. The three captives also stared wide-eyed when they recognized it. Mongo unwound the red and green reinforced rubber tubing hanging on the side of the rolling dolly. He raised the stainless steel welding torch, connected by the tubing to twin 150 cubic foot tanks—one filled with acetylene, the other pure oxygen.

Chapter 44

PAT HAD CROSSED LINES of moral conscience before in a soldier's world where rules were scarce. Blind obedience. He'd killed and worse. They'd taught him creative ways to get information. The violence was brutal, often choreographed in sheltered tents and rooms, but the inevitable conclusions were almost always drenched in blood.

He'd left it behind, unable to deal any longer with a shredded conscience, one that had mercifully pulled him back. Now Mongo seemed to be drawing them into ethical territory he wasn't sure he could visit again.

He'd never seen this dark side to Montgomery "Mongo" Eugene Willett, a bear of a man, calloused by a life of hardship. A casualty of an emotion-deficit backwoods clan that knew nothing outside their generational life of crime and rural poverty, his bulk and mountain-man countenance disarmed everyone he met. It was obviously having that chilling effect on their captives. But other than a few unavoidable bar fights over the years, all of them victorious, beneath the facade stirred a gentle soul as insecure as the next man, a friend for life, loyal in his own crude way. This latest version of Montgomery Willett, however, was unsettling. An unexpected wildcard in a situation that may have already gone too far.

Mongo unhooked the metal flint striker from the dolly and opened the top valve on the tank of acetylene. He made a point of facing the bound men when he struck the flint. When the acetylene gas shot from the tip of the torch it caught with the distinctive 'whoomp' and the three bound-and-gagged men jumped. Their eyes swelled as they began to squirm, their screams unintelligible behind the gags, heads shaking violently.

The mountain man calmly opened the valve on the other tank, releasing a stream of pure oxygen and converting the acetylene jet into a 5,000 degree flame. He adjusted the manual knob on the torch handle while a captive audience watched the flame change from orange, to yellow, then to the familiar intense blue. A color that signaled terror.

Granny shot a desperate look at Axle and Pat shifted in place, unsure how to diffuse a situation that was getting out of hand. The tension in the trailer had maxed out, a drama with dangerous consequences. Axle reluctantly moved toward the large man and placed his hand on a tattooed arm.

"That's too far, man. We can't do this," he whispered.

Mongo turned his back to the captives still shouting muffled screams behind the gags. In full panic they tried to wrestle themselves up off the boxes but Mongo reached back with his leg and placed a cobbled boot in each crotch, one by one forcing them back down onto the boxes groaning in pain.

He turned back to Pat and Axle and raised the torch to chin level to better illuminate his face, throwing fractured light onto his full beard. As he triggered the torch three times in succession, each pull generating a sharp hiss, they caught a telltale sign—an unmistakable bold country wink, one they had seen before after too many rounds of Jack Daniels. He discretely placed the index finger of his free hand vertically in front of his puckered lips and shushed them. Right before he unleashed the drama.

He erupted into a spontaneous, rambling oratory, spitting

out the fake dialog of a madman, his arms flailing for effect, solely for the benefit of their prisoners. He spun as he rambled, the torch cutting through the air like a holiday sparkler. He railed against subversives, against weakness, against communist cowards who would sneak up on a man in the middle of the night, three on one. Axle swallowed a grin.

The rant behind the beard grew louder as he recalled imaginary encounters in imaginary wars in which he never fought. He drew Pike's silent approval when he brandished deep emotional scars from altercations down in the mountains where vigilante justice prevailed and from which he had triumphed victorious. A lesson he assured them they were about to learn.

Granny stifled a smile as the mountain man's voice swelled with inflection, deep in the moment, a Shakespearian spin on Cool Hand Luke, performed in front of an attentive audience. Toward the end of his performance he turned back to his friends and caught their attention with an exaggerated wiggle of his eyebrows to reassure them, proud of his first stage work.

With his back to the captives he flashed a second subtle wink, then turned to his real audience. He triggered the torch in spurts of blue heat and delivered a powerful closing line. "Let's see how important that information is to the gents."

Mongo motioned to an object on the rough wood floor of the trailer and Granny, now in the role of supporting actor, followed his lead. Granny picked up a three-foot piece of steel re-bar and held it out in front of him, wrapping a rag around his end to absorb the heat. In full view of the captives Mongo triggered the torch and held it to the bar. The blue flame spit an incendiary shower of orange sparks and smoke, accompanied by a sickening, static crackle and the industrial smell of melting steel. The bound men watched wide-eyed as a piece of 60,000 psi reinforcing bar, within seconds, was reduced to molten metal. The cut-off piece of steel dramatically dropped to the floor with a clunk and the cut end began to cool from hot orange to gray.

Wild-man Willet held the tip of the torch up in front of his face, this time in full view of the bound men, pretending to examine it. He made a professional muttering to himself about the temperature before he studiously turned the adjusting knob on the side of the torch a quarter notch and triggered it again.

"That's better." He calmly turned to the seated trio and. concocted the most diabolical grin he could muster.

"Who's first?"

A urine puddle was already spreading beneath the associate on the left, uncontrollable whimpering, his eyes closed. Pat figured this one would be easy to turn but would he have enough useful information? Maybe, but not his first choice.

The other sidekick, sitting in the middle, also appeared to be an easy target. His eyes couldn't get bigger and his heels kicked violently against the floor, begging. It was clear he had no interest in the excruciating pain waiting at the end of the acetylene torch, no matter what fee he had been promised. Hired hands with no emotional investment. Like the first man he was screaming through his gag, a child begging them to let him talk. Another backup choice.

"Why don't we start with this smart-alec little fellow," Pat said, pointing at Mo. As he stepped around Mongo he discretely looked back at him, eyes wide and eyebrows raised, seeking one final assurance from his friend that this whole scene was purely for show. He got it, a brief, imperceptible nod.

Game on.

He kneeled down to Mo, then reached back and gently pulled Mongo by the front of his shirt down with them. The short man's swagger had disappeared. It was replaced by an involuntary trembling as he stared, transfixed, at the live acetylene torch a foot from his face, gripped in the powerful paws of a madman, hissing with each pull of the trigger.

Pat let him squall behind the gag. Another lesson he had learned—let a victim's fear escalate until desperation takes over and he begs for the chance to talk. Unless the victim was a fanatical zealot anxious to meet his 72 virgins, it usually resulted in reliable feedback, unclouded with misinformation or missing details. Before he untied the gag he looked the man square on.

"I want you to understand I'm not playing with you. What do you know about this address?"

On cue, Mongo triggered the torch. Mo violently nodded his head in agreement and screamed in his throat. Pat untied the binding and pulled the gag out of his mouth.

Mo gulped several breaths of air and with the gag Pat wiped the man's red face, covered in perspiration. "It's just . . ." he gasped, between deep breaths, ". . . your friend's address."

"I know that. Why do you have it? You going after them too?"

The man avoided eye contact, terrified at delivering the truth, and looked away. Pat grabbed his jaw. The bruises from the earlier beating were already making appearances. "Is that it? Are they next?"

Mo hesitated too long. Without warning Pat grabbed Mongo's hand and leaned the stainless steel shaft of the live acetylene torch down against Mo's pants leg, just for a second. It was long enough. The blue jet burned a hole in his pants and seared a dime-sized spot into Mo's flesh beneath it. He bellowed a cry of agony, an uncontrollable, rapid-fire series of high-pitched squeals while the singed edges of the fabric continued to smolder against his skin. The unmistakable stench of cooking flesh drifted upward. Pat tamped out the frayed edge and waited until the pain subsided.

"Don't . . ." the man cried, "Please . . . don't."

Pat hooked the man's chin and pulled his face back up. "Who's setting this up? I know you're not the one."

"They'll kill me."

Mongo hit the trigger on the torch again and Mo jumped.

"Ok, Ok, Ok," he stuttered, full submission. "One guy . . . Tom Garth . . . team leader . . . please don't."

"He the one with the green truck?"

A fast nod.

"He works for Masters. Masters is behind it, isn't he?"

"Yes," the man said, defeated.

"OK, you're doing great. When were you supposed to hit my friends, the ones at this address?"

Mo stared at the torch hovering inches from his face. "We weren't."

"You said they were the next target."

"They are," he said, between choppy gasps, "but not by us."

"Then by who? Garth? Does he have another team in town?"

"Yes."

"And when's it supposed to happen?"

"They're on the way now. A simultaneous operation."

"Shit!" Pat screamed. He pulled one of the silenced Glocks out of the pile that Pike carried to the trailer and grabbed Mo's collar and slammed him against the wood cribbing on the trailer's metal wall.

"How's it supposed to happen?"

"It wasn't my idea." He was desperate to deflect liability and his words spilled out in a torrent. "I wouldn't have done it that way."

"What way?" Pat was in the man's face. "What way?" He forced the barrel of the Glock under the man's chin.

"They're gonna burn 'em!" Mo cried, his will broken. Then a second time, the words barely audible, dribbling out through a flood of uncontrolled sobs. "They're . . . gonna . . . burn 'em."

Chapter 45

PAT WAS ON HIS FEET, a quick glance as his watch. "I can get there in 25 minutes. Hold 'em here. I'll call you."

Granny grabbed Pat's arm. "Buddy, maybe it's time to call the law."

"As soon as I know they're safe." Pat pulled away and dropped back down in front of Mo, limp against the trailer wall. He jammed the pistol hard against the man's temple. "How? How were they going to do it?"

It spewed out in quick bursts. "An explosion . . . C-4 in the electrical panel . . . remote detonator."

Pat lurched back up, his fear at critical mass. For the first time in his life he felt helpless. He released the magazine from the borrowed Glock, a quick check on rounds, and rammed it back into the grip.

Pike tried to block his path. "Pat, c'mon, man. The police? Let's call 'em."

Pat's cold stare left no doubt he had already considered it. "A show of force, things get out of hand. People die. These guys are professional killers . . ."

Pat stopped, gripped in a blinding thought, and his eyes closed. His right hand tightened on the grip of the Glock, an involuntary reflex, while he studied it, the pistol tapping an anxious beat against the side of his leg. When his eyes opened he turned in slow motion toward the man on the floor, his words cold, without inflection.

"Was Tom Garth on the team that burned my house?"

Mo turned away. He stared at the floor until he heard the sound of the Glock's slide ratcheting back, engaging the first bullet. His breath left him.

Pat asked again, counting out the words, "Was Tom Garth on the team that burned my house?"

Mo looked up at the barrel of his own pistol pointed at his forehead, his eyes wide with fear. No choice.

"Yes."

Pat's next question was already on the way.

"Were *you* on that team that killed my wife?"

Mo stared into the open barrel, unable to speak. His refusal to answer was answer enough. Pat calmly approached the sitting man and placed the Glock against his temple while the demons urged him on.

"Pat, don't do this," Granny said.

Pat heard nothing. His finger tightened against the trigger. He'd come so far from out of nowhere and now he'd found the truth. Time to even the score, one at a time. He was on autopilot now, relentless, unfeeling, like in the old days. Blind obedience, only this time for Allison. The thought of her watching made him hesitate. He blinked, unsure. The dark forces clawed at him, their talons digging deep. They were close. But Allison's call was pure, unwavering. He felt his finger relax and the demons slithered away, cursing, making plans for their next opportunity.

Pat pulled the gun away from the man's head and stood up. He took a deep breath and cleared the cobwebs from his own mind, then pulled out his cell phone and stepped around Pike.

He jerked open the lift door, the clatter of rollers rumbling in rusty steel tracks, and hit the ground running. He dialed

Randy's number while he rushed toward the parking lot. After five rings he heard the ringtones stop. Pat halted, no words, no background noise, and listened, waiting for the response that should have come from the other end. When none came he disconnected and began running again, faster.

* * * * *

The dissonant sound broke the tense silence in Randy Oliver's kitchen, a treble-heavy tune calling out from the pack of three mobile phones lying on the counter. An oldie from 1966, a song that made Randy's stomach ball up in a knot: 'Wild Thing' by The Troggs. The ring tone on Randy's iPhone. On a whim he'd had Brad program it for him, a self-depreciating disconnect from his own mild-mannered personality. It had been the source of good-natured ridicule from friends and associates. Tonight it wasn't funny. Tonight it threatened to trigger a bad ending if the incoming call was from Pat. Especially if the man across from him griping a semi-automatic Beretta realized it.

Storming the Oliver house a few minutes earlier had taken seconds. Two men with pistols barged in through the front door while Garth tore through vertical blinds covering the family room's open patio door. For the Oliver family the siege was terrifying, a traumatic ordeal that only happened in the movies.

The men quickly tied them up with rawhide boot laces and rounded up cell phones, Randy's from his pocket, Julie's lying on the side table. They found Karen's in her purse when they unceremoniously emptied it onto the coffee table in front of the couch where she sat. An all-American family trapped in a real-life nightmare, a front page headline Randy was afraid he would never get to write.

Despite the limited quality of the phone's tiny speaker, the ring tone held the room's attention. Garth stared at it, then back at the Oliver family sitting on the couch and recliner, their arms bound behind them. He picked the phone out of the pile and frowned as he struggled to pronounce the name on the screen.

"Lachesis? What the hell is that?"

Randy felt his heart fall. Following their fateful encounter at the rest area in Georgia and their ensuing bond with Pat, Randy had playfully anointed Pat with the nickname Lachesis, the apportioner. In Greek mythology, the second of the three Fates, white-robed incarnations of Destiny that controlled the metaphorical thread of life of every mortal from birth to death. After Julie's rescue it only seemed appropriate. Pat had accepted the honor and proudly made it his new screen name.

Garth answered the call and waited without speaking. He heard nothing from the caller. Finally the connection shut down. Confused, he held the phone up to Randy.

"Any idea who this is?"

"Must be some crank call," Randy said.

His mind churned, running through bits and pieces. *Pat called, didn't speak, I didn't answer. He has to know something's wrong. Buy some time.*

While Garth stood guard Randy watched the two associates make their way through the kitchen. The short one, portly with brown-tortoise-shell framed glasses, backtracked out the front door. The taller one, slim with a ruddy complexion and a buzz-cut appeared to be scouting for something. He slipped out into the garage. The leader paced in the kitchen, glancing back at them at intervals.

Randy checked the clock on the kitchen soffit above the refrigerator. Pat's call came at 9:23. Two minutes had elapsed.

Garth picked an apple out of a bowl on the kitchen counter, then sat down in front of them and took a bite. Randy eyed him.

"You going to shoot us?"

Garth took his time with his mouthful of apple and swallowed before he answered. "Not unless you force me to," he said, wagging the pistol. He had no intention of shooting anyone. A bullet in any of their bodies, even the forensic trail of a bullet, would take 'accidental fire' off the table.

The short man returned with a small nylon carry bag. The buzz-cut intercepted him at the door to the garage. "Out here." Both men took one step down into the garage. Garth tossed the apple in the kitchen sink and backed over to the door. He kept his pistol pointed at the family while he involved himself with the scene unfolding in the garage.

With the gunman 20 feet away Randy ducked his head and whispered to Karen and his kids out of the corner of his mouth. "I think Pat's on the way. We have to buy some time."

"How, Dad?" Brad whispered.

"I don't know. A diversion. Anything."

"We try to escape," Karen said, "they'll shoot us."

Randy kept his voice low. "If they wanted to kill us they would have already done it. Something else. Think."

Karen racked her brain as she stared blankly at the coffee table in front of her. The contents of her empty purse were scattered across it: lipstick, mascara, car keys, nail clippers, billfold, compact, flashlight, pens . . . Then her eyes returned to one object. The man was watching them from the kitchen. With her hands bound behind her back there was no way she could get to it without him seeing.

Julie was on the end of the couch, her eyes sweeping the room. To her right the family room opened into the formal dining room, one they only used for holidays. In turn it adjoined the house's central core—the front foyer and the stairway to second floor bedrooms. The gunman in the kitchen had his own angle to the front door through the living room. With her hands tied behind her there was no way she could get the front door open before he intercepted her.

Brad was watching her. "My cell phone," he whispered.

Her brow wrinkled. Then a latent thought crept into her head. When the men searched them earlier Brad's response had puzzled her. Now it made sense.

"You didn't leave it in your locker at school, did you?" she whispered.

"On my study desk upstairs."

Chapter 46

JULIE JUDGED the distance and waited. When the man in the kitchen glanced into the garage again she bolted off the couch into the dining room. At the sound of running feet Garth turned back and saw the newly-vacated seat on the couch.

"Hey!" he yelled to the garage, "get in here."

The buzz-cut appeared immediately and Garth lunged into the living room. He expected the girl to try the front door. Instead he watched through the banister railing as a pair of blue-jeans disappeared up the stairs. He chased after her, the tall man behind. The third man in glasses abandoned his work in the garage and stood guard over the remaining family members. In the confusion he never noticed when Karen twisted and snared something off the table and slid back onto the couch.

At the top of the stairs Julie turned right two steps toward Brad's bedroom, kicked the door shut, and twisted the button on the cheap lock. Brad's iPhone was there on his desk. She backed up to it, flipped the ringer to 'silent', slipped it into her back pocket, and waited for the door to break open. A second later it did, the door jamb splintering behind the force of the tall man's shoulder. They manhandled her out of the bedroom and carried her kicking back down the stairs.

They slung her face-first down onto the couch. When she

tumbled on top of her brother, Garth noticed the outline in Julie's hip pocket. Before she could right herself he pulled out the iPhone and held it up to the tall man. "Miss something?"

"She didn't have it when I checked 'em," he said, glaring at Julie and Brad.

Garth pressed the On button and the screen lit up. Behind the icons was background wallpaper, a full-color photo of Brad on the basketball court, releasing a jump shot over a lunging defender. Garth raised his eyebrows at Brad with a mock question. "I thought you left it in your locker."

"I guess I forgot," Brad said, defiant.

Garth mulled it over and turned the screen toward them so they could see the image. "Did you make the shot?" He didn't wait for an answer. He handed the phone to the buzz-cut. "Put it with the rest."

He glared at Julie, tapping the barrel of his Beretta into the palm of his hand. Her little dash had failed but it still angered him. He had to remind himself a bullet was out of the question. He gave an order to the tall man.

"B.J. doesn't need your help in the garage. Stay with them, watch every move. If any one of 'em gets off that couch again, hurt 'em."

"Even the girl?"

"Especially the girl."

Randy homed in on the clock in the kitchen: 9:41. Eighteen minutes since Pat's call. Out of the corner of his eye he watched Karen busy behind her back, fingering her ring of keys and the car's pushbutton remote. The Suburban parked in the front driveway was at least forty feet away, maybe more.

The short man had disappeared back into the garage while the buzz-cut kept his full attention on the Olivers. Karen manipulated the ring, careful to silence the keys, and aimed the plastic remote-control fob in the direction of the driveway. The man in the garage had started up again. She mentally crossed her fingers and pressed the large orange button.

Two seconds later any question about the effective range of a keyless remote was answered. The Suburban broke the silence of a quiet residential neighborhood settling in for the evening, blaring out a barrage of loud, intermittent honks at three-quarter-second intervals, repetitive, unmistakable, metallic blasts, one after the other, piercing the night.

The short man in glasses appeared in the doorway to the garage, agitated, his open arms begging the question. The horn continued to bellow, unabated, relentless obnoxious bursts with no end. Garth ordered the tall man to stand watch while he rushed across the dark living room to the front windows. When he parted the blinds there was no mistaking the lights on the blue and gray Suburban parked in the driveway, the flashes of yellow and white synchronized with each repetitive burst of the horn.

He bolted back into the family room. The contents of Karen's empty purse scattered across the coffee table confirmed what he already suspected. He shoved the coffee table aside and grabbed Karen by the back of her neck, jerking her forward. He checked her hands. Empty. The horn outside continued to blare, steady, unforgiving staccato blasts.

He rolled her into the floor and pulled the seat cushion off the couch. Wedged into the space between the couch base and the back he saw the key ring and the black plastic remote fob. He pulled it out of the crease and pointed it toward the driveway and pressed a button. The horn went silent.

He slipped back into the darkened living room and parted the blinds again. No sign of nosy neighbors. They were probably peeking out front windows or grinning in front of their TVs, making plans for some good natured ribbing tomorrow. Unfortunately, after tonight their plans would be meaningless in the aftermath of a raging fire that would disrupt the routine calm of their upscale neighborhood and take four lives.

His captives had tested him but retaliation would be a waste of time. They were almost ready. As he headed back to the family room, in his own twisted way he respected their resourcefulness. They had no training and still they had created disruptions. Admirable. Especially from amateurs. The task in the garage was nearly complete. In a few minutes the family would understand why they never had a chance against a professional like him.

Karen was still lying on the carpet, dazed but unhurt. Garth lifted her up and gently propped her up on a stool at the kitchen counter. He slipped into the kitchen and with his left arm he swept the pile of cell phones and pocket knives into the sink. He whispered in Karen's ear, "Don't want to tempt you."

Without prompting the buzz-cut moved to the sliding glass door and locked it. Randy checked the clock: 9:47. Twenty-four minutes since Pat's call.

"How much longer?" Garth asked, as the short man headed back to the garage.

"Couple of minutes if I could stay on it," he said, adjusting his glasses. He gave Garth a sarcastic smirk. "You think you can keep this bunch of commando's under control that long?"

"Just finish it."

A little over two minutes later the short man stepped back into the kitchen, a satisfied grin on his face. He carried a device slightly larger than a pack of cigarettes and handed it to Garth. It had a lever-activated hand-grip and a short rubber antenna. "Safety clip's on but be careful. I've got two blocks of plastic packed around the mains, blasting caps in place. I left the panel cover off. It'll improve the blast spread."

Chapter 47

"CLEAN UP," Garth said under his breath. He tipped his head toward the family room. "We'll get them ready."

The electric panel was embedded in the garage wall common to the house. The short man knelt in front of it gathering up loose items on the concrete floor—six-way screw driver, needle-nose pliers, small flashlight, black electric tape, scrap wire cuttings—and stuffed them into his bag. As he prepared to zip it up he heard a distinct sound behind him. A soft whistle. Manmade. Intentional.

He stopped and listened. He felt someone's presence, light breathing. Then the mottled sound of crickets and the subtle drift of neighborhood noises not found inside a garage. Through an open door he heard the swoosh of a car passing on the next street.

He was kneeling. Slowly he turned toward the sound. With his body as a shield he casually let his right hand fall inside the nylon bag, feeling for the Beretta under the clutter of tools and scrap. When his body turned enough he saw a man braced and pointing a silenced pistol at him.

Pat shook his head and whispered a warning.

"Don't do it."

The man's hand had found the Beretta. Even with a pistol

pointed at his forehead, he felt a surge of bravado, partly because of his perceived deception, partly from the false courage that came from the feel of a gun in his hand. He slowly got to his feet. As his body raised so did his arm, drawing the gun out of the bag with it.

Every man picks his time. This was his. His move was swift but Pat's finger was already snug against the trigger. As two shots plowed into the man's temple, his arm continued its swing in a wide arc, an involuntary muscle response, and the Beretta discharged a round into the opposite wall. He fell, dead weight. His glasses jarred loose when his skull cracked against the slab, and the Beretta clattered across the concrete floor.

In the family room the buzz-cut had bound Julie and Brad's ankles with rawhide laces while Garth leaned back against the kitchen sink going over the final sequence. Both men recognized the familiar sounds at the same time—three distinct shots discharging through sound suppression devices. They wheeled toward the garage in time to see a gun skidding across the concrete and the arm of the dead man flopping into the picture. The buzz-cut drew his weapon and crouched, using the kitchen island as cover. Garth backed up to the refrigerator on the wall next to the garage, his weapon in a two-handed grip.

From his seat in the recliner Randy could see nothing, but his captors' unexpected shift into fighting stance was a giveaway. *Pat? The police?* He barked an order to his son and daughter, "Get on the floor." Brad used his knees to overturn the coffee table and he and Julie dropped onto the carpet behind it while Randy shifted to the couch.

Randy shuddered at the bigger problem—Karen perched on the stool in the line of fire. The armed man was using her for cover. As Randy scanned the room, out of the corner of his eye an unexpected movement caught his attention. Between two missing slats in the vertical blinds to his left, a glimpse of something outside on the darkened patio. The light from the family room picked up shadows of a face, hands, finally enough to make out the features of Patrick Grainger testing the locked sliding glass door.

Randy glanced at the buzz-cut in time to see him staring back. Randy's stomach tightened when the armed man turned toward the door. He felt sure Pat was armed, but a gunfight, with Karen and the kids ten feet away was something he couldn't risk.

Adrenaline is an amazing thing, part of the human body's stress response system. Heart rate increases, blood vessels contract, air passages dilate, all of which increase blood and oxygen flow. That's the scientific explanation. It doesn't fully explain why ordinarily sane people abandon rational thought when loved ones are in mortal jeopardy.

When the armed man moved from Karen toward the sliding door, Randy lurched off the couch, his hands still bound behind him. He stepped over the overturned table, then lowered his shoulder and charged from behind, a low guttural cry rising in crescendo to the point of impact. Like a linebacker tackling an unsuspecting quarterback, his body struck the man in the lower back, forcing the man's arms upward and the gun with it. Randy plowed forward, legs churning. With nothing to check their momentum both bodies slammed into the sliding glass door and through it, bursting out onto the patio.

The explosion of tempered glass fragments sprayed across the concrete and lawn like buckshot, hailing down on Pat as he ducked from the onslaught. Randy's dead weight landed on top of the man, cushioning his fall but knocking the breath out of him. The armed man wasn't as lucky. His face-first impact against the concrete was brutal. Pat checked the unconscious man, then whirled back toward the house, pistol raised, prepared to engage the final assassin.

Chapter 48

PAT QUICKLY CUT AWAY the rawhide strips binding Randy's arms and Randy rolled off the unconscious body, his own chest aching as he gasped for breath.

"Two more . . . one in the kitchen, one in the garage," he groaned. "Both have guns."

"Garage is dead," Pat said, his focus on the doorway. He leveled his weapon and stalked toward the opening where the patio door had been. Behind the overturned table in the family room Brad and Julie had risen to a sitting position, their backs against the couch, pleading to someone in the kitchen.

Pat darted his head into the opening and back. The third man had already pulled Karen off the stool, using her as a shield. The barrel of his semi-automatic pistol was jammed against her head.

"Shut up!" he screamed at the boy and girl. He silenced them with one round over their heads into the back of the couch.

Pat had no choice but to make himself a part of it. He inched his way into the opening, his gun rigid in front of him. The man was backing his way out through the kitchen. Pat stepped up into the room, his gun aimed as close to Karen's head as he dared.

"You know I can't let you take her," Pat said.

R A Y   P E D E N | 223

"Forget it, Grainger." He pressed the gun barrel tighter. "Don't make me shoot the lady."

A thick silence passed between them. "You must be Garth."

It caught the assassin off guard. "How do you know my name?"

"Had a nice chat with your boys in Lexington. They felt like sharing."

"I assume they're out of the picture?"

"Toast."

"I underestimated you, Grainger. Five out of six. Not bad."

"I'm going for a perfect score," Pat said. "Actually I was thinking eight for eight. I still have some unfinished business with your boss back in Richmond."

"I figured you were on to 'em. Snooping around the farm, and all. How'd you find out?"

"I'll tell you all about it over a cup of coffee. You up for that, Tom?" He inched forward a step, his pistol steady.

Garth's own Ranger training hadn't completely gone to waste. He knew Grainger was playing him, trying to disarm the negotiation with casual banter. He decided to tip the scales.

"How'd it feel, talking to your daughter after all those years? After another man raised her for you?"

"After this is over, I think I can catch up."

Garth's eyes blazed cruel. "Too bad your wife can't say the same."

Pat shuddered, a deep tremor. They'd taught him the hardest part of negotiating was blocking out personal attacks. *Win the mind games.* He felt his gun teetering slightly, and he adjusted his stance, trying to regroup. He couldn't let the voices of revenge make him lose his poise. He thought better of pursuing this thread, but his curiosity wouldn't let him hold back.

"You know anything about that?"

An evil smile crossed Garth's face. Even though he'd been

unsuccessful in eliminating his prey, an emotional knife to the throat seemed like the next best thing.

"I was there."

Pat always assumed if he followed the trail to its final conclusion he'd eventually wind up facing the man who killed his wife. This was the moment. *Win the mind games.* He inched forward, his skills front and center, and changed the direction of the conversation.

"How you plan on getting away from here?"

"Only one option," Garth said.

"You really think I'm gonna let you take her?"

"You got no choice. She's my insurance plan."

"Can't let you do it, Garth. You'll kill her."

"Use your head, Grainger. My big payday was killing all of you. Just a tragic accident. A single body gets me a lifetime manhunt. I don't know how much you've got on the Colonel but it's safe to say he won't be around long enough to give me a goddamn dime." He gave it a final thought. "I've saved a few bucks. Not much, but it beats three squares a day on death row. I'll let her out someplace safe."

Garth backed up. He kept his profile protected, showing only a shadow line behind Karen's head. With his gun tight against her head he figured a hero shot by Grainger was out of the question.

Pat matched each step, following them through the darkened living room, 15 feet apart, his pistol ready for the slightest opening. Garth used his gun hand to unlock and open the front door. He backed through it, pulling Karen with him onto the front porch. He continued to back up, off the porch, across a front lawn illuminated only by one tall post light next to the driveway. His dark green pickup truck was parked at the curb.

"Garth!" Pat shouted as he stepped off the porch. "You know we never kill innocents."

Garth stopped by the post light. "Weren't you listening? I don't want to kill her. But without a hostage I wouldn't make it to the county line."

"Take me," Pat said. "I'm the one you wanted in the first place. I lay my gun down, you let her go."

It was a desperate plea and Garth silently ridiculed the folly of trading a harmless hostage for a dangerous one. Then it came to him: a perfect way out. Grainger's offer was made to order. The original scheme was off the rails. Now Grainger was going to let him back on. Garth grinned in the dark.

"Slide your gun over and I'll turn her loose."

Chapter 49

"Here we go, baby," Pat whispered to Allison in the dark. He took a deep breath, then stooped and slid his weapon along the sidewalk in Garth's direction where it caught on the edge of the grass. He stood up.

"Let her go."

A few tense seconds later Garth's arm loosened its grip on Karen's neck. He shoved her away and re-directed his aim toward Pat. Karen stumbled as Pat guided her past him.

"Get in the house," he said, his eyes fixed on Garth.

Once the storm door closed behind him, Pat spoke.

"Did I make a mistake, trusting you?"

"It'd be so easy," Garth said, drawing a lazy figure eight in the air with the pistol barrel. He was almost disappointed Grainger couldn't see the smile spreading across his face. "You didn't think I was a man of my word, did you?"

"I had my doubts," Pat said. "Now what?"

Garth waited a few seconds before he answered.

"Actually, I don't think I'll take you with me after all." He backed up toward his pickup and wagged his gun. "On the porch please."

This unexpected turn of events caught Pat off guard. *Something wasn't right.*

"No hostage?" he asked, as he backpedaled up onto the porch. Over his left shoulder he saw Karen and Julie watching through parted blinds in the living room. Randy and Brad were not with them.

"No need," Garth said. His left hand reached into his jacket pocket and pulled out an object that Pat couldn't make out in the shadows. "Taking the lady as a hostage actually screwed up my plans, Grainger. But you, my friend, so obliging, gathering everybody inside."

An alarm went off in Pat's head but he didn't put the pieces together until Garth held up the hand-held remote detonator. In the glow of the post light he flipped off the safety clasp and backed away.

"Just my way of saying goodbye."

Pat recognized the device, standard issue like those they'd used in northern Iraq. Then he recalled the conversation with Mo on the floor of the trailer. *An explosion . . . C-4 in the electrical panel . . . remote detonator.*

His eyes widened. He turned and howled a desperate warning scream to the Olivers inside the house, one he knew would be too late. Over his shoulder he watched helplessly as Garth ducked for cover behind the Suburban and squeezed the trigger-grip, bracing himself for the magnificent, fiery explosion that would rock the neighborhood and make headlines tomorrow.

Nothing.

Only the empty click of the remote's mechanical trigger.

Garth stabbed the remote in the direction of the garage. Again nothing. He knew line of sight had no bearing on radio waves but still he scooted to the other side of the Suburban and gave the handle a third hard pull. No response. He jammed the heel of his hand against it, an attempt to jar some loose connection back in place and tried again. Nothing. Over and over, frantic squeezes, all of them coming up empty. He was slipping into panic overload, his desperation giving in to child-like whimpers. The only sounds in the calm quiet of the neighborhood were the harmless clicks of the remote handle and the innocent throbbing bass from a bedroom stereo three houses down.

With his mission in total collapse, Garth's inner demons saw their chance and took him. He rose from behind the Suburban and bellowed a primordial scream, and turned toward Pat. Driven by blind vengeance for an adversary who had gotten the best of him he charged Pat, unarmed on the front porch. He stopped past the porch light and raised his pistol.

Pat dived to the concrete but he was defenseless. The thin porch post and railing offered no protection against the semi-automatic pistol in the hands of an enraged madman. That's why it surprised him that he never heard the first bursts from a 15-round magazine emptying into him. Nor did he recognize the dull thump that took the place of shots that never came.

The post light behind Garth had placed everything in front of him in full shadow: outstretched arms in firing position, the Beretta with a chambered round, his crazed look of desperation. It wasn't until Garth stumbled, his body in a slight twist, that Pat and all members of the Oliver family now watching through the living room window saw it. A tri-blade arrow projected from the man's body below his right armpit. Blood pulsed in regular intervals from the wound, synchronized perfectly with each beat of his heart.

Pat pushed up from the concrete and whipped his attention toward the street. On the far curb one house up, in the dim glow of a street light he saw the red pickup truck, its familiar decorative detailing scrolling front to back. In the rear window was the gun rack with a hardwood, re-curve hunting bow conspicuously missing. A familiar figure stepped out of the shadows in the yard across the street and walked toward him. *Axle Morgan, Man-Whore.*

Garth was still on his feet staggering into the front yard when his knees began to give way. He stopped and looked in disbelief at the black carbon shaft protruding from his body, painted with blood. He grabbed at it, a natural reaction. The sharp sting of the arrow's three razor-edged blades sliced deep gashes into his right hand, his last conscious sensation before his eyes went blank and he tipped over, face forward, in a dead heap.

Pat quickly retrieved the pistol lying on the edge of the sidewalk and approached Garth's twitching body. Blood oozed from the gaping entry point under the left shoulder blade. The vein end of the arrow had disappeared inside his body. From the trajectory Pat guessed it had torn through the man's heart, shredded a lung, and from the amount of blood that had just stopped pulsing from the body, severed a major artery.

The tri-blade hunting arrow is an efficient thing, unforgiving, designed to cause catastrophic damage to interior organs and kill quickly. Its purpose is humane, to prevent a target from wandering into the woods suffering in agony, although the intended victim typically has four legs, a white tail, and an occasional rack of antlers. In this case it had done its job. And assassins were always in season.

Axle appeared in the yard, long, loping strides, carrying his bow by the maple-and-cherry hardwood grip like a briefcase. "Sorry, man, I wanted to take him when he came out of the house, but with the woman, that would've been a really tight neck shot, even for me."

Pat stared at his friend. "You were supposed to stay back in the trailer with the others."

Axle shrugged. "You could always fire me."

The front door opened and Randy slipped out, followed cautiously by the others. They huddled in a group and stared in shock at the body lying in their front yard, a red stain seeping through the grass. Pat recognized their confusion when they peered over his shoulder at the man with the bow and he offered a quick introduction.

He leaned down and carefully picked up the remote detonator lying in the grass next to Garth's body. He held it delicately with a thumb and forefinger and examined the contact points in the dim glow of the post light before he flipped the no-fire clip back in place.

"There's explosives in the electric panel. It's a miracle this thing didn't work," he said, as he held up the detonator.

Brad and Randy exchanged a knowing smile. It was subtle but it caught Pat's attention.

"What?"

Brad held out his hand. In it was a wireless receiver with two cut wires dangling free. He pulled a pair of wire-pliers out of his jeans pocket.

Pat stared, slack-jawed.

"I wasn't about to play around with those freaking blasting caps," Brad said, still shaking a little at the close call. "They're still stuck in the C-4. But I figured if I could cut the receiver loose at least the remote wouldn't work."

"But how'd you know what . . .?"

"The short guy had a big mouth," Brad interrupted. "Heard him telling this douche bag," he pointed to Garth's body, "about the plastic and the blasting caps. As soon as Dad cut us loose I didn't have time to think about it. The pliers were on the tool bench in the garage."

Pat stared at him, scratching his head in disbelief, his voice rising a half octave.

"How the hell do you know about C-4 and detonators?"

"I follow current events," Brad said, smugly, his confidence returning. He threw a self-conscious look at his dad. "Even read the paper once in a while. Suicide bombers, crazies blowing things up. And Google's there to show us how everything works."

Their conversation was interrupted by a passing car, slowing to a crawl. The woman driving was staring wide-eyed at one man holding a handgun, another with a hunting bow, and a body on the ground. Pat watched her raise a cell phone to her ear after punching in what he felt sure was 9-1-1, before she gunned the engine and sped away.

Chapter 50

PAT SLID HIS PISTOL into the small of his back. "I've got to get out of here."

"No, wait," Karen said, her hand grabbing his arm. "We'll tell the police what happened. You too, Mr. Morgan. I'm a lawyer. Kentucky recognizes the Castle Doctrine. You had a right to use deadly force."

Pat stooped to Garth's body and rummaged through his pockets until he found the dead man's cell phone and slipped it in his pocket. "When this guy doesn't check in, Masters and Wainscott will know the mission failed and they'll run. I'd be surprised if they don't have plenty stashed away in overseas accounts."

Randy connected the dots. "And they'll take Aimee with them."

"Yes," Pat said, "they'll take Aimee with them."

"When the police get here," Julie blurted, "just tell them where Masters and Wainscott are."

"The FBI doesn't have enough on them yet," Pat said. "By the time the confessions roll in from the foot soldiers, and the State Police put two and two together and verify the conspiracy, they'll be long gone. Besides . . ." He turned away.

"What?"

"Wyndham's the bigger problem. They're exposed. They've killed once, maybe more and they won't stop. They've got too much to lose."

"Why do they have to kill anybody?" Brad said.

"They're vulnerable. Masters and Wainscott will be first," Pat said. "Then my daughter. Then me, if they can." He looked down at the dead man and delivered the final blow. "And your dad knows enough to send them all to prison."

The group fell silent.

Pat pulled himself full upright. "Randy, they're not taking her away from me again."

"You know what they say about possession being nine-tenths of the law?" Randy said, his hand on Pat's shoulder. "I'm placing bets on the one-tenth."

Pat nodded. He nudged Axle's shoulder. "I owe you, buddy, big time, but I gotta go. They'll hold you until they sort things out."

Axle's expression was thoughtful as he rubbed his chin. "Three meals a day and I won't have to listen to Pike's bitching? Not so bad." He dropped the grin. "Us jarheads, honor first. Sometimes we make allowances for you Army pussies, too. Git on, now."

Pat turned to Randy. "The police will rake you over the coals, so don't tell any outright lies. I just need to buy a little time."

"The way I see it," Randy said with a straight face, "I don't *know* where you're going. That wouldn't be a lie, would it?" He looked back at Karen and got an affirmative nod.

Brad glanced at Julie. "You know anything, Sis?"

The Southern Belle drew her fingertips up against her cheeks. "It's just all so confusin' . . ."

Pat acknowledged them with a grateful smile and disappeared into the darkness. His motorcycle was parked six houses down the block. Within thirty seconds they heard his motor crank and rev twice before it roared away. A little over a minute later the Frankfort Police Department turned the corner from the opposite direction.

Two cruisers screeched to a stop at the curb and officers burst out of both, weapons drawn. Axle was disinterested in the newcomers. When they found him standing over a body holding a professional bow with a quiver of arrows strapped to his back, protocol was automatic. They forced him to the ground and handcuffed him. With no way to distinguish good guys from bad they restrained the entire Oliver family. Within a half hour, the Olivers' front yard was buzzing with activity, roped off with yellow crime-scene tape and illuminated with battery-powered light stands.

Officers from the second two cruisers found one body inside the garage, a third lying unconscious and bloody on a carpet of broken glass on the back patio. The Lexington Bomb Squad along with a member of the ATF arrived within the hour and removed the blasting caps and the C-4 from the electric panel. By the time the eleven o'clock news came on eight uniformed officers, two plain-clothes detectives, two paramedics, and one reporter from Randy's own newspaper had drawn most of the neighborhood out from their couches and beds.

All parties were transported to police headquarters downtown where they were questioned over the next several hours while forensics experts scoured the crime scene. Based on the damages at the house and the consistent independent testimony by each member of the Oliver family the detectives were comfortable identifying them as victims.

It was clear that Axle Morgan had released the arrow that killed Garth. His boastful claim that it was a 'pretty good shot' removed all doubt. Other details of the events and players were sketchier, and as the questioning dragged on, it became apparent that one other person was a participant in the evening's events and that person had left the crime scene.

* * * * *

Pat was an hour and a half down the road before he steered his bike off an exit ramp, and came to a stop on the shoulder of an unlit rural side road. The leather jacket he pulled out of the saddlebag would fend off the chill from the next several hours of night riding. He wandered a half-dozen steps away from his idling bike and made two calls.

The first was to Granny, who with Pike and Mongo were patiently baby-sitting the three stooges. Pat explained the turn of events at the Olivers' house. The part about Axle's timely Robin Hood rescue brought a smile to Granny's face.

"Granny, I'm gonna send the Lexington Police out your way. They won't know who's who, so they may hold you guys for a few hours. I'll try to convince them how it came down."

"Don't sweat it," said Granny, "Pike's already called Brannon to let him know we won't be on the job tomorrow." He had one more question, even though he didn't expect an answer.

"Can you tell me where you're going?"

"Better not."

"Does it have anything to do with your daughter?"

"No comment."

"Don't do anything stupid."

Pat's next call to the Lexington-Fayette Urban County Police dispatch was brief. When he clicked off he slid onto the leather seat, cranked the throttle, and settled back for a long night's drive to Richmond, Virginia, certain that neither Brent Masters nor Eddie Wainscott would be happy to see him.

Chapter 51

BRENT MASTERS leaned his arms on the four-board paddock fence and stared across an empty pasture faintly lit by the slim crescent of a new moon. He took another sip of bourbon and dangled the glass with two fingers.

They should have completed their mission by now.

He glanced at his watch—1:46. He'd lost count how many times he checked it over the last half hour. Garth should have called in at 1:00. Maybe things were still evolving. Maybe there had been a slight hitch. Still, he should have called.

Masters took another swig. His patience gone, he pulled out his cell phone and dialed again. It went to voice mail. He shut down before the recorded greeting had a chance to finish. He turned toward the house, a short trek across the gravel driveway to the kitchen where he scooped fresh ice out of the freezer and filled the glass again with bourbon, his third tonight.

His anxiety was getting the best of him. He drifted back outside and absentmindedly headed off at a brisk pace toward the back barn as he scoured possibilities. Even if Grainger had deviated from his normal routine Garth should have filled him in. Then again maybe Garth was flying by the seat of his pants. After his surprising infusion of courage last night the man may think he had a free hand. As soon as the teams got back to Richmond and the smoke cleared, new deal or not, he would remind Garth in no uncertain terms who was in charge.

By the time he reached the smaller paddock by the back barn the glass was a third empty. He wheeled and retraced his route back to the house. Near the steps on the side porch he stopped and repeated the call. Voice mail again. He drained the glass while he waited for the greeting to end. Against his better judgment he left a message: "Goddammit, Garth, call me. What's going on!"

When the call ended he slung his empty glass against the low brick wall behind the flower bed. Unable to keep it to himself any longer, he charged toward the main barn and slid open the large metal door. He switched on the lights in the front bay where a golf cart sat charging. It started immediately. He tore out across the gravel parking lot, around the front toward Eddie Wainscott's house 400 feet away, bathed in the yellow glow of a mercury-vapor pole light.

The golf cart skidded in the gravel when it came to a sharp stop. He bounded up three steps to the front door and jammed his thumb repeatedly on the doorbell button, then banged on the oak door with the heel of his hand. In less than a minute a light appeared at the second floor landing, followed by the foyer light downstairs. Eddie Wainscott, in bathrobe and slippers, tramped down the carpeted stairs with a 9-millimeter pistol in his hand. The porch light came on and Wainscott cautiously examined the intruder before unlocking the door.

"You have any idea what time it is?" Wainscott said, squinting at the clock on the living room mantle. "Almost two thirty."

The liquor had diluted any sense of decorum and Masters bulled his way in. "Something's wrong. I can feel it. Garth still hasn't called in."

Wainscott led his friend back into a large kitchen and clicked on one bank of recessed can lights. He laid the pistol on the counter and pulled a carton of orange juice from the refrigerator while Masters plopped onto a stool at the counter. Wainscott set two empty glasses on the counter and waggled the carton at Masters, an offer. It was refused and he poured a half glass for himself.

"OK, why are you worried?"

"He's an hour and a half late."

Only a few minutes out of a deep sleep, Wainscott looked haggard and he rubbed his eyes with the heels of his hands. "Things don't always fall into place like they're supposed to. Sometimes shit happens." He gulped some juice.

"Garth's been over-aggressive lately but he knows to keep the line of communications open. If things weren't hitting on all cylinders he'd let me know." Masters fidgeted on his stool. He grabbed the empty glass, pressed it against the ice dispenser, and slipped over to the liquor cabinet where he poured a short Glenlivet, straight up, and took a sip.

Wainscott shuffled across the red-oak kitchen floor to the garden window above his sink and stared out into the back yard as he thought out loud.

"He's winging it, picking his time and place. Hell, it could be going down as we speak. We're talking one big-ass explosion." As Wainscott waded through the possibilities a tinge of caution finally crept into his voice.

"Besides, if he's in trouble what can we do about it tonight?"

Masters stared into the scotch. "I don't know but if he—"

The ringing cell phone in his pocket interrupted him. He jerked it out, ready to tear into Garth, when the caller ID on the screen stopped him: Franklin Pentecost. He stared at the ringing phone.

"Well, answer the damn thing," Wainscott scolded.

Masters glanced at Wainscott, then back at the phone and

cautiously pressed the green button. "Yeah?"

"What's going on, Brent?"

Masters had no intention of revealing his concerns to Franklin Pentecost. He put the phone on speaker and shot back a detached response, unaware of the slur in his speech, "Haven't heard anything."

"Wasn't he supposed to check in at 1:00?"

"That was the plan, but things change in the field," he said, parroting the mini-lecture he'd just received from Wainscott.

"Have you called him?"

"Goes to voice mail. He'll get his messages."

"Brent, you said you had a crack team. Three guys for Grainger. Another three for a defenseless family. And you haven't heard from any of them yet?"

"I have a problem with that but I'll deal with him when he gets back."

"Look," said Pentecost, "Richard's got contacts in Louisville, an officer with Metro Police, I think. I'll see if he can find any activity on the Lexington or Frankfort police wires. If things didn't go well in Frankfort, like in no ball-of-fire-explosions, that'd be pretty hard to miss. I'll get back to you."

Masters stared at the dark screen and took another sip of scotch.

Wainscott fidgeted. "All this shit coming down, are we in over our heads with Wyndham?"

Masters looked up from his glass. "What the hell are you talking about? We're all in this together."

"May be but the way things are going down, with Grainger back in the picture? And now, Pentecost getting involved? I'm starting to get a bad feeling about Wyndham. Those guys play for keeps."

"They're taking care of business. They've got no choice if we want to stay out of prison."

Wainscott paused, a big exhale. "We did some bad things over there, Brent."

"Don't tell me your conscience is getting to you after all this time."

Wainscott dropped his head. "Now that Helen's gone I sit here sometimes, this empty house and wonder if it was all worth it. Tell me you don't feel a little guilty."

"Of course I do. We're talking people's lives here. But there's no way to turn back. If Fowler and the rest had just played the game we wouldn't be in this fix. It was them or us."

"I don't know," Wainscott said. "Sometimes when I think back I realize we killed people, Brent. And now we're killing more people. Innocent people. For money. For this," he said, spreading his arms out toward his leather furniture and luxury entertainment center, his pool and manicured estate. "Is it worth it?"

Masters rolled his eyes and killed the rest of the single malt.

* * * * *

Even beneath the steady drone of his motorcycle Pat felt Garth's cell phone vibrate in his breast pocket. He throttled down to a slow cruise and in the pitch-black of a nearly deserted interstate he pulled out the phone. Without answering he noted the caller and time on the lighted screen. Fifteen minutes later he quietly observed a second call from Masters. He slipped the phone back in his pocket and cranked the accelerator grip, his focus on Richmond and those who waited for him.

* * * * *

At 3:20 in the morning, pacing in his home office, Pentecost answered the phone. "Your guy find out anything?"

"Lexington's pretty quiet tonight," Richard said, reading from his notes. "Other than the usual 20 or 30 DUIs, they've got two assaults, both of 'em nightclubs, three domestic violence calls, a robbery at a convenience store, a couple burglaries, a prowler at a women's exercise club. The only curious item was the Urban-County Police picking up six men in a construction trailer. My guy can't tell what that's about yet. But no murders."

"How about Frankfort?" he said, settling in behind his desk.

"Even quieter."

"No residential explosion? No fire?"

"Nothing."

"Dammit! Have him follow up in a couple of hours, see if anything shows up." Pentecost rocked back in his leather chair, sock feet planted against the front edge of the desk. His list of options was getting shorter.

"You've got some men here in town, ready to go like we talked?"

"This very minute, only two I can trust," Richard said, "Two more coming in on the sunrise flight, should be at the office mid-morning. Didn't know you were in such a hurry."

"I didn't either, but things may have taken a turn for the worse. We have to be pro-active."

"You want us to take out Garth and his team?"

"Actually, that's the problem. They may have already been, shall we say, thwarted."

"So, you want to move on Masters and Wainscott?"

"Have your guys ready. If Garth surprises us and the mission is successful we'll wait until he gets back in town, let things blow over. If not we'll have to deal with our locals sooner."

"What's sooner?"

"Today."

"Saturday? At home?"

"If things have fallen apart in Kentucky it won't take the police long to tie Garth to Masters. Hours, maybe. Once they get to him and Wainscott, we're vulnerable." Then he corrected himself. "No, we're dead."

"I hate to piss on your plan, Franklin, but your sister and the girl will be home with Masters."

"I've thought about that. I'm pretty sure I can manipulate my sister out of the house with some fake family catastrophe. She's pretty gullible."

"And the girl?"

Pentecost paused, one last chance to reconsider something he had already decided. "Look, I hate it, an innocent girl. But she's Grainger's daughter, for Christ sake. A link to the past we have to eliminate. I should've never agreed to let Brent take her in way back then."

"That's pretty hardcore, Franklin. Your sister will never forgive you. She'll turn on you."

"If we do it the way I tell you she'll never know we were involved. Just be ready. I'll make a decision as soon as Louisville gets back to us."

Franklin Pentecost spent the next ten minutes going over details for a plot conceived an hour earlier while he was wearing a path in his Persian rug.

Chapter 52

EARLY DAWN and the night chill hadn't burned off yet. Pat's Harley cut across the pavement centerline onto a gravel shoulder and began picking his way up a steep, abandoned access road cut into a wooded hillside. Over time storm runoff and four-wheelers had gouged ruts, exposing pockets of field rock. As he climbed, his tires spun, losing and regaining traction. Despite the rugged terrain he'd chosen this vantage point two weeks earlier for a reason.

At the top of the incline the lane doubled back on itself into a small clearing. He pulled into thick pasture grass and hit the kill switch. The rumble of his motor dropped away, giving way to the silence of a rural Virginia morning.

He pulled a pair of high-mag binoculars out of his saddlebag and walked to the edge of the clearing overlooking the county road sixty feet below. In the distance the sun was in the early stages of a slow rise behind forested hills. With his binoculars aimed across the road, due east, he adjusted the focus. A few trees from the hillside below stabbed their way into his view as he scanned his target.

His position was centered on the entrance drive shared by Masters and Wainscott. On his left, to the north, was Masters' compound: the sumptuous country farmhouse, two large barns, black-fenced paddocks, 15 acres of mowed pasture fronting the county road, 20 more untended acres rolling up into wooded hills beyond.

On Pat's right, to the south, was Wainscott's 32-acre tract. His traditional brick home was an uninspiring twenty-first century Americana with steep, asymmetrical gables that dominated too many upscale suburban subdivisions.

He glanced as his watch: 7:16. He'd made good time, although at the expense of an aching lower back. The soreness in his buttocks was another painful reminder why a forced ride was always a bad idea. He went through full-body stretches, each one accompanied by a full-throated groan. When he finished he retrieved a styrofoam cup of coffee from the holder on his bike and sipped. Cold. He dumped the contents in the weeds and tossed the cup before raising the binoculars again.

Masters' white Mercedes was in the gravel lot just off the wrap-around porch. A silver Lexus was parked next to the large barn. Wainscott's driveway, on the other hand, was empty. If he was home his navy blue Cadillac would be stabled in the four-car garage. With no activity this early it seemed as good a time as any to make the call.

He pulled up the number for the Kentucky State Police. He didn't expect Detective Damron to be working on a weekend so he left a message and made sure the operator knew the importance of the call. Ten minutes later his phone rang. He smiled at Damron's name on the screen.

"We got some disappointing news, Grainger, that you might be involved in a couple of murders at Randy Oliver's house last night."

"Not murder . . . homicide. There's a difference."

"Don't split hairs. Frankfort Police are still sorting out details. Leaving the scene of a crime was not a good move."

"I had my reasons. Listen, you said if we could prove the

conspiracy in Kuwait we'd have a legitimate motive for my wife's murder?"

Damron's interest level shot up. "You told me the evidence burned up in the fire."

"I found the CD."

"You have it?"

"It's in my motel room in Lexington, taped behind my sock drawer. Best Western, Room 214. Everything's on it. It's all yours."

"Where are you? There are a lot of people looking for you."

"Just get the CD." He clicked off.

At 7:55 Pat's patience paid off. He watched Brent Masters descend the steps from his porch and get in his car. At the end of the entrance drive the Mercedes turned south on the county highway toward town. Betty and Aimee apparently were still in the house. Pat decided to hold his ground.

* * * * *

"My guy called back."

Franklin Pentecost checked his watch: 8:20. "Any news?"

"Yeah, and it's not good," Richard said. "Those six men in Lexington in that construction trailer? Three of 'em are ours. The other three work for the steel erection company that owns the trailer. The report says they caught our guys breaking in. Holding them until the cops showed up. Our boys are taking the Fifth so far but the cops have their wallets which mean drivers licenses, cards, documents that tie them to Richmond. The kicker is the police got a call last night from a man identifying himself as Patrick Grainger. My guy's information is sketchy but Grainger claimed our three were there to kill him."

"And Frankfort?"

"Close, but nothing. The police found two blocks of C-4 in the electric panel. One man dead in the garage, another with a concussion on the back patio. They'll interrogate him when he's conscious. Garth was killed. Some cowboy nailed him with a freaking bow and arrow. It won't take long to link Garth to Masters."

Pentecost let the words sink in. His list of options had shrunk to one. "Your two men ready to go?"

"Drinking coffee at McDonald's, waiting for my call."

"They have everything? The spray paint, the candles, the drugs? It's got to be believable."

"They've got it all."

Richard hesitated before he asked the obvious question.

"What'd you decide about your sister?"

"I'll call you right back."

Showtime.

He pulled her number up from his contact list. A few seconds later Betty Masters answered.

Pentecost faked a voice in panic. "Sis, we need to talk."

"Well!" she said, spreading the sarcasm thick as butter. "You finally found time to grace us with a call?" Sibling scolding dripped off her tongue. "I haven't heard from you in, what, six months?"

Pentecost had mastered the art of lying with a straight face. Fending off chirpy regulators in contentious Senate hearings had given him plenty of practice. Dealing with an insecure, weak-willed sister would hardly be a challenge.

"Something serious has come up. I need to see you, Sis."

Her naiveté had always been her failing. As expected, her attitude slipped instantly from critical judgment to familial concern. "What's wrong, Frankie? What's the matter? Is it Joanna?"

"I can't talk about it over the phone," he said, injecting urgency and false emotion into his voice."Please. Can you come out to the house?"

"Well . . . sure. When?"

"Now, Betty. Right now."

"Now? But I'm not dressed . . ."

"Just come! I need to talk to you, Bet. It's important. Can you leave in twenty minutes?"

"For heaven's sake, what's the rush, Frankie?"

"I'll tell you when you get here. Twenty minutes? Promise me."

Hook, line, and sinker. "OK . . . twenty minutes."

He called Richard back.

"Tell your boys to finish their happy meal and then head out. I just sent my sister on a wild goose chase. She'll be out of the line of fire for a little while but we've got a narrow window of opportunity. If they see her silver Lexus in the driveway tell them to back off until she leaves."

"I've been thinking about the girl, Franklin. We've done a lot of things but killing an innocent girl, I'm not sure we're up for that."

"Are you up for death row, Richard? I'm no monster but I don't intend on spending the rest of my life in prison waiting for the appeals to run out. End this thing now."

* * * * *

At 8:36, Pat watched Betty Masters scramble across the gravel parking lot to her silver Lexus. Even from a distance he could see gravel dust spewing from under spinning tires. She barely stopped at the county road. This sudden burst of activity seemed odd, the Colonel and his wife leaving minutes apart, and she in such a hurry. If Aimee was home they'd left her alone.

Four minutes later, as he mulled over the unfolding events Pat watched a black Chevy Tahoe turn off the county highway. The muscles in his neck tensed as he followed the vehicle with his binoculars, then relaxed when it turned right toward

Wainscott's house. Two men got out, one with a box under his arm, and lumbered up the steps to the front door. Moments later Wainscott let them in. Pat tried to make out the license plate but he was too far away and there weren't any marking emblems on the car.

Thirteen minutes later he observed the men getting back in their car. But instead of heading back out to the highway they drove 400 feet to Masters' house and stopped at the front door. He couldn't see in the shadows of the front porch but someone, apparently Aimee, let one of them in while the second man moved the Tahoe around to the back out of sight. The dodgy scene unfolding in front of him was too suspicious to ignore.

He double-checked the magazine in his Colt, then mounted his motorcycle and hobbled his way down the rutted access road. The steep grade, coupled with a rugged profile and loose rock made the descent treacherous and he nearly lost his balance more than once.

At the bottom of the hill he turned right onto the paved road heading south. A hundred and twenty yards later he abruptly turned left into a private farm lane belonging to Wainscott's neighbor, a discovery during his reconnaissance on Aimee a week and a half earlier. There was no gate and the trees that lined the left side of the lane offered cover while he motored back to a spot with a good angle to the rear of Wainscott's house.

He dismounted and slipped into the sparse tree cover. For a full minute he tried to pick out activity in the rooms that backed onto the patio. Even with binoculars he detected no movement. Getting closer was risky but the black Tahoe had left him with an uneasy feeling. He weaved through the trees back toward the highway. When he reached a spot where Wainscott's four-car garage shielded him from the house he abandoned tree cover and took off across the pasture. At the back of the garage he pulled out his Colt. He slipped around the back corner and approached the expansive brick patio marked by a large rectangular swimming pool and a generous inventory of lawn furniture and potted plants.

The rear wall of the house was dominated by atrium doors and tall casement windows. All were dark except for an odd flickering of soft light. No signs of activity, TV, sounds, no lamps or ceiling lights on in the family room and kitchen.

When Pat stabbed his head into the corner of the first oversized window, he saw something he didn't expect: walls despoiled with spray painted graffiti, crude graphic images, pentagons, heretical phrases in block lettering. Scattered on tables around the room were lit candles, the source of the flickering light.

The warm glow from the sunrise was enough now to illuminate Eddie Wainscott, spread-eagled in his leather recliner at the far end of the room, a red streak trailing down his face from a single bullet hole in his forehead.

Chapter 53

PAT EXPLODED LIKE A SHOT toward Masters' house more than a football field away. Eighteen seconds later he pulled up short at a mock orange hedge on the property line, gasping for breath. Other than one white trellised arbor with a latticework gate, the eight-foot tall hedgerow ran unbroken from the front of both houses several hundred feet toward the rear. He picked a spot in the leafy undergrowth with a good view of the back of the house 150 feet away and forced his winded body into the tangle.

Looking past the kidney-shaped pool he trained his binoculars on a set of large patio doors. Lights were on in the family room and despite the glare on the glass he noticed movement. His heart rate spiked when he recognized Aimee cowering on a floral couch. Two men stood a few feet away with automatic pistols—professional assassins sent for Eddie Wainscott and Brent Masters. She was a hostage for now.

He processed the implications. Word of the failed plot back in Kentucky must have found its way to Richmond. Wainscott's murder meant Wyndham was in play. As he had guessed, the two men he considered his most hated enemies had become targets. He smirked at the irony. Mice hunted by cats, cats hunted by dogs, the predators growing more dangerous. It was time, he decided, for someone to step in as head of Animal Control.

The man nearest the door was slim, maybe 5'-10", a lightweight, but fit. His lean, muscular body filled out a tan, long-sleeved t-shirt and jeans. Wavy, blonde hair curled around his ears to his collar. As he patrolled back and forth next to the glass door he seemed too young, maybe a high school jock lured into a world of danger and money disguised as intrigue. The other man, the leader, was several years older, shorter with a powerful, stocky build. The shaved head, black t-shirt, and camouflage pants suggested classic ex-military, most likely a mercenary.

Aimee hunkered in the corner of the couch, her arms crossed, legs curled under her. The younger man stood guard while the smooth-headed one disappeared into the depths of the house. When he returned he was disconnecting a call on his cell phone.

"I let him know Masters wasn't here. So, we wait."

He ordered the blonde man to an observation post in the front parlor and sat down in an armchair opposite Aimee, expressionless, tapping the barrel of his silenced Ruger in his off hand.

A half minute later a dog began to bark outside. The mercenary sprang from his chair to the sliding glass door. He took a quick survey of the yard, craning his neck over to the leading edge of the door to get a better angle but saw no one. He turned to the girl. "Your dog?"

"Yes," she said, her first word since the break-in.

"He do this much?"

She squeaked a timid response. "Sometimes when he sees a rabbit or something."

He scanned the yard again, slower this time. Nothing. Without looking back he yelled to the front parlor.

"Hey, Ace, get in here."

When the young man appeared in the hallway the bald one tipped his head in the direction of the back yard.

"Check out the mutt. Probably nothing. Just wanna make sure."

The man strained to hear the barking. "It's a fucking dog."

"I know, but I don't take chances. You got nothing better to do until our guy shows up."

Annoyed, the young man slipped around behind the couch that separated the family room from the kitchen. He slid the glass door open and stepped down onto the slate patio. With his weapon raised, he walked to the edge of the pool and did a full 360 sweep of the yard. The barking had eased off to a whimper, coming from the side of the house.

The mercenary stuck his head out the sliding door. "Anything?"

"Don't know, maybe a critter." The younger man moved farther out into the grass and tilted his head to get a better angle into the wide side yard. Concern gave way to relief, then mild irritation.

"The little bastard's got his collar caught on a bush, over there by the gate." He lowered his weapon, muttered an inaudible curse at the dog, and ambled toward the gate, disappearing around the corner of the house.

The mercenary waited at the open sliding door, half in, half out, one eye on the girl. A minute later he watched as the dog wandered into the back yard and dropped into a sunny spot in the grass. When the younger gunman didn't follow, he called out. No answer. He raised his weapon, leaning out the door, and called out again, louder. Nothing.

"What the hell . . ." He felt a twinge of caution. He pulled out his cell phone and hit a programmed number. It answered after one ring. "Richard, those two new guys show up yet?"

"They just got in. Sitting here in front of me. Why?"

"I don't know. Something feels wrong. I sent junior out to check on—"

The tranquil composure of the house was interrupted by a violent crash from the front room, an unmistakable explosion of shattering glass and splintering wood and the thud of dead weight landing hard on the floor. He slung the live cell phone into a cushioned armchair and snatched his squealing captive off the couch. With his left arm tight around her neck he pushed her forward, pointing with the Ruger.

At the French doors to the front parlor he discovered the source of the crash. An intruder had blasted through double front windows, lying sprawled on the carpet, covered in shattered glass and wood blinds. His arms groped as he struggled to get up. The mercenary fired two quick rounds into the man and the arms stopped moving.

He kept his pistol leveled and inched toward the still body. When he peeled back the blinds with his foot, under a layer of glass and splintered wood he recognized, too late, the long blond hair and a tan, long-sleeved t-shirt. As he backed up the first thing that went through his mind was the barking dog and the realization that their plan had been compromised. The next thing that went through his mind was the 45-caliber bullet Pat Grainger fired point blank from behind.

A single shot. The hollow-point slug opened a small hole when it entered the back of the assassin's head, mushrooming and expanding inside the soft tissue of his brain. It exploded out his forehead in a larger shape, dragging with it helpings of blood and organic matter, along with skull fragments and skin.

The brutal engagement had taken place behind the girl out of her line of sight. Other than the shock of the Colt's loud blast, her horror didn't register until she began to associate the colorful spray of blood and nuggets of brain tissue stuck like warm oatmeal to the ceiling and walls. She felt the assassin's muscles instantly relax and release his grip, and she let out a single shriek. The dead man dropped to the floor like an anchor while Pat grabbed at the gun still clutched in a lifeless hand.

In the empty family room twenty feet behind them, the open cell phone in the armchair squawked questions no one heard. The sound of the crash was troubling but it wasn't until Richard heard the crack of the gunshot followed by a high-pitched squeal that he knew their plan had gone to hell.

He disconnected the call and ordered the two new arrivals over to a door. In the walk-in closet was a small but carefully-stocked arsenal—semi-automatic pistols, M16 automatic rifles, grenades and launchers, dozens of assorted weapons, all loaded, spare ammunition stacked neatly in the right slots. He tossed a pistol and an automatic rifle to each man along with extra magazines and the three rushed out the side door to a black Chevy Tahoe in the parking lot.

Chapter 54

"WHERE THE HELL IS HE?"

"How would I know?" Richard said. "They just called. The girl's home alone."

"Goddammit!" Pentecost kicked a wastebasket across the study. "And my sister?"

"They watched her drive off. Whatever you said, it worked."

Pentecost ran his hands through graying hair and closed his eyes. Detectives back in Kentucky were probably making connections as they spoke. This was no time to piss around waiting for Masters to return home.

Richard interrupted his train of thought.

"I got a call coming in, Franklin."

He disconnected and took the call. He listened patiently until he heard the breaking glass. Then a gunshot and a girl's faint scream.

* * * * *

Brent Masters wiped nervous perspiration with the back of his arm and swung open the stainless steel door. The fire-proof safe, slightly smaller than an under-counter refrigerator, was set into a built-in walnut credenza behind his desk at Wyndham-Lynch's corporate offices.

He pulled six vinyl pouches from the upper right compartment and stacked them on the carpet. Each one was stuffed with enough documents to make it pucker against the binding cord. He tilted out a separate cigar box and checked the bundled microcassette tapes inside before placing it next to the pouches. He worked quickly.

On a lower shelf he reached behind a stack of letter-sized files and retrieved a large manila envelope, sealed to protect the photographs inside from moisture. He added it to his batch.

On one knee he scooted to the left hand compartment, half as deep as the first. With one arm he raked a stack of irrelevant files onto the carpet. He tapped on the false back panel and removed it, exposing a navy blue nylon carry bag turned on end. He dragged it out and set it beside his stack, then climbed into his swivel office chair and took a breath.

It had been awhile since he had examined the contents of the pouches. He knew what was in them, but a twisted desire to reflect one last time on the evidence wouldn't let it pass. He picked up the first one, untied the binding cord, and ripped at the Velcro tab. His hand grabbed a handful of documents and slid them out on the desk. As he paged through the stack it flooded back, the invoices, contracts, memos, diagrams, hand-written notes: the only copy of the incriminating documents SSG Patrick Grainger had entrusted to Eddie Wainscott in Kuwait.

In a separate packet clamped together with two large metal spring clips were multiple bundles of emails—hard copies. Scores of incriminating interoffice communications between him, Wainscott, and the players who had directed the show from Wyndham-Lynch's comfortable offices back in the States. It had been careless of them, he knew that now, leaving a trail documenting the names, dates, precise operational plans, every change in direction, every clandestine directive. Every murder. Even though they had used token metaphors to soften the cynical ruthlessness of their crimes, these pieces of evidence would be deadly. Wanton emails, all conveniently signature-annotated, none of which in hindsight should have ever been sent.

He'd done his best to erase his computer back when he left the service, deleting emails and electronic documents and files. But who could know for sure what sneaky little micro-bytes might still be hiding on a hard drive somewhere, waiting for some high-tech wizard to electronically resurrect them and reveal their crimes to the world? Assuming, of course, those hard drives still existed, and if so, whether the United States Army could ever find them boxed away in some obscure warehouse in who-knows-where, USA.

Even if he managed to wiggle out of their mess he couldn't leave this treasure trove of information behind. He might as well draw up a typed confession and drop it in the local newspaper's inbox. On the other hand if the grand scheme wound up collapsing around him, everything in these pouches and boxes might turn out to be useful. From the outset the plan had been hatched by others in high places. Perhaps this library would be valuable if he had to negotiate his way into a plea bargain or a lesser sentence.

His curiosity satisfied, he stuffed the documents back into the pouch, retied the binding cords, and stacked all of them on his desk blotter.

He glanced down at the full blue nylon bag on the floor. As with the other packages he knew what was inside but the almost erotic power that came from touching it one more time made it impossible to pass up. It wouldn't take a second. He unzipped the bag and laid it open on his lap, then pulled out one stack and fanned it, admiring the currency like a love letter. He held it up to his nose, the rich smell of crisp fifty-dollar bills still invigorating. He'd debated using hundreds but they would be easier to track and harder to spend. This bag of salvation would be his short-term ticket out of the country. It might even tide them over in case anyone found a way to tap into any of his carefully-constructed off-shore accounts.

His ringing cell phone jolted him out of the daydream. He glanced at the screen and cursed out loud, a child caught with his hand in the cookie jar. Then he remembered he was alone. He stuffed the pack of fifties back into the bag and dropped it onto the hard plastic mat under his chair. He cleared his throat into the phone.

"Did Louisville find something?"

Franklin Pentecost's experience in deception was considerable—with government investigators, with his business adversaries, and the last few years with his wife, now that she had made a less-than-graceful transition into middle age. Just off the phone with Richard it was clear his plan was already off script. This call might tell him where Brent Masters was at this moment instead of lying at home with a bullet in his head.

"Not yet. You hear from Garth?" Pentecost said, trying to dismiss the mental picture of the dead assassin with an arrow through his gills.

"Not a word." Masters was sweating again. It had been a long time since he'd been outflanked. He checked the blue bag to make sure it hadn't grown legs and walked away. It was beginning to look like he'd need it sooner than he thought.

"Brent? You still there?"

Masters recovered and gasped an uncharacteristically weak response.

"I'm here."

Pentecost dialed up the pressure, a calculated emotional strategy now. "Why don't I drive out to your house? We need to come up with a contingency plan if this thing blows up. Have you told Betty?"

The mention of his wife jolted Masters back into focus. "Betty doesn't know anything. You know how she is. She'd overload."

Pentecost pictured his sister on the road to his house in an emotional panic. "Let me talk to her. I'll tell her I'm coming."

A noticeable hesitation as Masters looked around his office. "She, uh . . . she can't come to the phone right now."

"Why not?"

"She's . . . she's back at the house."

"I thought you were at the house," Pentecost said, feigning surprise. "Where are you, anyway?"

It didn't seem prudent strategy, letting Franklin Pentecost know that he was sitting in Wyndham's corporate office, cleaning out files, gathering evidence that would implicate them all. Pentecost's piercing interest in his whereabouts nicked his attention, sounding a tiny alarm.

"I ran out to get some cash from the ATM," Masters said, "in case we had to move fast."

"So you heading back to the house?"

"Um . . . yeah. Why?"

"No reason." Pentecost searched for a convincing response. "I just thought you might want to get Eddie involved when Garth calls in."

"Yeah, maybe I should."

Once they hung up, Masters pondered the faint signals that seemed to be gaining strength. Pentecost pressing him about his location? Urging him to return home? And why hadn't their contact in Louisville turned up anything yet? An explosion, fire, dead bodies? Those details would have been all over the police wires. His suspicions were climbing.

He called Wainscott and waited six rings before voice mail kicked on. He shut off, a second try, again no answer. The voice of doubt was getting louder.

He snatched a leather briefcase from the credenza and stuffed the pouches and cigar box into it, and placed it on the desk next to the blue nylon bag. Then he made one last call.

"Betty, you up and moving around yet?"

"I'm halfway to Franklin's house."

"Wha . . . Franklin's house?" This wasn't the answer he expected. "Why?"

"I have no idea," she said. "He called me this morning right after you left. Some kind of emergency. Said he needed to talk but wouldn't tell me why."

"But I just got off the phone with him. Said he wanted to talk to you but . . ."

His brain recorded the shrill clanging as the final alarm went off. Why hadn't he seen it earlier? It came to him now how compelling a billion dollars and avoiding federal prison could be for a ruthless player like Franklin Pentecost, even if it meant turning on the rest of the team.

His instincts kicked into high gear. His whole life he'd been a high-octane player. Over the last 24 hours, as the scheme closed in around him he had grown timid. It put him and his family in a bad position. This bucket of cold reality splashing in his face brought him back and his fear dropped away, replaced by a resurgence. Now that he could see the field, he recognized his enemies. The rush was invigorating.

"Is Emily at home?" Masters asked.

"Yes."

"I'm heading back to the farm. Call her, make sure she's OK. Tell her to get out of the house, immediately. Go hide in Garth's apartment over the barn. She knows where the key is."

"What are you talking about?"

"I'll explain later. Just do it."

"Brent, what's going on?"

"Betty!" His voice exploded, not in anger, but in fear, as a clash of unpracticed emotions came to a head. Everything he'd worked for, all those he loved but couldn't show it, were in jeopardy. Uncharacteristically he softened his hard edge so she could understand.

"Emily may be in danger. I know I've kept you in the dark more than once but please, just do this one thing for me. For Emily."

Silence filled the phone line while she struggled to understand the cryptic message coming from her husband. Wisely he didn't give her a chance to debate it and shut down the call.

Slipping over to the locked wardrobe cabinet in the corner of the office he punched in a keyed code. He pushed aside two hanging suits and dress shirts and pulled out an object from the back, along with the necessary accessories. He grabbed the blue nylon bag and briefcase from the desk and disappeared out the back door.

Chapter 55

THE GIRL made a frantic retreat away from Pat and the dead man lying at her feet. She scrambled past the younger man's body to a corner of the room and dropped into a wingback chair that had escaped the bloodbath. Her fingers probed her hair, followed by high-pitched squeals each time she pulled her hands back wet with blood and brain matter.

Pat grabbed two terrycloth towels from the powder room off the foyer and tossed them to her. A second trip and he soaked two white, monogrammed washrags in hot water. When he returned he handed one to her. Despite her recoil, with the other he washed her face and arms, then began swabbing foreign material from her hair while her eyes wandered across the room. He felt her trembling.

She was disoriented as she attempted to make sense out of a deadly chain of events that had landed in her world on what should have been just another calm Saturday morning. Pat draped a towel around her shoulders and made her drink some water. Her legs bounced with nervous energy as she stared in disbelief at the traumatic scene in her home.

Pat tried to imagine her spending Christmases in this room scouting around a live tree heavy with pine scent, hunting for presents with her name, shaking them, giggling with anticipation.

Then after a hearty Christmas breakfast with seasonal music in the background, stuffing piles of shredded wrapping paper and ribbon into plastic garbage bags with her mom while she counted and stacked the spoils.

The scene staring back at her now was surreal: two men lying dead on the same carpet where she had crawled as a toddler. A room littered in the aftermath with shattered glass, splintered pieces of window frames and grid, broken blinds, and drywall, all marinating in a carpet-soaked pool of crimson, turning darker by the minute.

Pat sat on his haunches and leaned back against the French door across the room, waiting. His forearms dangled loosely across his knees while he gave her time and space to gather herself. He watched her without speaking and it wilted him. He had no way to make it easier.

It came as no surprise to him, the striking similarities with another scene eight weeks earlier in a deserted barn on a Georgia back road. The setting was different, even the method of the kill, but the reasons were identical. And the outcome. Despite a stable of good intentions he'd been forced to take lives again.

He left it behind a long time ago, hoping time would erase haunting memories, yield forgiveness for reckless decisions made during the hubris and seeming invincibility of his youth. But the only thing that seemed to change was the cast of players. He couldn't avoid the implications that a higher power may have other plans for him while he waited for some elusive extension of grace. He closed his eyes and buried his face in his hands, a brief, temporary escape from whatever might come next.

It was maybe a minute before he heard her speak. "Who are you?"

Unlike her panicked response to the assassin's violent death minutes earlier, her voice was firm. Fear and indecision had given way to a simple need-to-know. He cringed in the darkness behind his hands when he realized that in the confusion she had not gotten a good look at him. *Who am I?* He wanted to blurt the words out. *I'm your father.*

It had been a given back when he returned from Kuwait, accepting that she was gone forever, even though he dreamed of her during nights and years of fitful half-sleep, drenched in sweat. Now, a moment in time that could never be—even in his wildest dreams—had appeared. He had never been more scared, not even during precipitous moments of conflict and human anguish when long odds had brought death close enough to taste.

He found himself unable to move, afraid to show his face. Hiding like this behind trembling hands was no way for a practiced killer to act. He slowly dragged his palms down his cheeks, uncovering his eyes. She was staring at him. After everything he had been through in a troubled life, the death and brutality, the horror of war and despair, the disarming ease with which good men slipped into evil for the sake of victory, very little disarmed him anymore. This was different and he felt his stomach slip a notch.

He ran through the script. He was confident his charade with her five days earlier in the riding ring had been successful. In a few seconds when he emerged from behind his hands he felt sure she would recognize Pat Cooper, family man from Tennessee scouting the Richmond countryside for a farm and riding stable for his family. He had no way of knowing that her world had already been shaken by a different truth.

Following Brent's outburst in their kitchen Betty had pulled herself together. Once she managed to recover from her own shock she spent two candid days with Emily revealing an unlikely tale of family duplicity that a girl of thirteen could never have imagined. About Colonel Brent Masters, the well-intentioned imposter, a man Emily had always known as her father; and about Pat Cooper, the man who really was. Betty did her best to tell the story the way her husband had explained it, back when Emily first came into their lives: the chance opportunity, the scandal, the unholy negotiation, the final bargain. Betty spoke truthfully, as far as she knew it. She had no way of knowing that the story she relayed to her adopted daughter was a deception of the highest order.

The girl rocked in the wingback chair, her arms wrapped around legs pulled tight to her chest. Her eyes made an unapologetic survey of the stranger hiding behind his hands, of his jeans and sweat-soaked t-shirt stained with blood.

"Are you some kind of policeman, or special agent or something?"

An ache knifed through his heart. So many years. A daughter lost to him forever. Now here she was, alive, fifteen feet away, scarred perhaps by brutal events, but alive.

He'd already made a calculated decision to wait for an appropriate time to reveal his identity. This was not that time. Too many deceptions would have to be overcome, patiently, with professional help from counselors. For now he had to get her out of harm's way before Masters returned. A confrontation could turn ugly. He decided her first impression of him was as good a cover story as any. He slid his hands away from his face and eased into an adlibbed monologue.

"Emily, I'm Pat Cooper. I'm an agent with the FBI. I wasn't honest with you the other day. I can't say why yet, but . . ."

He stopped at her sudden audible gasp when she recognized him. She pulled one hand over her mouth and her eyes widened while the other hand gripped the arm of the chair tight enough to make her arm shake.

"But you . . .?" she said, pointing at him with the hand that had covered her mouth. Tears welled up and she turned away sharply, staring through the gaping hole in the front wall. She picked up the towel on the edge of the chair, the one not stained with blood, and found a dry spot and wiped her eyes before she looked back at him.

"You're . . ." She couldn't finish it.

"Yes. With the FBI."

She cleared her throat twice and wiped her eyes again with the towel. As she regained her composure her eyes fixed on his face, examining every feature. Finally she lowered her pointing hand and relaxed her grip on the chair. After a long pause she raised her chin, a gesture of growing confidence, and let out a long sigh before she spoke, almost matter-of-factly.

"My Mom told me my Dad is not really my Dad."

A lump formed in Pat's throat. It surprised him that they had confessed anything to her. He tried to choke back feelings and gamely moved forward in the role he had set up.

"We know. That's part of what we're investigating."

A long silence hung between them. Neither knew how to take the next step into the conversation. Her eyes cleared a little. She glanced down at her hands, then back at him, and opened a door, unsure what was on the other side.

"They told me more stuff."

Pat's eyebrows arched. "Good stuff, or bad?"

She tightened her lips, resolute, and began shaking her head, gently at first, then with nervous energy. Her emotions swelled, transforming her from a scared young girl into someone empowered. The fear that held her hostage a few minutes earlier had dissipated, replaced by a growing anger. It was unmistakable and her eyes narrowed to slits when she finally spoke.

"Why?" she said, defiantly.

"Why . . . what?"

Her eyes blazed with a fierce indictment.

"Why did you give me up?"

Chapter 56

THE ACCUSATION caught him between the eyes, a direct hit.

Nothing in his Green Beret training, brutal as it was, had prepared him for this. Their cadre had taught defensive measures against all the obvious weapons: a razor-sharp knife slashing wildly through the air, a shattered beer bottle in a dimly lit bar, a loaded pistol just out of reach. This was one they missed. The assault staggered him. Even if he had seen it coming he had no defense against one simple sentence, straight to the heart: '*Why did you give me up?*'

He found himself unable to move, dead weight against the French door, stunned at six piercing words his lost daughter had thrown at him like acid. It was a cruel distortion for her to think he had abandoned her when he had spent the last twelve years limping through the aftermath of a father's hell? Yet there she was, hatred burning in her eyes like hot coals.

The confusion was overwhelming and it took a few seconds to regroup. He knew the gulf of enlightenment would be mined with lies, but he had no choice but to dive in and see where it took them.

"What makes you think I gave you up?"

"It doesn't matter," she snapped, shifting in the chair. "Just tell me why."

He leveled his eyes at her, hoping for the right combination of compassion and tough love.

"Your mother and I never gave you up. *Never.*"

"Liar!" she screamed at him before he finished, leaping out of the chair. He allowed her response to bounce off onto the floor, no damage done, while she raged on.

"I knew you'd lie. I knew it! My Mom told me . . . I mean . . . my mom. . ."

She was stumbling over the unavoidable disconnect, this new parental reality that would inhabit their conversation from this point forward. He watched her slump back in the wingback chair, confused, trying to decide what labels to give the players. As he expected, the voices of habit and heart were too strong and she clenched her hands.

"Yeah, my Mom, OK? My Mom. She told me everything."

"And 'everything' is . . . what?"

"You *know* what!" she screamed at him, slamming her fists on the arms of the chair. "Admit it!"

Pat flinched. *Admit what?* Betty and Brent Masters had obviously crafted a caustic tale of abandonment with him and Allison cast as heartless villains. How could he counter the untruths if he didn't know what they were? So he allowed her to pile on the accusations.

"Just admit it. You and my 'mother'," she said, her fingers gouging the air with angry air quotes, "thought more about your get-out-of-jail card than you did your daughter." Sarcasm spilled out like venom.

Get out of jail? Pat stared at the floor, speechless, trying to connect the dots. He rose from his squatting position and paced. Obviously this wasn't the best time to balance the scales of truth, not with time at a premium, but her story was incredulous, painful, and he couldn't let it go.

"So, you think we abandoned our own child so we could,

what, somehow keep from going to jail?"

"Oh, let me guess," she said, her words thick with condescension. "You don't remember getting caught, you and my mother, stealing all that money during the war? My Dad should've turned you in instead of . . ."

She hesitated, unwilling to speak of the illegitimate alliance, one that changed her life in ways she still couldn't wrap her head around. She put the thought behind her, gathering herself, and forged on.

"He and Mom couldn't have kids, and *you* didn't love me enough." She stumbled over her words, visibly shaken. "It was screwed up. How could you . . ."

He watched her sliding between anger and despair as she struggled, her eyes wandering around the room, trying to make sense out of something senseless. Her shoulders fell under the weight of betrayal and loss at the desperate thing her adoptive parents had done, even if it had been with good intentions. Then she turned to him, her chin high and prideful, and the largest burden finally came out.

"How could you trade your daughter for your freedom?"

There it was.

Not enough to dredge through the details. But definitely enough to destroy a young girl's faith in parents of blood and parents of opportunity. Pat felt his stomach clinch at the impossible place where outrageous lies had placed them.

"You don't have *anything* to say?" she asked.

He turned to her, physically and emotionally spent, reeking of sweat and dirt, blood and desperation, the pistol still hanging loosely in his hand, an image unlikely to command respect or admiration. And he heard his own voice, calm and unwavering, making his own brief statement.

"Your mother and I loved each other more than I could ever explain. When you were born it completed us. It was all we wanted."

To his surprise she didn't interrupt him. He looked away, a dramatic hitch in his voice as he searched for Allison somewhere in that vast void behind his eyes where she always lived. His head dipped before he groped for more.

"We never gave you up," he said softly. "Someday, maybe not today, you'll know."

Chapter 57

SHE STARED AT HIM. His response offered no hint of apology, words uncharacteristic for a man that might have traded her for his freedom and some cash to boot. She hadn't expected that.

Then another thought appeared, raising the level of confusion. He had been an absentee father, yet somehow he showed up out of nowhere. How did that come to be? Killing two men was problematic for sure, but he *had* saved her life. The clutter of possibilities rolled around in her head like marbles in an empty coffee can. Without acknowledging it, her anger dropped a notch from boiling to a medium simmer and her curiosity overrode the call to hate, at least for a minute.

"But my real mother *did* give me up," she said, pulling her legs up against her chest again.

The grief in his heart was heavy enough to sink ships.

"No she didn't." His head dipped again, and he repeated it, barely above a whisper. "She didn't."

"Then where is she?"

His shoulders fell and he looked off into space searching for Allison again, for help and counsel with their precocious daughter, full of questions. He imagined a voice in the background urging him on. So he told it, as much as he thought she could handle.

"She died. In a fire while I was away in the war."

She took the answer in, not automatically as fact, but for what it might be. A chapter in her life, one she hadn't read yet, and she found it important. She exhaled and rested her chin on the top of her knees. Regardless of this man's past and the frightening abilities he had with taking life she could see that their conversation was taking a toll even on him. But her stream of consciousness was on a roll and she couldn't leave it there.

"Then after that war . . . why didn't *you* come back for me?"

"I thought you were dead too," he said.

She cocked her head. "Why would you think that?"

"The farmhouse in Kentucky where you were born, where you and your Mother and I lived, it burned down while I was away." He hesitated, unsure whether to reveal more details. He decided she was entitled to know at least some of it.

"They found two bodies inside, hers and a child's. We had no reason to think that child wasn't you."

Hard-boiled details. A tragedy for sure, possibly fact, possibly not, firmly planted in front of her. It was a troubling visual. She couldn't accept it as truth yet, but with that much detail it was impossible to ignore. Her emotions stepped to the back of the stage while she took a turn to the analytical.

"It wasn't me," she said, arms spread wide as proof.

When he didn't fill in the blanks she continued.

"So who was it?"

"We don't know."

As soon as the answer was out of his mouth he felt an unexpected tinge of shame. The true identity of the child killed in his farmhouse had been completely lost in his quest to find Aimee. She was somebody's child, not simply a statistic on a Medical Examiner's report. And of course another damning truth was tied to it, one he couldn't share with her yet. Her adoptive father knew who the child was.

Pat leaned against the door frame, a respite from the drama. "It sounds like I'm avoiding your question."

She looked away, debating a myriad of conflicting stories, before she turned back to him.

"They told me you gave me up. My Mom . . . you know, my adoptive Mom . . . why would she lie to me about that."

"Maybe she believes it."

An exaggerated exhale and a groan as her head swung toward the ceiling in teenage frustration. "Who am I supposed to believe, her or some stranger who says he's my real father? You've been gone my whole life."

"In a way I haven't, not really."

He pulled out a well-worn wallet, lopsided with loose corners of leather stubbornly hanging on. He opened it to the faded plastic windows, ones that he had flipped through hundreds of times in quiet motel rooms or lying in a lonely tent in front of a campfire. He held it out and she hesitated, as if it might be contaminated, before she took it.

The first picture was a bundle of fleshy pink cheeks and green eyes, all framed with a Pooh t-shirt. Pudgy arms reached for the camera, a face exploding with laughter and innocence, colorful rings and shapes scattered on the carpet. Aimee stared at her own picture, mesmerized, and her clipped anger dissolved into a broad smile before she caught herself in what she sensed might be an act of disloyalty. She pulled back into a defensive posture.

"You're saying this is me?"

Pat's index finger urged her to turn to the next window, another picture of a toddler, this time lying face down in a crib. A bare bottom was prominent in the shot and she grinned and blushed at the same time. Pat pointed to a spot in the picture.

"Look familiar?"

She drew the picture closer and found the tiny purple

birthmark in the shape of a bow-tie above her left hip. Like hers.

She turned on her own to the third window. She was greeted by a grown woman in her early thirties in a white tank top, looking back at the camera over her right shoulder. She had no makeup and a wisp of hair hung loosely across a face sporting an infectious grin, as if the cameraman didn't know what she was up to. There was no pretense other than to offer herself to the camera, which made her that much more stunning, a woman in her element, ready for the next adventure.

Aimee stared at the picture, engrossed, her fingers playing across the plastic window. She made light strokes over her mother's face, her hair, her smile, her complexion, before she looked up at Pat. The question in her eyes required no words and he simply nodded to her as he admired the picture for the millionth time.

Two more pictures, one of mother-holding-her-child, and the last, husband-and-wife, blue jeans in a wicker settee, Allison nestled into his arms, her hand lying on his bare chest, content and grateful for a life she would never get to finish.

Aimee flipped through the pictures a second time, then a third. She closed the wallet and held it for a long time before she handed it back. She leaned back in the chair, then turned her face toward the gaping hole in the wall and thought for a time before she faced back toward Pat.

"What was her name?"

"Allison."

She smiled her approval, a slight nod and turned away again, her thoughts running free, trying to feel her way through a minefield of premises that changed who she was and the direction her life was about to take.

Finally she turned back to him.

"What was mine?"

Chapter 58

BRENT MASTERS jerked the steering wheel and whipped the white Mercedes back into his lane as a Dodge pickup in the oncoming traffic swerved to avoid the collision. The driver leaned hard on his horn and flipped him the finger, shouting an unintelligible curse as he passed. Masters' panic behind the wheel was running 70 miles an hour in 45 zones, passing everything on the two-lane county road to his house.

The moving parts to the unfolding crisis had become obvious to him in short order. Franklin Pentecost may have been a ruthless corporate tyrant that long ago lost his principles to greed and power but he was one hundred percent white-collar, a consummate delegator that ruled from the sterile safety of the boardroom. He never allowed his own hands to be stained with the blood of his enemies. Any final order to kill may come from him but the brute reality of taking a life would be handled through one man only.

He slowed down and scrolled the Contact list on his phone. Alternating eye contact between the screen and the road, he selected a number he'd never dialed before.

A frown creased Richard's brow when he noted the incoming call and he waited until he steered out of a curve before he answered.

"You know you're not supposed to call this number. Ever. Emergencies only."

Masters was in full attack mode, his weapons of strategy still sharp, even after years of inactivity. He had no hard details about Kentucky but Garth's failure to call in and the not-so-subtle signals from Pentecost made it clear there had been a total breakdown. He'd have to make educated guesses about what happened and wade through it.

"Richard, I just got off the phone with Pentecost. Kentucky was a complete failure. I'd say that qualifies as an emergency."

Richard studied his caller. "He talked to you about this?"

"Just now," he lied. "He said you'd fill me in."

"I don't know, Brent. You're not in my chain of command."

"We've got a cluster-fuck of epic proportions on our hands here," he shouted, turning up the heat. "We're about to be exposed . . . Pentecost, me, Eddie. Which means you're in deep shit too, old boy. I can't work in the dark here so fill me in, goddammit. Did *any* of our crew get out?"

He wavered before he gave in.

"No."

"We eliminate *any* targets?"

"Afraid not."

"Grainger?"

A brief hesitation and a clearing of his throat. "Nobody knows where he is."

Masters felt his jaw tighten. If he was any judge of character Patrick Grainger would be on his way to Richmond, if he wasn't here already. He'd deal with that later. His bigger concern fell with the head of Aurora on the other end of the line, the man who implemented Franklin Pentecost's not so delicate matters of life and death. He had to steer this killer and his crew away from Emily and it was too late in the game to beat around the bush.

"I'm guessing Pentecost's given you your marching orders?"

"Not sure what you mean."

"Garth's in custody or dead. It's not hard to figure out who they're gonna come looking for next."

"No idea."

"Let's cut to the chase, Richard. Me and Eddie are one Grand Jury indictment away from your boss and you know it."

"I guess I do."

"So, you coming after me, Richard?"

All the cards were on the table now.

"Where are you, Brent?"

"At the office waiting for you," Masters lied.

A strong silence.

"Hmmm, I don't think so," Richard said, confident he knew how to draw Masters home. "I think I'll make a quick side trip to your place first."

It was Masters' turn to fall silent. He terminated the call and stepped on the gas.

* * * * *

On the way to her brother's sprawling country estate Betty Masters dialed her daughter's number a fourth time. Again it went straight to voice mail, not surprising since Emily's iPhone was resting peacefully on the bottom of the pool in their back yard. She gave up and pulled up her Favorites list for her husband's number.

"She won't answer her phone, Brent."

Masters tried to disguise his fear as he stepped on the gas.

"Maybe she's in the shower. Keep trying."

"She's always close enough to hear her phone."

"I know. Keep trying."

Betty heard the alarm in Brent's voice and fell into anxiety mode, right on cue.

"I'm turning around."

"No!" he shouted, "*Do not* go back to the house, Betty."

"Why?" she said as she slowed down and pulled into a farm entrance.

Betty was helpless under pressure, sometimes a few steps away from the edge of sanity even during the best of times, but he never questioned how much she loved their daughter. If he didn't give her some credible reason, at least part of it, he'd never be able to stop her.

"There's a man, maybe more than one, on the way to our house, Betty. They'll be waiting for me. But if Emily's there . . ."

"Brent!" she screamed, full panic.

"Calm down. I'm on my way."

"Why do they want you?"

"Some things that I know, Betty, important things they don't want to get out."

Her mind was scattered but not completely shot.

"Does this have anything to do with Emily's real father? Is he coming back to take her away?"

"He's probably already back," he said as he stomped the pedal and accelerated around a delivery truck, "and he's not trying to take her. He's trying to protect her."

"From what? Protect her from what?"

"From these men, Betty." He didn't know how much she could handle. "They're mercenaries, from back in Kuwait. They're capable of anything."

"Please tell me they wouldn't hurt a child."

"Betty, they killed lots of people over there. If we get in their way they'll kill us . . . even Emily."

It was like a stun gun to the head. She lowered the phone into her lap, trying to wrap her mind around an impossible truth. She raised the phone.

"How could he protect her?"

"He's not just some family man looking for a horse farm."

He edged into the passing lane, into a flurry of brakes and horns coming around a curve, and swerved back to avoid another head-on.

"He's a Green Beret from my old Brigade. A trained killer, but he'll do anything to protect Emily. I'll get there as quick as I can. *Do not* go back home." He clicked off and passed three cars on a straightaway.

She sat stunned in her idling Lexus. Like so many times in the past, a helpless wave swarmed her. Then something came to her, leaping out from the hazy muddle of her mind.

* * * * *

In the blood soaked parlor Pat and Aimee were tiptoeing their way through delicate questions-and-answers when he pulled his ringing phone out of his jeans pocket. He stared dumbfounded at the screen, in shock at a name he never expected to see: Betty Masters. He threw a cautious glance at Aimee before he answered.

"This is a surprise."

"Is this Pat Cooper?" she said, on the edge of hysteria.

"Yes," he said, honoring the alias.

"Mr. Cooper, or whatever your real name is, are you in Richmond? *Please* say you're in Richmond."

The question and her tone caught him off guard. The repercussions from this call were limitless, the possibilities all bad. But he recognized the panic in her voice and decided to follow it to some conclusion. "Yes, I'm in Richmond."

"Thank God," she gasped. "Are you anywhere near our house?"

"Why?"

"Good Lord, I don't have time to piss around," she screamed at him. "Please, how close are you?"

"I'm pretty close," he conceded, glancing around the room.

"I'm begging you, please get over there right away."

"Why?"

A long pause while she tried to regain her poise.

"I don't have any choice. My daughter . . ." She halted, trying to bring herself to say words that seemed impossible. ". . . your daughter is at our house alone. My husband thinks some men are going there and she might be in danger. Brent says you can protect her."

He glanced at the two dead men on the floor. "Go on."

"Take Emily to the apartment over the back barn. She knows where we hide a key. He says she'll be safe until he gets there."

"He's coming here?" Pat said, a glance at Aimee. She was staring back at him while he struggled to disguise the one-sided conversation.

"Yes. Just hide her until he gets there."

"Look, I really think things will be OK."

"You don't understand. Brent says these men kill people. They *kill* people! They could kill Emily." She was losing her grip. "You *have* to get over there, Mr. Cooper. Please. For her sake."

At least he could reassure her.

"All right, I'll check it out. Would that make you feel . . ."

He stopped when he saw a black Tahoe turn off the county road and accelerate down the entrance drive.

"Shit!"

Pat disconnected and grabbed Aimee by the arm and began dragging her through a room littered with glass and dead bodies. His abrupt change in behavior was frightening and she retreated into hostage mode, resisting him. He stopped and with his hands planted on her shoulders, he glared into her eyes, his nose inches from hers, then pointed with his pistol.

"There's a car coming down your driveway filled with men that want to kill us. Where's the key to the apartment over the back barn?"

She shot a frightened look out the windowless opening in the wall. Halfway down the driveway she saw the approaching car, identical to the one that pulled up to her house an hour earlier driven by the two men lying dead in the living room floor.

She bolted toward the sliding glass door in the family room, Pat behind her, out past the pool and redwood gazebo. They angled across the back yard toward the smaller barn, an older timber-framed hay barn with oak plank siding stained black, a sturdy relic from the former farm operation.

"Where's the key?" he shouted as they scaled the black four-board fence and hit the gravel parking lot running. She didn't bother to answer, sprinting, taking dead aim on the small personnel door a quarter of the way down the sidewall of the barn. Athletic as Pat was, he had to dig hard to keep up with her. The last forty feet offered no cover, exposing them as the Tahoe pulled up in front of the house and the three passengers got their first glimpse of the gaping hole in the front wall.

Pat and Aimee came to a stop at the metal door, the top half glass with a snap-in plastic grille. She retrieved a rusted key from over the drip edge and unlocked the door as a bullet from Richard's Glock plowed a gash in the oak siding inches away. They ducked into the small vestibule and a second bullet shattered the door glass behind them. A stairway ran a straight shot up to a second level. They took the stairs two at a time while Pat scrolled for KSP Detective Phil Damron's personal cell number.

Chapter 59

AT THE TOP LANDING Pat and Aimee bolted through the unlocked apartment door and raced to a double window overlooking the parking lot. Sixty yards away three men were gathering automatic rifles and spare magazines from the Tahoe.

Pat's call had gone straight to the KSP detective's voice mail. "Phil, where are you, buddy?" he pleaded, eyes fixed on his attackers. "I'm in Richmond at Masters' place with three killers knocking on the door. We need a little help here!"

The armed men were already running diversion routes toward the barn. He tossed the phone to Aimee. "Call 9-1-1."

He checked his Colt—the eight-round magazine was a lousy choice for a long-term firefight and all his spares were back in his saddlebag. Thankfully he'd only spent one round and it was buried in Masters' wall, slathered with brain matter. He'd have to make his shots count.

He raised the aluminum sash on the left window and jammed the screen out with the heel of his hand. He took aim at the man closest to them, on the left. The attacker swerved at the last second, dodging behind a large tree at the edge of the yard as Pat's shot kicked up dust in the gravel. Pat shifted his attention to the man on the right and fired again as his target jumped behind a hay truck. The slug ricocheted off a metal fender.

Where was the third man? Pat froze when he spotted the shooter leaning out of the open garage door of the front barn, an automatic rifle aimed at the window. Pat body-slammed Aimee away as a thirty-round salvo exploded into the apartment, shattering glass and shredding the barn siding and drywall like paper. They were sitting ducks.

Aimee cowered in the hail of bullets. When the gunfire stopped, she grabbed the cell phone lying on the floor. "I'll call Uncle Eddie. He'll get help."

"He's dead," Pat said, as he dragged her away from the front wall.

He scanned the efficiency apartment. Other than a bathroom and walk-in closet near the stairs, it was one open space, maybe 20' x 30'. The original oak columns and beams were left exposed, supplemented by minimal framing and drywall at the sidewalls. A TV and living area occupied one side, a queen-sized bed with sparse furnishings the other, and the compact kitchen adjoining the living room backed up to the stairwell.

He had five rounds left. The three attackers each carried automatic rifles with spare 30-round magazines, and the apartment floor was nothing but carpet and vinyl on plywood. If the killers made it to the barn he and Aimee had no chance. He pointed to the back wall of the apartment.

"What's on the other side?"

"A hayloft. Supplies and chemicals."

"Back stairs?"

She nodded.

He rushed to the back wall. Several violent kicks broke through the drywall and insulation, opening a hole large enough to crawl through. He motioned to her.

"Get to the back stairs, quiet as you can, and wait. When you hear gunfire get the hell out. Run for the woods at the back of the farm as fast as you can."

"What are you going to do?"

"Buy some time."

"But you can't—"

"Don't argue with your father." He shouted, forcing a grin. "I know what I'm doing. Now go or I'm grounding you for a week."

She couldn't avoid a half-smile before she reluctantly disappeared through the hole. Pat only had seconds before it would begin. He slipped off his boots and crept over to a spot near the refrigerator. He picked up one of the cheap tubular kitchen chairs and waited. When he heard the metal rollers on the garage doors slide open he waited a few seconds before he launched the chair across the room into the bedroom area and backed up, ready for all hell to break loose.

As soon as the chair landed, the deafening roar of three M16 automatic rifles erupted at the same time. A firestorm from 45mm NATO cartridges riddled the bedroom side of the apartment in a non-stop fusillade. Slugs capable of penetrating 1/8-inch steel at three hundred yards found zero resistance from the plywood floor. Other than a few rounds that burrowed into the 6" x 8" oak beam, bullets slashed unimpeded at three thousand feet per second through the roll insulation and metal roof of the barn, turning it into a virtual sieve. Pat glanced at the perforated ceiling, unable to suppress a fleeting thought. *I'll bet that voids the warranty.*

While the non-stop barrage of bullets continued to engulf one half of the apartment, Pat readied himself, inching closer, and picked his spot. Once the magazines emptied and the men stopped to eject and reload new ones, Pat slid soundlessly in his sock feet into the shredded bedroom area, right before the shooters began discharging fresh magazines at full automatic into the living room and kitchen that Pat just abandoned. The ear-splitting blitzkrieg of bullets and smoking gases from the volley filled the apartment.

When it stopped one hundred and eighty rounds had shredded the floor, some holes as large as a softball. He slipped over to one of them near the middle and hovered over it, motionless, his Colt aimed at the opening. As soon as he detected movement he fired one shot and lurched away. The unsuspecting killer below dropped to the dirt floor like an anchor in still water when the Colt's slug drilled into the top of his skull. The remaining two men reacted, emptying new magazines into the ceiling above the dead man before dodging for cover behind hay bales in the side stalls.

The second mercenary made a nervous move toward the door when Richard halted him with an arm signal. He squinted, peering through the haze thick from the automatic fire, into the dimly-lit depths of the barn. With all the smoke from the firefight he could barely make out stalls on both sides of the aisle stacked full with baled hay. The one exception was a single stall behind him next to the door. There, bolted to a concrete slab, was a metal safety bin for hazardous materials and containers of gasoline and diesel fuel. His mind flashed back twelve years. The irony seemed appropriate.

They scurried to the bin and pulled out two yellow diesel fuel containers. With their eyes trained on the floor above they sloshed fuel on the hay in a half-dozen stalls. It took less than twenty seconds. Richard dropped his can and lit the nearest bale. The gathering fumes caught in an audible flash.

The other man pulled out a disposable lighter and did the same on his side. They backed up as the flames escalated, devouring the fuel-soaked bales like a ravenous animal, spreading, quickly attacking tinder-dry, 90-year-old seasoned oak columns and beams. It only took seconds for the blaze to begin charring the floor joists of the apartment above. The smoke limited visibility to a few feet. They backed away and slid the barn doors open, ready for the rush of oxygen that would feed the monster.

They weren't prepared for the lone man 20 feet away, stalking toward them, his hands gripping a brown and tan Shrike AWS automatic rifle with a thirty-round magazine. Brent Masters' eyes grew wide at the sight of flames raging inside his barn. He halted and looked past the two men. The fire was doubling its fury as fresh air from the open door swept through the aisle.

"Where's my daughter, Richard?" he demanded over the growing crackle of flames. The head of Aurora International never got a chance to respond. Masters glanced up at the apartment and recalled his instructions to Betty: . . . *tell her to go hide in Garth's apartment, over the barn . . .*

"Nooooo!" he bellowed.

The Shrike turned vicious. His finger locked hard on the trigger, his rage out of control, as he unleashed a salvo of bullets that ripped two torsos nearly in half.

He dropped the rifle and charged past the dead men into the open garage door, calling to his daughter, but he had no chance. The hay and the barn itself made a perfect fuel. It had gained momentum, too far gone, an inferno now, eating into the wood floor joists and plywood of the apartment. The heat was overpowering and forced him out. The smoke rolled thick and low through the aisle as the draft carried front to back, a perfect air tunnel.

He reversed course and ran around to the side door. Through the broken glass he saw that the stairway was already engulfed in flames. Black smoke boiled up into the apartment like a chimney. Again the heat drove him back. In a feverish panic he ran back to the front where the floor joists had begun to give way.

The heat was intense, forcing him away from the barn, and he collapsed in a heap in the gravel as he watched the flames licking behind the front windows, consuming the apartment. He managed feeble, plaintive gasps, calling to her, and clamped both hands against the side of his head, a futile attempt to hold back the horrifying image of his daughter trapped in the fire.

He never heard the sound of Betty's tires skidding in the gravel behind him. He didn't see her running past him toward the tower of flames, wailing a mother's desperate cry, before the blistering heat drove her back too. She flailed the air with her arms, a hopeless attempt to fan the fire into submission as the roar of the flames and the ominous pop of burning wood overpowered the countryside pastoral. She turned back to him for a sign that her worst fears were wrong, but the agony in Brent Masters' tortured expression told her everything. She collapsed on her knees in front of him and closed her eyes to block out the torment before her body toppled onto the gravel and rolled over, begging for anything to end her grief.

The once-proud timber barn shuddered and began its loud collapse inward. As the flames swelled, the metal roof panels took on their inevitable deformation, no longer even worth their weight as scrap.

In their distraught state of mind neither Brent nor Betty Masters noticed Pat Grainger as he emerged from behind the hay truck parked beside the front barn. It had been his point of refuge after he slipped through the hole in the drywall into the loft and wound his way to the ground, all while Brent Masters was cutting two men in half with his rifle and scrambling to save his daughter. A stolen daughter that Pat knew was safely hiding by now in the forested hills at the back of the farm.

Chapter 60

PAT EYED the roaring tower of flames consuming the barn. The billowing plume of smoke and orange-hot embers were disappearing into the glare of the sun. He heard an explosion, then another, the last two plastic gasoline containers.

He took a quick inventory. He felt sure the adjacent farms had reported the blaze by now. The main house was far enough away so probably not in jeopardy. The large front barn was closer but the metal roof and wall panels offered temporary protection against drifting embers. He had already responded to the stamping and neighing from two horses inside and released them into the front paddock. The farm's diesel and gasoline fuel tanks were too close for comfort but if the pumper trucks arrived soon they could cool them down. Nothing to do but wait.

He turned his attention to Betty and Brent Masters writhing in agony in the gravel thirty feet away. He sat down on the running board of the hay truck and watched with callous indifference two despicable child-robbers, consumed by disabling grief over the unbearable loss of a second 'daughter.'

He briefly considered if he should have the decency to relieve their misery. Just go tell them the truth, that she managed to escape. But each time the muscles in his legs tensed, ready to lift his body from the running board, his memory grabbed him by the collar and pulled him back in place. *Twelve years* dragging around his own agony. Trying to find some way to get through each day. And then another.

Twelve years trying to deal with the loss of a wife and daughter whose blessed existence had saved him from his own tortuous past. It was a put-me-out-of-my-misery agony that had forced the Colt up to his mouth more than once, always stopping short, refusing to grant him release.

The longer he waited to share the good news with two contemptible life-thieves, the longer they would have to suffer. As it should be. It was only fair. A fitting justice for the terrible crime they and their empty consciences had committed.

He had always second-guessed whether he might have deserved his own personal torment, a just punishment for arrogant times in his youth when his conscience deserted him and allowed him to touch the dark side. But his wife and daughter were innocents and they deserved a chance to live.

As he waited, while one minute dragged into two, then into five, as the fire's relentless march through the barn stamped an end to another unheralded chapter in the book of life, the satisfaction he had long anticipated from this primal eye-for-an-eye justice seemed to grow hollow and weaken, like the wood and metal losing ground to the fire.

It was replaced by something else, what he couldn't tell. The hand-wringing joy of revenge, that hateful, poisonous thing he had dreamed of for so long, had somehow managed to dial itself down into a simpler, less satisfying sense of regret. Or possibly acceptance. A long-overdue acknowledgement that neither their suffering nor his, whether dispensed by the wheels of justice or delivered by invisible demons, would ever make things right. And at once it seemed pointless to carry it further.

He had expected more.

He stood and moved away from the hay truck toward Brent

Masters, now little more than an overweight bundle of heaving arms and legs doubled over in the gravel, gasping for breath. Betty Masters was still lying face up, motionless. Other than shallow breathing, her eyes were empty, her mind buried in a place of lost hope. It was a place he knew too well.

Even though Pat's conscience had confronted his demons thirty feet earlier and come to a merciful understanding, as soon as he got within five feet of the Colonel the evil furies of the man's crimes once again raised their heads, slashing their way back into the picture. They refreshed Pat's hatred and he found himself unable to acknowledge the man, even in his misery. Over the growl of the fiery tempest, he spoke to the burning barn instead.

"She's alive."

Masters seemed not to hear him at first. Finally the presence of another person registered and he turned his head toward the voice.

"W-what?"

Pat continued to stare at the mountain of flames. "She got out. Aimee's alive."

Masters was virtually blind from his tears, the first ones he had shed since the death of his real daughter. He wiped his eyes with the heels of his hands, then with his shirtsleeves, clearing them enough to see who was responsible for the voice. When he twisted on his left hip in the gravel toward the shadowy figure standing next to him he recognized Patrick Grainger. Other than a hardened countenance for both men, little had changed in twelve years. Masters' paternal instincts briefly overrode his hatred for an adversary.

"How do you know?"

Pat could only talk to the fire.

"I got her out the back. She's in the woods. Safe."

All the breath left Masters' body and he dropped his head

and muttered a silent prayer of thanksgiving. Then his grief seemed to leave him as quickly as it had come. He cast a sideways glance up at Pat, a practiced leer.

"I figured you'd show up."

Pat ignored the comment. He was watching Betty Masters fifteen feet away, beginning to stir. She had rolled over on her stomach, her arms out in front, her chin inches off the gravel. She was peering up at him from under the top rims of her eye sockets. He stepped toward her when the Colonel's next comment stabbed him in the back.

"Is that what you named her? Aimee?"

Pat stopped. He turned and looked down at Masters and the cruel smirk clinging to the man's face. The ranking officer once again pretending to hold court over his subordinate.

"She'll always be Emily Masters," the Colonel said, "no matter what you tell her."

Even with the curtain of fire raging behind him Pat recognized the baiting as soon as the words were out of the man's mouth. *Never react. Win the mind games.* But Pat felt his hand tighten on the Colt hanging loose in his hand and he couldn't hold back.

"You'll never be her father, you sonofabitch. Just one lonely, disgraced ex-army, rotting away in federal prison."

"You got no evidence, Grainger."

"You and Sergeant Major got careless."

"That information you gave Eddie? It disappeared." He forced a laugh, weak cover as he recalled the legion of incriminating documents hiding in the trunk of his Mercedes forty yards away.

"It's amazing how much data can fit on a CD, Colonel. Did I forget to tell you about that copy I made in Kuwait?"

Masters' arrogant smile vanished, twisting into a smug frown. "Even if you did, the statute of limitations is up."

"Only on the fraud. There's no statute of limitations for arson, kidnapping, murder. You kidnapped my daughter, murdered my wife, Fowler, his wife, and whoever that little girl is you burned up in the house. Every one a capital offense." He shook his head. "You, ol' buddy, have paved a wide trail to the electric chair. How's that fortune working out for you now?"

The sum of truths was too much. Masters lunged, a desperate wave of fury, before a kick from Pat's boot sent him sprawling. Pat was on him as soon as his head bounced off the gravel, the Colt planted tight against Masters' forehead and he pulled the hammer back. He felt the grip of a powerful force. His hand shook with the rage of years and he heard himself screaming over the thunder of the fire.

"You cause so much damage. Do you just turn away so you don't have to look at it? Did it make you lose sleep, even a little?"

"Listen to yourself, Grainger. I did what I had to do, just like you did. It was war. People get killed. And, yeah, you walk away from it."

"I'm nothing like you." He stared into the hard eyes of the man who had orchestrated Allison's death and robbed him of a daughter's childhood, all for the sake of a house with four chimneys. The force swelled, growing stronger, and he felt his finger closing on the trigger when Allison made another appearance, whispering in his ear, refusing to let him forget there were others. She was closer than she'd been in awhile and he thought he felt her breath on his face, cooling off his anger. He pulled the Colt away from Masters' forehead.

As he rose and backed away he heard a light crunch in the gravel behind him. He turned, startled to see Betty Masters walking toward him with a weak grip on the Shrike automatic rifle her husband had dropped in the gravel minutes earlier.

Chapter 61

PAT RAISED HIS PISTOL. He had no idea if any rounds remained in the Shrike's magazine.

"Betty. Please. I don't want to shoot you."

He'd observed her minutes earlier, lost in another world, unable to cope with another tragic loss. Standing in front of him now her glazed expression told him not much had changed. Pat backed away, his finger against the trigger, when he realized she wasn't approaching him. Her expression was empty but her line of vision was clear. She was walking toward her husband lying in the gravel. In the fallow field of her mind she seemed to not notice Pat. She came to a stop in front of her husband and raised the rifle.

Masters stared at his wife. His voice shook as he feverishly tried to back away from the barrel.

"What the hell are you doing, Betty?"

She stood there, mute, looking at him through vacant eyes and her finger trembled as it eased down the side of the frame to the trigger. Pat had witnessed emotional shock many times over the years. Trying to out-talk a distraught person always drew long odds.

"Betty, please, I do not want you to do this."

Her finger didn't move, hovering in front of the trigger.

"Betty?" Pat said again.

Her husband cowered in the gravel beneath her blank stare. She was dealing from an empty chamber of thought, or so it appeared until she slowly turned her head toward Pat, her lips trembling as she tried to get the words out.

"He killed your wife, Mr. Grainger."

"He'll have to pay for that. But not here."

Her eyes were filled with regret and a plaintive plea for forgiveness seemed to rise up out of her.

"I didn't know," she said, barely more than a whisper.

"I know you didn't. Let me have the rifle."

Her mind was wandering, lost in the wilderness, and her lips quivered, looking for the right words.

"I just wanted my daughter back," she said finally, and her eyes closed as she slipped into a vague, long-lost remembrance of a terrible time. When her eyes opened a few drops trickled down her cheeks.

"Betty, when you called me awhile ago, you said you had to trust me. Remember?"

A nod, barely perceptible.

"So trust me, Betty. It's important that your husband live no matter what he's done. There are others involved and he can testify against them. They've got to pay for their crimes too."

He watched her confusion building as she struggled to process his words. He suspected she could filter out only so much of the truth, especially under extreme duress, before she broke down. For that reason this was definitely not the time to let her know that her brother was responsible for it all.

He sensed a faint spark of acceptance. She was trying to find her way back. She turned to her husband, the Shrike still aimed at his chest, and wailed a question heavy with pain.

"Why?"

Pat suspected Brent Masters felt little regret for forty years of arrogance and greed. Even now during this emotionally-charged confrontation with his wife, he seemed to be searching, not for apology, but for justification. Beneath the bravado and exaggerated pride Masters was going to have to accept a hard truth soon, that it would never be right for them again.

"I did it for you, Betty. For us." he said. "For Jenny."

Pat glanced at Betty as she slowly shook her head at his response.

"Jenny would never have wanted this." Betty didn't take her eyes off her husband. "If you know who's responsible you have to make it right, Brent."

Masters reflected on the leather briefcase in the trunk of his Mercedes, all the parts and pieces that could make it right bundled together in one handy spot. And he thought, wistfully, about the nylon bag next to it crammed full of fifty-dollar bills he would never get to spend. The farm would be swarming with cops soon. They'd find it all. He looked at his wife and nodded his head, a weak final surrender, and secretly wondered if there was some place in the middle of such a fucked-up finale to find redemption.

Pat took two slow steps over to Betty Masters, eased his left hand under the hand guard, and gently took the Shrike from her. She breathed out and Brent flopped back on the gravel, unable to comprehend the shit storm that was about to come next when it got considerably more complicated.

"Who's Jenny?" said a voice. Aimee Grainger stepped out from the rear door of the big barn.

Chapter 62

ALL HEADS TURNED toward her, rooted in place with one hand on the fender of the hay truck.

It had only been a few hours since she crawled out of bed, slipped on the robe draped across a chair, and popped a frozen waffle into the toaster. Everything in her life was orderly, familiar, few questions other than who would be on Facebook this morning. Now she couldn't think of anything that wasn't a question. Three people staring at her, all strangers: a mom and dad who weren't her real family, and a newcomer who was. Even worse, she didn't know who *she* was anymore. Another stranger. On top of it all, a new name had popped up.

Betty rushed to her, arms outstretched. Instinctively Aimee reacted, tentative with her half of the embrace, one they had shared thousands of times. This time it seemed different. Not false, not diluted, but different.

Betty pulled back to get a look at Aimee's face and saw the confusion that was weighing her down. Despite Betty's fragile psyche her mothering instincts took over, digging deep, and she managed to pull it together during this moment of family crisis. She put an arm around Aimee and walked her over to where Pat and Brent waited.

Pat's arms were crossed. Despite his shock at seeing her he

delivered a mild, disapproving look. "I thought I told you to head for the woods."

She answered with a shrug.

"How long you been listening?" he said.

"Long enough."

The depth of her despair was impossible to miss. She turned tentatively toward Brent Masters, a man she had always known and loved as her father. He reached to her, touched her arm, and she recoiled slightly before she relented and moved to him and returned a hug they had shared often. When he released her he tipped her chin up when he spoke. "You know I love you."

"I know."

He hesitated. "Did you hear much of our conversation?"

She pulled back and dropped her chin again so she wouldn't have to hold his gaze. She thought about the question, whether to answer or not, before she looked into his eyes.

"All of it."

Brent turned his head and ballooned his cheeks with a huge breath, then let it seep out slowly. As a successful, brute-force military commander over a 30-year career he'd never let emotions get in the way of a good decision. Every problem always had an answer.

Until now.

He searched for a strategy, some way to salvage what was turning out to be a cluster fuck of epic proportions. Everything was perched on the edge of disaster, in complete jeopardy, and for the first time in his life he had no answer. Aimee's stare confirmed the fragile nature of the situation and he shook his head, searching for words that wouldn't come easily. "I don't know . . . things just . . ."

"Did you know her, my real mother?"

He recoiled and his brow furrowed at the sudden recognition of a cold-blooded truth that even he had never even considered.

He never knew her.

He shifted uncomfortably but she refused to let him off the hook. Her steady stare made it clear that she recognized his answer, even as he tried to recover.

"Emily..."

She jerked away, anger blazing in her eyes, as hot at the raging fire that continued to ravage the barn eighty feet away.

"You didn't even know my real mother and you killed her?"

His mouth opened but nothing came out and his chin began to quiver.

Unconsciously she glanced over at Pat and realized he was following her every move, watching her open doors to her own past, one at a time, confronting the demons behind each one. This man who had killed to save her.

She turned back to Brent, a volatile brew of anger and confusion and fear. Then finally a sense of despair that she didn't see coming.

"I never knew her either."

He reached for her, but she stepped back. "No!"

"Emily, listen . . ."

"Who's Jenny?" she asked, defiant, turning back to Betty.

Betty tried to summon the strength to answer but the words were difficult coming. Pat helped her.

"Jenny was their birth daughter." He looked at Betty to confirm his guess as sirens from the approaching fire department pumpers began to sound in the distance.

Betty struggled with the final piece. "She only lived a few weeks past her first birthday."

Aimee shot an accusing look at Brent and moved another step away from him. "Did you kill Jenny too?"

Before Masters could protest Betty placed her hand on Aimee's arm. "No, honey. She was really sick. He did some bad things but that wasn't one of them."

She pulled away from Betty and took three determined steps toward the front paddock before stopping, her hands clasped on top of her head. She stared into the distance, over the top of the board fences while her mind wandered deeper into the story. The sirens from the fire trucks were getting closer. When she wheeled around she looked at Betty, her eyes still fiery.

"What did you mean when you said he could make it right?"

Her attention whipped to Brent, the question directed at both of them.

Chapter 63

BRENT MASTERS DODGED Aimee's piercing stare and looked to Betty for help. It was a wasted gesture. He wasn't ready to give up, not yet. He turned away, still looking for a way out, refusing to accept the surrender that was inevitable. All of those war games in a long and distinguished career and he'd never once waived a white flag. Now what choice did he have?

Aimee's hand on his elbow brought him back to the present and he heard her ask it again, softly from behind.

"How can you make it right?"

He turned to face her. He knew that was a mistake even before he did it.

Pat broke the silence. "Colonel, you're going to spend time away no matter what you do. Maybe this is a chance to salvage something." He looked at Aimee. "Some things are worth saving."

Brent Masters waited for what seemed like the longest time. He glanced at Betty and Aimee, then slowly reached into his pocket and pulled out his car keys and took a long look at his lost future as he tossed them to Pat. "In the trunk. Everything you need."

"If you're talking about evidence of the fraud," Pat said, "we've already got that."

"You want the rest of them, don't you?"

Brent looked away, lost for the first time in his life, and caught a glimpse of a hawk soaring through smoke-free air one farm over. He let his mind relax while his eyes followed its glide path. Once it disappeared behind the far tree line he rattled off a brief summary of documents and emails and photographs that validated the conspiracy and the capital crimes that followed. Everything that would make it right.

"Everybody. Top to bottom." He didn't reveal names, not with Betty there. She'd find out soon enough about her brother.

Their conversation was interrupted when two pumpers from the fire department made a wide sweep off the county road into the driveway. Within twenty seconds they barreled into the gravel parking lot while Pat herded the others over to the open door in the front barn. Within minutes three sport utility vehicles from the local FBI field office skidded to a stop in the parking lot and field agents spilled out, their efforts concentrated on four people huddled in the metal barn.

Phil Damron had done a thorough job briefing the FBI team leader in Richmond. Once everyone was identified they Mirandized Brent Masters and handcuffed him and placed him in one vehicle. While he was being escorted to the SUV he made sure Betty and Aimee heard his redemption speech as he opened up about the leather briefcase and the bag of cash in the Mercedes.

Even though Betty had no knowledge of the murders or kidnappings her role in taking a child outside the boundaries of a legal adoption, depression or not, was up in the air so they also handcuffed her and loaded her into a separate vehicle.

Pat had given up his Colt and the empty Shrike as soon as the agents rolled in. His status in the eyes of the law was not as clear cut. While two agents stood guard over him and Aimee together on the golf cart, the lead agent got on the phone to Phil

Damron to discuss protocol and detainment options for Pat. He wasn't under suspicion for specific crimes back in Kentucky, other than leaving the scene at the Olivers' house, but the dead bodies in Masters' living room was another matter.

Pat carefully watched Aimee staring at the floor of the cart, overwhelmed by the enormity of the situation developing around them. She had been emotional when Brent and Betty were handcuffed and put in patrol cars. It was all closing in on her, the disorienting chaos of law enforcement and the fire department working to get the fire under control.

He leaned over to her. "It's a lot to handle. I know it's hard to see them being taken away."

She nodded.

She finally looked at him. "You hate them, don't you?"

Pat clasped his hands and looked away, better to collect his thoughts.

"Your adoptive father—let's call him that for lack of a better term—may have been a good father to you, but he did terrible things, and he'll have to pay for them. He arranged the murder of my wife—your mother—someone I loved very much. Someone you loved very much. And he took you away from me. I'd be lying if I said I didn't hate him for those things. Your adoptive mother, other than the cockeyed way she got you, I'm guessing she probably didn't know about any of the rest. So, hate her? No, I don't."

He weighed his words before he continued. "They've always been your parents. You've never known any different. You have every right to love them. If you do, and I expect you do, you shouldn't feel guilty about it."

"I don't know what I feel. It's hard," she said, shaking her head. She waited in silence a bit before she finished her thought. "And I have no idea what I feel about you."

"I'd be surprised if you did. Why don't you let it come to

you in its own time. OK?"

She didn't answer.

"You scared?" he asked.

She looked absently out into the parking lot at the hustle of people before she responded.

"What's going to happen to me?" She swung her eyes up at him, not waiting for an answer.

"My mom . . . I mean my 'adoptive' mom and dad are going to jail. You're my real Dad, unless you've got another surprise for me. But I don't know anything about you, other than you kill people."

Pat winced.

"Besides, you'll probably go to jail too. Uncle Eddie is gone. They probably won't let me stay with my friends. I mean, what do I do . . . live under a bridge or something?"

He finally understood. This wasn't his area of expertise but he considered before he spoke. "You're right about them taking me to jail. Those two guys in the living room, obviously."

His mind flashed back to another time and the sharp irony that went with it. "Another young lady about your age once gave me a good recommendation when I needed it. I'll tell you about it sometime." He raised his eyebrows in a mock plea. "I'm hoping I can count on you for one?"

She smiled at him and nodded.

"I won't tell you about the bow and arrow part, at least not yet," he said. Her eyes widened and then she sighed and shook her head with an 'it-doesn't-surprise-me' look.

"As for you," he said as his eyes swept the parking lot and the milling FBI agents, "they'll probably find a foster home here in Richmond for the first few days, maybe a week or so. I'm not really sure how that works." He didn't have to look to know she was making a face.

"They might let you stay with friends, I don't know. But

that's all temporary. The bigger problem is where you'll live after things settle down."

"Great. If that's supposed to make me feel better it's not working."

"I'll tell you what. Just go with the flow, ride it out for a few days. When they finish processing me I'll make a call. I might have an idea you'd find interesting."

Chapter 64

THE HALF-OWNER of Two Sisters Cafe dropped two menus on the table and Randy and Mike Turner offered their cups while she poured.

"We've got one more coming, Sheila," Randy said, as he tore open a package of sweetener.

"How's the extended family thing working out?" Mike asked.

"Better than we hoped. Julie's in eighth grade, Aimee's in seventh, so they're in the same middle school. School hadn't started in Richmond yet when everything blew up so that made it easier. Julie took Aimee under her wing, introduced her to her friends. A little tentative the first two weeks but who wouldn't be? We've got her in counseling. Same lady who worked with Julie."

"Any issues?"

"The hardest thing's been getting used to a new name. Pat let her decide. At first she wasn't sure but now she says she likes it."

"She and Julie getting along?"

"They've got a lot in common. It's like having a new sister without the growing pains. The guest bedroom came in handy. I get the feeling they talk a lot, bounce personal things off each other. So far, so good."

"It didn't take the Feds long to let Pat off the hook," Mike said. "If there ever was a justifiable homicide, Richmond was it. I'm not sure how he managed to get the authorities to go for this daughter deal though. He's her natural father. Why didn't he push for immediate custody?"

"He'll get custody. But he knew a new environment was going to be a huge change for her. Asking her to live with a single father that's been drifting around the country for twelve years was a little intimidating for both of them. So he ran it by Karen and me, just an idea. At first it seemed a little off the wall but when we discussed it with Julie and Brad they were cool with it. When Aimee found out what the connection was between us and Pat, especially Julie's rescue, she warmed to the idea."

The bell on the front door tinkled when Pat entered. He winked at Sheila and ordered coffee on the way to the table. "Sorry I'm late. We're buttoning up our steel package."

"Have your boys forgiven you for their little trip to jail?" Mike asked.

"Forgiven me? Hell, they keep buying me beer for putting a little excitement in their lives. Especially Axle. He's a legend now. All the ladies want a piece of Robin Hood." He laughed and offered his cup to Sheila who poured and winked back at him when she laid a menu down.

As soon as they scanned the breakfast specials and ordered, Pat opened up. "What's the latest?"

Randy had kept up with the details of the investigation, as much as Phil Damron was authorized to release.

"Investigation's underway. Indictments filed soon. The documents in the trunk of Masters' car were damning, especially the emails between Franklin Pentecost and others high up in Wyndham-Lynch. The Feds weren't sure Masters would follow through and testify against the rest of them. I'm guessing they offered him a life sentence and immunity from death row in exchange for full disclosure."

Pat took another sip of coffee. "I honestly think he wanted to find some sort of redemption with Betty and Aimee. He was a cold-blooded, greedy asshole but I believe he still loved his wife. And Aimee, too, in his own way."

"It looks like Betty Masters didn't know about any of the serious stuff," Randy said. "She's going to be spending a lot of time in a psychiatric center in Louisville trying to work through it. Aimee visits her every week."

"I can't tell you how much it means to Aimee," Pat said, "Julie going with her. You've got one special daughter, Randy."

"We both do."

They waited while Sheila made a special trip to drop off maple syrup and containers of butter and jelly and top off coffee cups that were still nearly full.

Mike looked at Pat. "We better not get too attached to this guy," he said, thumbing toward Randy. "He's been working on a story about this whole logistics/conspiracy/murder/kidnapping thing. He'll be famous soon."

"Yeah?" said Pat.

"DoD and the Army aren't too happy about it, but it's a powerful story," Randy said. "Had to break it up into parts, like a series. I've gotten serious interest from the national wires. Think I might be able to get it to the syndicates."

"That's great," Pat said. "No names, I hope."

"After all this, you want to remain anonymous?"

"I prefer to fly under the radar. Give me a code name." He thought for a second. "Is Lachesis still good?"

"Perfect," Randy said, grinning at Mike Turner's bewildered expression.

"Have you been able to get any more details on how they pulled off the fire?" Pat said.

"Like you figured, the space heaters were brought in to

throw everybody off. Masters finally conceded that even though Allison died from carbon monoxide her death was no accident," Mike said, almost afraid to broach the subject.

Pat stared at his coffee. "Mike, if the drug screens never showed any chloroform or knockout drugs in her system why couldn't she get to Aimee before the carbon monoxide got her?" He recognized a noticeable hesitation from both of them. Then he guessed the only logical answer and sagged. "They held her?"

"Until she was unconscious. Masters verified it."

Pat continued to stare at his coffee. "Did it take long . . . ?"

"No," Mike said quietly, "it didn't."

The table went silent for a full minute before Pat seemed to regroup. "Did the sonofabitch ever ID the baby that died in the fire?"

Randy was glad to be moving to a less emotional topic.

"He did. Sadly, the orphanages in the Middle East are overflowing with children and a lot of the operators are poor or corrupt. It doesn't take that much money to buy a deceased or dying child that nobody claims. Wyndham made hundreds of flights back and forth from Afghanistan and Kuwait to the US, so bringing a body back on one of their daily runs wasn't hard. The timing had to be perfect. They were counting on the body being so badly burned in the fire that testing for CO in its lungs would have been impossible. And it was."

"Jesus Christ," Pat said.

Sheila brought a tray with three breakfast plates. She placed an obvious hand on Pat's shoulder when she asked the table if they wanted anything else.

When she left Mike changed the subject. "What're the odds of Pentecost and the others going to jail?"

Randy ran down the list he had discussed with Phil Damron. "We knew the statute of limitations on the fraud in Kuwait was up. That's six years. But even though arson, murder, and kidnapping have no statute of limitations, the practical matter is that Wyndham has so much money and enough manpower in their stable of attorneys that no matter who's arrested they'll post bail and drag this thing out and delay prosecution indefinitely. The older ones like Pentecost, could outlive a verdict, go on with their lives of luxury, maybe even die of natural causes before they're ever convicted."

Mike peeled the cover off a plastic tub of grape jelly and angrily began plastering it on his toast. "I used to think we lived in a country where justice prevailed."

Randy noticed Pat calmly pouring syrup from a small stainless steel pitcher held at eye level. He seemed distracted, intently focused on the honey-brown column of maple syrup that he was letting ooze onto his waffle.

"You OK, Pat?"

"Yep," he said, staring into the trail of syrup, tightening it to a thread.

Randy's cell phone rang in his pocket and he checked the screen. "It's the office. Sorry."

He listened without talking, then his face turned serious. He disconnected the call and laid the phone on the table and stared across the table at Pat.

"What?" asked Mike.

Randy continued to stare at Pat, busy forking bites of waffle and sausage links into his mouth.

"What's wrong," Mike asked again.

Randy didn't take his eyes off Pat when he answered. "Ten minutes ago Richmond FBI notified Phil Damron that Franklin Pentecost's Mercedes exploded in the driveway of his house."

Pat crammed in another bite of waffle and his eyes casually dropped to his plate, then to Mike. "Pass the butter, please?"

Chapter 65

PAT SQUINTED at the bedlam from 2,400 pubescent voices screaming in competitive disharmony from opposite sides of the hardwood floor. Disparate sounds of hands clapping in rhythm, feet stomping on wooden bleachers, the itchy squeak of rubber on polished wood. An occasional brash whistle cut through the noise like a knife, then an occasional flurry of brass, woodwinds, and drums revving up the faithful. All coupled with the distinctive, pungent recollection of burnt popcorn, hot dogs, and the sweat of boys in athletic combat.

He was having second thoughts about his date, whether she would be able to tolerate the discord and the harsh glare of white metal halide. He could almost anticipate her displeasure before she got around to expressing it.

But tonight she surprised him. A rare chance to escape Briarwood Estates seemed to override the perfect opportunity for premeditated griping.

He glanced at Margie in her wheelchair taking it all in, a smile plastered on her face. She caught him looking. "What?"

"Nothing, I was just wondering how you were doing."

"Peachy. You think all this excitement is too much for an old lady don't you?"

"No," he said, setting up in defensive posture, "I just didn't know if you could deal with the noise and people, that's all."

"I love it. It'd be a sad state of affairs if everybody in here sat on their hands mumbling wouldn't it? It's been a long time since I've been around this many people with a pulse. Back at the home I'd be wondering who'd be the next one to fall over in their plate."

She turned back to the game and began clapping bony hands to the beat of a fresh round of snare drums.

"Uh, Marge, that's the other school's band you're clapping to."

"Don't care. It feels good. I don't think it'll change the outcome any, do you?"

After the timeout and teams returned to the floor Pat pointed him out. "That's Brad. Julie's brother. He's a freshman at Eastern Hills."

"He's a good ball handler but he's got a funny shot."

"What do you mean funny shot?"

"He guides the ball. Needs to use more wrist with his shooting hand."

Pat stared as her, dumbfounded. She cut him off when she noticed him looking. "You ever hear of March Madness? Besides, I played when I was in high school."

"*You* played basketball?"

"Girls basketball had different rules back then, but I played. I was a scoring machine."

Pat continued to stare at her until she swatted him with her program. "Watch the game."

When they first arrived, because of Marge's wheelchair, the school had positioned them near the stage where they had a clear view of Eastern Hills' fans. He quickly located Randy and Karen near the center, half way up.

On the second row, tucked in the middle of a boisterous cheering section, he found Julie and Aimee, their arms moving in unison. Before the game started he pointed them all out to Marge. When he identified Aimee he let Margie focus on her while the cheer rambled on. "That's your great-granddaughter, Marge."

He felt her hand tighten on his arm while she beamed at the only remaining blood link to her daughter.

"After the game," he said, "I think it's time you met her." When she turned to him her face held hope for the first time in twelve years. That and an unrestrained smile.

Pat tried to keep his mind on the game so he could pick it apart with Brad after it was over but he found himself drifting to Julie and Aimee. At one point in the second quarter he caught Julie looking over at him and she flashed a smile and a wave. Then she nudged Aimee and pointed and Aimee caught his eye too.

Aimee had taken the couple of months he'd suggested, peaceful, valuable time to regroup. Aimee and Julie each had their own personal wounds to deal with. Their time together, a two-person mutual support group, made it easier.

For Pat and Aimee there would be time enough to start over, when the time was right. The plan would seek its own level, when they were both ready. For now she was at peace, comfortable broadcasting a loving smile back at him and a discrete wave in front of her body, just between the two of them.

As he waved back, his subconscious took over and the cacophony of the crowd seemed to dial down, drifting into a shallow buzz, folding in on itself, the voices and sounds bleeding gently into a slow, mellow blend, finally little more than an indistinct murmur. The bright lights dimmed, then faded, and the sounds and smells and even the game itself found another place for a minute while his thoughts started an inescapable drift inward.

How did I wind up here? In this place, with these people?

All the lost chapters in a life, scenes brimming with vibrant colors that somehow fade to gray, then disappear right before our eyes, the special people in our lives caught by a wave of circumstance and swept out to sea. And after that, what? Do we pull out blank pages and start drafting a new manuscript, recounting our memories, perhaps only the good ones, or do we wrap them all in sailcloth and slide them off a plank, give them up to a bottomless sea of regret and let it swallow them whole, not to be seen again.

How do you put the pieces of your life back together when something terrible and unexpected slams into you? You analyze and rationalize, tell yourself that good will eventually triumph over evil. Maybe you even convince yourself that a total re-boot will eventually make things right.

But there are no sure things. In the end the person you once were is gone. You have no choice but to become someone else, a stranger. You can't reclaim that other person, the one you were before things changed. Maybe the stranger is a better person, who knows. But it doesn't matter.

He's all you have now.

Spes

ACKNOWLEDGEMENTS

Writing a story is a singularly isolating experience, just you and the keyboard and your thoughts. Researching and publishing that story is the opposite. Without the help of gracious individuals, many of whom I didn't even know, this story wouldn't be. If I've missed some, please forgive me and know that I'm grateful.

Lots of technical advice kept my tale, hopefully, from being full of holes. Mike Wilder, former Executive Director of Kentucky's State Medical Examiner's Office, guided me through the anatomy of a fire scene and how an ME's office functions alongside other agencies. Douglas P. Lyle, cardiologist, forensics expert, technical advisor for TV, and award winning author of more than a dozen thrillers and non-fiction texts (including three reference books on my desk), provided invaluable guidance on forensics and DNA.

Jon Keller endured a noisy McDonald's next to a kid's birthday party and shared background on how a military base in Kuwait looked, smelled, sounded, and functioned. Don Salchi shared vivid experiences as a veteran and explained the effects of combat on soldiers. Bob Foster, FBI agent (ret) filled in lots of gaps about procedure and jurisdiction. Keith Meador told me more than enough about the deadly options of bow-hunting.

Major Fred Deaton (ret), Operations Director at the Frankfort Police Department, guided me through the workings of a local police department and the anatomy of a crime scene. In the Frankfort Citizens Police Academy I learned about their sophisticated programs and facilities, and the way professional behind-the-scenes police work functions in my hometown. I gained a far greater respect for local cops. Those guys know their stuff.

As an inaugural member of the FBI Lexington Citizens

Academy, dozens of instructors, seasoned pros every one, overwhelmed me with the many sophisticated programs, methods, procedures and so much more about top-rung crime fighting than I could absorb. I learned how interconnected we are with a dangerous world. I learned that FBI pros are really fine folks. Mostly I learned that we are in good hands.

Killer Nashville is one of the pre-eminent writing conferences in the US. Clay Stafford organizes an annual buffet of lecturers, authors, crime fighters, agents, and publishers, which has led to dozens of friends and contacts otherwise unavailable. Two of those buds, prolific wise-guys and partners in crime, spur me on. Terri Lynn Coop, who beat me out of the Claymore Award, is never short on sarcasm, advice, and support, and Tim Caviness, website developer first class and my annual conference roomie, shared his moonshine and ubiquitous sense of humor, and schooled me on how to format my novel.

The whole exercise in developing my book cover seemed to fall together. With a concept in my head I was blessed to wrangle the professional talents of Gene Burch, my former dentist, now photographer of high repute and a Photoshop devil. Our friendship has benefited from the exercise. Local businessman Mike Barnes, another friend, was the perfect protagonist on the cover. His support is a joy, his enthusiasm contagious. And when another local photo pro, Bill Rodgers, offered his studio and lighting expertise, the four of us kids jumped in and created something. We had fun that day.

My appreciation to so many tolerant and supportive friends. MaryAnn Burch and Pat and Phil Huddleston were my first Beta readers and cheerleaders, and later Jack Damron. To my benefit Lacey Roberts, despite her obsession with commas, told it like it was. I apologize to all for my early drafts being so lame. To the endless list of pals that, in good fun, teased me mercilessly in the beginning, thanks for the ribbing and then for finally coming around. My brother Don, PhD and former Mr. Universe finalist, was always there with encouragement. And of course to my loving and loved extended family: Tiffany and Elmer, Hailey and Tom, and Layne, none of whom ever doubted me (at least until I was out of hearing distance).

Deelie Dunstall was way above my awkward social status in high school. Now a close friend, she did a meticulous page-by-page line edit and provided on-target suggestions when my story had holes and curious timelines didn't add up. Her catches made my book better. I can't thank her enough.

Regina Wood endured many evenings during the three years we dated reading weak manuscripts and offering encouraging comments when we could have been watching Breaking Bad and drinking cheap wine. In those early years, when my writing was trash, before I began to learn how to write, she was my biggest fan, refusing to let me give up. She's followed my journey, page by page, and holds me accountable to this day. Thanks, Gigi.

I'd be remiss if I didn't give props to my Mom, now departed. She was my spot-on inspiration for Margie. Her lively spirit literally wrote that chapter, most certainly the dialog, while I simply listened and operated the keyboard. More importantly, she raised two sons under trying conditions, her unconditional love and determination teaching us that nothing is impossible. I wish I had listened more.

Finally, thanks to the Almighty for whatever meager gifts he may have provided, but more importantly for giving me the nerve to drive toward an ambitious goal when a more rational person would have quit.

Victorian novelist George Eliot may have prophesized this project for me and thousands of other new writers when she said:

"It's never too late to be what you could have been."

Ray Peden's professional career spans 43 years as a Civil Engineer, General Contractor, Home Builder and Designer, Land Developer, Project Manager, and Public Relations Copywriter. Along the way he found time for other pursuits: magazine editor, R&B guitar, painter of fine art and some not so fine, drill sergeant, carpenter, stone mason. Throw in three ex-wives, three amazing daughters, four grandchildren and counting, and it was time to retire to a new career, the thrill-a-minute life as a novelist, counting bodies, conspiracies, and emotional upheaval while he sips bourbon and watches the Kentucky River roll by.

Website – www.writerontheriver.com
Email – raypeden101@gmail.com
Available @ Amazon and select independent bookstores.

Made in the USA
Lexington, KY
20 April 2017